SYMPATHY
FOR THE DEVIL

TERRENCE McCAULEY

BOOKS BY
TERRENCE MCCAULEY

Prohibition
Slow Burn

Available from Polis Books

The following is a work of fiction. Names, characters, places, events and incidents are either the product of the author's imagination or used in an entirely fictitious manner. Any resemblance to actual persons, living or dead, is entirely coincidental.

Copyright © 2015 by Terrence McCauley
Cover and jacket design by 2Faced Design
Interior designed and formatted by Tianne Samson with
E.M. Tippetts Book Designs

ISBN 978-1-940610-34-4
eISBN 978-1-940610-47-4
Library of Congress Control Number: 2015939006

First trade paperback edition July 2015 by Polis Books, LLC
1201 Hudson Street
Hoboken, NJ 07030
www.PolisBooks.com

POLIS BOOKS

To Paul Lomax

Photographer and Friend

CHAPTER 1

New York City – Present Day

THE MAN WHO called himself James Hicks checked his watch when he reached the corner of Forty-second and Lexington. It was just past eleven in the morning; more than an hour before he was scheduled to ruin a man's life.

And plenty of time to smoke a cigar.

He braced against a sharp wind as he crossed Forty-second Street. A cold humidity had settled in over Manhattan and the weather reports had done a great job of whipping everyone into a frenzy over the coming storm. TV stations and websites hawked it as 'The Big One' and 'Snowmageddon' and the ever popular 'Snowpacalypse.' The experts were predicting over two feet of snow with high winds and freezing temperatures for the next few days. It was too early to call it the Storm of the Century, of course, but that didn't keep the media from building it up that way.

Based on the data Hicks had been able to draw from the University's OMNI satellite array, he predicted the snow would be about a foot; with wind and ice being more problematic than the snow itself. He could remember a time not too long ago when New York would barely notice eight inches of snow, but panic was en vogue these days. Welcome to the post-9/11 world where preparation was paramount.

He understood why meteorologists exaggerated snowfall predictions. They were covering their asses against being wrong. If it was a little more, then they were close enough to claim accuracy. If the snowfall was a little less, at least it wasn't as bad as everyone had feared. Accountability took a backseat to relief and everyone went on with their lives. Either way, the weather folks had covered their respective asses.

Hicks hadn't worried about covering his ass in a long time. He didn't need to. Because in his line of work, small mistakes were forgotten and big mistakes got you killed. Such harsh, immutable constants brought a certain resignation to Hicks' life that he found almost peaceful. Danger can be a comfort as long as you know it's there.

Hicks headed for the concrete ashtrays placed in the alcove of the Altria Building across from Grand Central Terminal. There were a few cigar stores in the area where he could smoke indoors in warm comfort; maybe stir up some conversation with his fellow smokers on such a cold and blustery day.

But Hicks didn't want comfortable and he sure as hell didn't want conversation. He was working and needed the cold air to keep him sharp, especially before rolling up on a new Asset in less than an hour.

He stood out of the wind in the alcove of the Altria building and lit his cigar. It wasn't a cheap cigar, but far from the most expensive stick on the market. There was a time for savoring good tobacco and now wasn't it. Today, the cigar was merely a tool to help him stay focused and calm while killing time before his appointment. Because although Hicks had flipped hundreds of people from being regular civilians into Assets for the University, he still believed that changing a man's life forever deserved some pause.

Most of Hicks' colleagues didn't give much thought about the Assets they forced into the University system. They focused their efforts on researching the right prospect to turn; digging deep into the person's past for that one knife they could hold to their throat to make them comply. Past offenses and indiscretions they didn't want to see come to light. Current mistakes that could get them fired or ruin their marriage. Hicks' colleagues ran checks and analyses on a potential Asset's personality profile to make sure he or she could stand up to the passive pressures of the University's constant influence in their lives. If they passed all the OMNI simulations, then an Asset was approached, broken, and put to work. If an Asset cracked and killed himself or had to be eliminated, then OMNI was simply directed to change parameters to account for the shortcomings in the analysis model. It was all as simple—and inhumane—as that.

OMNI was the University's Optimized Mechanical and Network Integration protocol. The name was a relic of the group's past and had been around almost since the University's beginning. It was a term that had long since been outdated, but had managed to remain in use. When new hires asked details on which network, they were told 'All of them.' They soon saw the powerful reach of OMNI for themselves.

But Hicks had been running Assets long enough to know human beings never fit neatly into a computer program, no matter how advanced it was. Turning an Asset was like adopting a stray dog or a blind cat. They were being brought into an established environment and made to go against their own nature for your own benefit. The pet owner expected companionship and affection. The pet was expected to respond in kind or catch a rolled up newspaper in the nose.

Assets were expected to provide the University with information or access or options it needed at the time, but didn't have. If the Asset played along and did what was asked of him, he made out well. If he refused or got cute, they got the University's equivalent of a newspaper in the nose: a bullet in the brain.

From the shelter of the high alcove, Hicks checked the clock high above the façade of Grand Central across the street. The clock was; flanked by the stone images of a strident Mercury, a sitting Minerva and a lounging Hercules. The gods of speed and industry and commerce all concerned about time. Just like everyone else. Hicks found it a refreshing scene. Not even the gods were free of mortal troubles.

And in about forty-five minutes, Hicks would attempt to enroll a money man named Vincent Russo into the University system.

Hicks took a good draw on the cigar and let the smoke slowly escape through his nose. The frigid wind caught it and blew it across Forty-second Street. The streets were empty thanks to the impending storm, so there was no one around to complain about the stray smoke.

He wondered what Vincent Russo was doing just then. He could've pulled out his handheld device and used OMNI to hack the security cameras Russo had installed in his to watch his office, but there was no need. He knew Russo was a creature of habit. At this time of day, he was probably working away as diligently as he always did; verbally glad-handing clients over the phone about the status of their investments; convincing him that the fund he was buying them was a steal at the current price.

He probably rolled his eyes when he looked at his calendar and saw his twelve o'clock appointment with a prospective client. The new one with the name he didn't recognize. He might even think about postponing it, but realize it was already too late for that. Then he'd remember the statement that Hicks had sent him; the one detailing five million dollars he was looking to invest with Russo's firm. Greed would get the better of him as greed tended to do and he'd keep the appointment.

Greed had made Russo vulnerable to blackmail in the first place. And greed was going to be the reason why Hicks enrolled him in the University.

Hicks didn't feel sympathy for people like Russo or for any of the men and women he'd turned into Assets over the years. They'd all done things that had opened themselves to University pressure. Any dirt he had on them was their own fault. He'd sooner have sympathy for the devil himself than for any of his targets.

Still, becoming an Asset changed ones life and no matter how much they deserved it, the transition deserved at least some commemoration; hence the cigar.

Hicks was about half way through his smoke when a homeless man trudged into the alcove. He was pushing a creaky shopping cart as he escaped the wind of the coming storm. Given the man's weathered appearance, Hicks couldn't tell how old the man was except to see he was black and had a shaggy beard streaked with white and gray. His layers of tattered clothes looked liked they kept him reasonably warm and his cart was overflowing with plastic bags filled with other people's garbage. They were the things people discarded, but this man found valuable.

Hicks could relate to such things. He decided he liked this man already.

He watched the man push the cart into the far corner of the alcove. Hicks was ready to shake him off if he asked for money or a cigarette, but the man surprised him by saying, "Hey, mister. You trustworthy?"

Hicks hadn't been asked such a direct question like that in a very long time. "As far as it goes, I guess. Why?"

"Because you look like a trustworthy man to me," the homeless man said. "The kind of man I could leave my things with and find them here when I get back."

Hicks looked back at the cart overflowing with garbage, then at the man. "Why? Late for a board meeting?"

"Nope," the man said. "Just got to find a bathroom is all, and I need someone who can watch my stuff while I'm busy." He looked at Hicks' cigar. "Looks like you'll be here a while, and I promise I'll be back way before you're done smoking that thing."

Hicks admitted he was curious. "Why so particular? I mean, why don't you just…"

"Just find a doorway somewhere to piss in?" The homeless man shook his head. "Because it's against the law and breaking the law just ain't my style, mister. Besides, just because you are a certain way doesn't mean you have to act the way people expect."

Hicks liked the man's attitude and felt bad about the board meeting crack. "You take as long as you want, my friend, but I've got an appointment at noon."

"Funny, so do I," the homeless man laughed as he shuffled off. "Got that board meeting you was talkin' about. On Fifth Avenue, no less."

Hicks watched the man trudge back into the growing wind and head west, leaving him alone with the pushcart filled with things only of value to him. We were all like that, Hicks thought; pushing our own cart filled with shit we thought valuable through the world. Some valued love or comfort or money. Most wanted all three and thought money could lead to the other two. And if money didn't lead to it, then it certainly could buy it.

The formula varied, but Hicks knew everyone had at least one thing they valued most in this world. To that homeless man, it was his cart. But most of the people Hicks dealt with had their valuables stashed elsewhere in encrypted files on hard drives or in safe deposit boxes in banks no one was supposed to know about. They kept their secrets buried deep within themselves and prayed that no one ever looked for them. But someone always found out because part of every secret kept was the yearning to be discovered. To get caught. To tell. To let someone in on it. To confess.

Hicks had been in the intelligence game for over twenty years. He'd seen damned near every aspect of the human psyche known to man and yet it still managed to surprise him. No matter how many ops he'd run in any part of the world, he'd always learned something new from each one.

Even from a homeless man while he smoked his cigar on the street of a city bracing for Snowmageddon. He flicked his cigar ash into the concrete ashtray next to him. Or maybe it wasn't that deep. Maybe all of it was just unrelated bullshit.

Hicks' cigar had burned down to a nub when the homeless man came toddling back for his cart, looking more refreshed than when he'd left. A cup of hot coffee piped steam through its plastic lid.

Hicks dug his hand into his pocket, came up with a twenty and held it out to the man.

He expected the homeless man to take it. Instead, he just looked at it. "What's that for, mister?"

"Storm's coming," Hicks said. "I was thinking this could help you buy something to keep you warm."

But the homeless man backed away from the money, back toward his cart. "No thanks. I got all I need in this cart right here. Being prepared is what you might call a motto of mine."

Hicks put the twenty back in his pocket. "Mine too."

Hicks ground out his cigar in the ashtray. A light snow, barely a flurry, had begun to fall. The day was almost too pretty to ruin by threatening someone into working for him.

Almost, but not quite.

CHAPTER 2

Vincent Russo's office suite was a modern space in the Helmsley Building that straddled Park Avenue on Forty-fifth Street. Russo had gone with a chic minimalist décor: gray walls and glass desks; sleek telephones and computer screens. The paintings on the wall were equally chic, bland swirls that had just enough color to make them interesting. The receptionist Russo had hired matched the décor: pretty, but inscrutable.

The reading material in the reception area had obviously been placed there for specific effect. Lifestyle magazines showing wealthy white people of a certain age with good hair and better teeth living the life they'd always imagined. Golfing. Yachting. Sitting on a beach. Biking through woods. Boarding a private jet with grandkids in tow. Not a bald spot or a pot belly or a loud Hawaiian shirt in the whole bunch. Walmart had no place in the world Vincent Russo could provide to his customers. A great big dream there for the offering.

And since Hicks had been tracking every email into and out of Russo's firm for the past six months, he knew it was all one big lie. The office looked like it was trying too hard to be something it wasn't; just like the man whose name was on the door.

Hicks looked up when he saw Vincent—never call him Vinny—Russo walk down the hall to greet him. From hacking into the firm's security cameras, Hicks knew that Russo normally sent his secretary out to bring prospective clients back to his office, but not this time. After all, not every client walked in the door with five million in cash.

Vincent Russo was a large, solid man, a shade over six feet tall and just north of fifty years old. He moved like a man who was used to being given his way due to his size, which made it all that much easier for him to disarm you with his charm. He still had all of his hair and most of it was black, combed straight back from his broad sloping forehead.

"Mr. Warren, I take it?" Russo asked as Hicks stood to greet him. "Vincent Russo. Very happy to meet you, sir."

Russo went to shake Hicks' hand, but stopped when he noticed Hicks was still wearing his black ski cap and black gloves.

"Bad bout of rosacea, I'm afraid," Hicks lied; playing it mousey. "Makes everything I touch that much more sensitive, so the gloves help minimize my discomfort."

Hicks wasn't sure if Russo knew what rosacea was, but it

made him forget all about shaking hands. "Of course. I'm... sorry. Please, come back to my office where we can talk more privately."

Hicks let the larger man lead him back to his office, although Hicks already knew exactly where it was. As they walked, Russo provided a narrative of the dozens of people on the phone in the low cubicles.

"As you can see, we're a small but mighty shop here, Mr. Warren. And if you give me just a few moments of your time, I think I'll be able to prove to you that everyone in this firm is dedicated to giving each and every customer our undivided attention. And, as I'm sure you've heard, most of our customers have been very happy with the results."

Hicks offered a simper that fit the character he was playing. "I've heard nothing but great things about your company, Mr. Russo. I'm sure we'll get along just fine."

Russo ushered Hicks into his office and closed the door behind them. It was a corner office, with no windows out into the cubicle farm outside. There was no way anyone could see what was going on inside, either. The windows behind Russo's desk faced north onto Park Avenue. There was no way that anyone could see into the office from that angle, either.

Hicks sat in one of the chairs facing Russo's desk, which was as sparse as the rest of the office. No knick knacks on the walls; no mementos. Just a slim computer monitor, a sleek phone, and an old fashioned metal stapler engraved as thanks for speaking to an accounting group three years before.

The only visible hint of a life beyond his business was a picture of his son posing for a Little League portrait in full uniform. It was a cute pic, but Hicks knew the smiling boy in that photo had grown up to become the greatest heartache in Russo's life.

Hicks noticed Russo didn't display any pictures of his wife or daughter. That might have told Hicks something about Russo family life, if Hicks hadn't already known the whole story.

"Now, how might we help you today?" Russo asked when he was seated.

"You can help me get rich, Mr. Russo."

Russo laughed. "That's always the ultimate goal, of course. Given that you've told us that you have a substantial amount of money to invest, we have a variety of options available to us. It would help if you could give me an overview of where you're currently invested so I can help chart a course for your future."

"Chart a course for my future." Hicks let the words sink in. "I like the sound of that. Very nautical. Paints a nice picture." He reached into his nylon messenger bag and pulled out a thick file of papers bound by a precariously thin rubber band. He'd wanted Russo to be underwhelmed by the initial presentation. All the easier to overwhelm him at the right time.

"I've held many of these investments for a long time," Hicks explained as he handed the bundle over to Russo, who reached to take it with both hands. "I didn't feel comfortable emailing or sending all of this stuff by courier. I wanted to give it to you in person."

"That's understandable," Russo said as he took the bundle from him and laid it on the desk. "But we should probably start with some preliminaries. For example, what kind of

12

business are you in?"

Hicks nodded down at the pile. "You'll see. It's all right there."

Russo picked up the bundle again and gave an exaggerated grunt. "There's quite a bit here to review all in in one sitting." The thin rubber band snapped as he tried to remove it. "It might take me some time to go through it in order to get an accurate picture of your portfolio."

"It's not as intimidating as it looks," Hicks said as he took off his ski cap. "Besides, I think you'll find much of it familiar."

Russo gave a good natured shrug as he dug into the pile. "Let's see here."

But three pages into the pile, Russo began flipping through entire sections of the file; jumping from one page to another. "There must be some mistake here."

Hicks pulled his black gloves tighter and dropped the mousey act. "No Vinny. No mistake."

Russo rifled through the file now, finding one more familiar financial statement after another. Every dirty job and crooked transaction he'd pulled since he'd moved the firm to Manhattan five years before. Every name and account number of every cent he'd skimmed, thanks to the powerful reach of the OMNI network.

"Where the hell did you get all of this?" He looked at more and more sections before finally slamming the paper folder shut. "And what are you bringing it in here for? I've got this whole place wired for audio and video."

"I know," Hicks said. "But don't worry. I disabled them. At least what you've got in here anyway."

"Bullshit. All that's controlled remotely by…"

"By a security firm in Paramus, New Jersey, owned by a client of yours. They even gave you a break on the installation fees, but they're still over charging you. Their network firewall is shit. A drunken monkey could hack their system."

Russo's eyes narrowed. "What is this, anyway? Who the hell are you?"

"I'm the guy you need to listen to very carefully, because I'm only going to say this once."

But Russo was already way past listening. "Who are you? The Treasury? IRS?"

"If I was, you would've been arrested the moment you stepped out of your house this morning."

"Then I don't have to talk to you or listen to you or do anything except throw you out of my office."

"Calm down," Hicks warned. "This doesn't have to get nasty. And I'm not going anywhere."

But the finance man began to push himself out of his chair. Hicks reached over the desk and fired a straight right hand that nailed Russo in the center of the forehead just above the bridge of his nose.

The bigger man dropped back into his chair like a sandbag. Hicks normally didn't like hitting a prospect, but Russo was different. He was an alpha male and used to being in charge. The sooner he accepted the new order of things, the better everyone would be.

Russo sat spread eagle in his chair, dazed. He blinked and shook his head; trying to shake off the cobwebs, but Hicks knew they wouldn't clear that easy. "Keep your head still and breathe," he told him. "It'll pass quicker that way."

14

Russo cradled his head in both hands. "What did you hit me with?"

"A straight right hand in the right place," Hicks said. "And I won't hit you again unless you make me. I know you think those Mixed Martial Arts classes have taught you a few moves, but you still ride a desk all day. I don't."

Russo seemed to forget how dizzy he was. "How the hell did you know about those classes? They're..."

"Off the books, I know. A favor from one of your friends in the Nassau County Police Department. His brother in law owns a dojo near your house and he owed you a favor, so he set you up with a few free lessons for you. Not that you couldn't afford them, of course. It's the fact that they're free that's important to you, isn't it, Vinny? The principle of the thing. A sign of respect."

Russo sank even lower in his chair, legs spread even wider. "Who the hell are you? How do you know so much about me?"

"Who I am isn't important. How I know so much about you isn't important. But the fact that I know a hell of a lot about you is of the utmost importance because that knowledge is going to be the basis of our relationship from here on out."

"Relationship?" Russo blinked. "What are you, a fag?"

Hicks grabbed the commemorative stapler from his desk and threw it; hitting him in the balls. Russo stifled a scream as he shot forward to cradle his manhood.

"We don't do sarcasm here," Hicks told him. "Next crack like that gets your nose broken."

Russo looked up at him; his face red and his eyes watering. "What the fuck is this, blackmail? You want money, you little son of a bitch? If you know so goddamned much, then you know who I am. You know who I know. Shit, one phone call from me and you don't walk out of this building alive."

"Now you're embarrassing yourself," Hicks said. "The mobbed up guinea act might play with the pensioners you reel in here, but I know better. You're a nice Italian boy from Ronkonkoma whose old man provided sound financial planning for cops and firemen and teachers until you took over the business and moved to the big city five years ago. You move money for some really nasty people, but you don't have enough juice with them to have anyone killed on your say so."

Russo forgot all about his sore balls. "How did…"

"Your father died from a bad heart almost seven years ago," Hicks went on, "but mom's still doing well, though. Works at the library three days a week and volunteers with the Don Bosco Society on weekends." Hicks smiled. "I wish I had her energy. You're about as mobbed up as I am Chinese and, in case you haven't noticed, I'm not Chinese."

"No," Russo went back to cradling his head in his hand. "You're just another asshole trying to put his hand in my pocket. Fine. Fuck you. Just tell me how much it'll take to make you go away."

"Vinny, Vinny, Vinny," Hicks shook his head. "There's more to life than money. I'm not here to blackmail you. I'm here to help you."

"Great. Where have I heard that one before?" Vinny said. "You're just another asshole looking to take a bite out of me. Just like every other parasite in my fucking life. My wife, my kids, my partners." He lifted his head from his hands.

16

His face was flush and pale in all the wrong places. The spot where he'd punched him was an angry red and on its way to being a hell of a bruise. "But I've dealt with pieces of shit like you before in my time." He pushed the big file back toward Hicks. "What'll it take to make you and all of this mess just go away?"

"I just told you I'm not looking for money, and I'm not looking to add to your troubles." He pushed the folder back toward Russo. "You're right about there being a price for keeping the material in that folder quiet. The price is you. Or, to put a finer point on it, your agreement to work for me."

"Why in the hell would I go to work for you? I don't even know who the hell you are or what you want."

"I'm someone who can make your life very easy if you're smart enough to let me."

The damage to his ego brought the old Russo back to life. "I'm not interested in working for anyone. I've already got a boss and you're looking at him. I'm not just going to roll over for you or anyone just because they walk in here with a pile of paper."

Hicks ignored the bluster and laid it out as simply as he could. "From this day forward, you and I are going to help each other. My presence in your life and your business will be negligible, so long as you do exactly what you're told when I tell you to do it."

"That's what you think," Russo laughed. "Because if you know anything about me, you know I didn't get this far by taking orders."

"And you won't get any further if I send that file to Vladic." Russo flinched.

Hicks went on. "You've ripped off a lot of people, my friend, but Vladic's the worst, isn't he? He might be an ignorant peasant who probably wouldn't understand what all of it means at first. To him, it's just a bunch of account numbers and transaction statements. Might as well be in Braille for all the good it would do that ignorant bastard. But when he passes it along to one of his money guys—and he will—they'll explain it to him. And when they do," Hicks shrugged a little, "well, I don't have to draw you a picture about what he'll do next."

Russo looked at him through his fingers. "You wouldn't do that. I'm not good to you if I'm dead."

"You're no good to me if you don't agree to work for me, so what do I care?"

Russo let out a heavy breath as he rocked back in his chair. Hicks didn't see the point in pushing him any further. To do so would only lead to more posturing on Russo's part, and they'd already had enough of that. Hicks had made his point. Now all he could do was sit and wait for the seed to take root.

Hicks had learned long ago to let Assets take their time in making up their mind. Rush them and they'd say anything just to get away so they could think of ways out of it. Hicks made sure they completely accepted the bit before he hooked them up to the plow. And Vincent Russo wasn't used to being a workhorse.

But he'd have to get used to it if he wanted to go on living.

Russo's chair slowly turned away from Hicks, toward his tenth floor view of the northern half of Park Avenue. The snow was falling heavier and had just begun to stick on the window ledges of the buildings in the area. "I don't even know your fucking name."

"You can call me Hicks."

Russo kept looking out at Park Avenue. "That's it? Just Hicks? No first name?"

"What difference does it make? It's not my real name anyway."

"Figures. Who do you work for?"

"I don't see as how that makes a difference, either."

"Sure it does," Russo said to the window. "If you were connected to one of my clients, I'd be dead already. If you were a cop, I'd be in a cell. So that means you're either federal or some kind of intelligence guy." He lolled his head back against the headrest of his chair. "So, you CIA? NSA?"

"None of the above," Hicks said. "All you need to know is that I know everything about you. I've been tapped into every corner of your life for months. I know everything there is to know about you, your company, your wife, your rotten marriage, your daughter who hates you and your son's nasty heroin problem. I know about the hundred grand you keep in your safe at home, your whore on Fifty-third Street, and about that nice Dominican girl you met at the Campbell Apartment last week. You should keep it up, by the way. Those selfies you texted her of your junior partner down there really impressed the hell out of her."

Russo closed his eyes and faced Park Avenue again. "Jesus."

Hicks went on. "I know about your accounts in the Cayman's and Belize and in Cuba. I've got all your email accounts, your cell phones, your passwords, your bank accounts, and every other secret you've kept from the world all these years. I know which clients you've stolen from, how much, and when. There's nothing about you I don't know." He leaned forward in his chair. "And none of that will matter as long as you do exactly what I tell you to do."

"Which is what?"

Hicks sat back in his seat. "Anything I know you can deliver."

Russo turned his chair to face him. "And what the hell is that supposed to mean?"

"Exactly what I said. It might involve you giving me information on one of your clients. Or moving money for me. I might need to borrow your boat or one of your cars or vacation houses. I'll never ask you to do anything you're not qualified to do. Whatever it is, whenever I ask for it isn't your concern. You do exactly what I tell you to do when I tell you to do it and your life goes on exactly as it has been until now."

"And if I don't," Russo said, "Vladic gets this file."

Hicks nodded. "So do all of the other clients you've scammed, but I think Vladic will get you first."

Russo drummed his fingers on the desk while he thought it over. "I know I'm no angel, but this is a damned dirty business you're in. Doing this to people trying to make a living."

Hicks smiled. "But it's fun. Especially when I get the chance to screw over a guy like you. But like you said earlier, you're used to being your own boss so let me give you a valuable piece of advice. Don't try to find a way out of our agreement."

Russo pointed at the file on his desk. "What can I do to

you while you've got this?"

"You're thinking that now, but in a few hours after the dust settles, your ego will start eating at you. You might think you can actually do something about this, so I'm warning you now. If you hire someone to investigate me, I'll know about it, and there will be a penalty. If you tell anyone about our arrangement—your priest or your shrink or your girlfriend—I'll know about it, and there will be a penalty. You try to run, I'll find you, and there will be a penalty. If you run, I'll find you," Hicks said, "and I'll drop you off on Vladic's doorstep with that file stapled to your chest. And don't think about killing yourself, either. If you do, that file goes to Vladic and your business partners. Your partners will bankrupt your family and we both know what Vladic will do to your wife and children, especially your daughter. What he lacks in brains he more than makes up for in cruelty."

Russo stopped looking out the window. "Don't threaten my family."

"I'm not threatening anyone, ace. I'm just informing you of what penalties will occur if you try to break our contract. And if you start feeling sorry for yourself, like you've been picked on unjustly, remember that you put yourself in this position by screwing around with other people's money. Vladic's just the only one capable of cooking you over a slow fire for a month before he starts to really hurt you."

Russo sank even further back into his chair. He ran his hands back over his slicked-back hair and let out a long, slow breath. Hicks knew he was still looking for that exit; that escape hatch that would get him out from under all of this. The OMNI profile said he would. The profile also said Russo would accept the bit in time, but he'd buck before he did it. "When does this special relationship of yours start?"

"It started the moment I walked into this office. I'll let you know what I need and when I need it. It might be tonight. It might be never. I'll never ask you for anything you can't deliver, so don't waste time by making excuses if I call. Vladic gets an email. And if I contact you, don't get smart by asking me any details about our discussion here today. I'll just assume you're trying to record me or you have someone listening in. If that happens, Vladic gets an email. Understand?"

Russo closed his eyes and nodded.

"That's not an answer," Hicks said.

"Yes, goddamn you. Yes, I understand."

Hicks slipped his ski cap back on as he stood up and went to the door. He didn't worry about fingerprints because he'd never taken off his gloves. He'd never handled the file he'd given Russo without wearing gloves, either.

He paused before he reached for the knob. "I know you're going to have some sleepless nights over this. But I've been doing this a long time and I know how to make this painless for all of us. Do as you're told and you'll make a lot of money in the bargain. And if it matters, you can find comfort in the fact that you really never had a choice." He finished it off with a smile. "I'll be in touch. And remember, I'll be watching."

Hicks made sure he gave the receptionist a furtive waive as he went for the elevator. He was sure she didn't notice, but it was good to stay in character.

CHAPTER 3

As soon as Hicks got outside, he saw the weather had taken a turn for the worse. Cold wind and heavy snow whipped around him as he crossed Forty-fifth Street toward the MetLife Building on his way to catch the subway at Grand Central. The storm was blowing in right on time, but Hicks didn't mind. The wind and the snow only made him feel more alive than he already did.

Hooking a new Asset always made his day. He imagined salespeople felt the same way after closing a deal. Only this was much better. Because Hicks' thrill wasn't just over closing a deal on a house or selling merchandise. It came from bending a strong person to his will and making them do his bidding. It was a power trip. A boost to his ego. And an essential part of the University's success.

As always, Hicks' happiness was tempered by reality. Despite all his threats, there was always a risk that an Asset might do something drastic like kill himself. Russo's OMNI profile showed a low likelihood of suicide, but not even the University's biometric analytics could predict what a man might do when blackmailed.

Either way, Russo's ego would require some soothing pretty soon; more carrot than stick to appeal to the same greed that had put him in a position to be blackmailed in the first place. Hicks made a note to let Russo move some of the New York Office's fund's money in a day or so. Maybe three or four million to start. Let him make some coin off the commission and see the benefit his new partnership with Hicks could provide.

Hicks had just ridden the escalator from the MetLife Building down into Grand Central when he felt his handheld begin to vibrate in his pocket. He stepped out of the flow of pedestrian traffic and tapped the screen alive.

To anyone passing by, he looked like any other man checking his email on a smartphone. On the off chance the phone was lost or stolen, whoever found it would see a phone with a regular passcode screen. Even if they managed to crack the passcode, they'd find all of the usual apps and features one would expect to find on such a device.

But in reality, Hicks' phone was unlike almost any other device in the world. It had been issued to him by the University and didn't operate on any cellular network available to the public. It only functioned on the University's secure OMNI network.

Hicks entered his four digit passcode that unlocked the

common features of the phone, then tapped on an ambiguous-looking icon that activated the device's camera. The camera scanned Hicks' facial features to verify that he was, indeed, James Hicks.

Another passcode screen automatically opened and asked for a longer twelve-digit password. He entered it and was allowed to access the University's server.

A text message appeared, formatted in the University's usual spare style:

> STUDENT 1357 REQUESTS IMMEDIATE INTERVIEW. 20:00 HRS TONIGHT. LOCATION FORTHCOMING. PLESE ADVISE AS TO AVAILABILITY.

Although the message was properly formatted and relatively short, Hicks still had to read it three more times to understand it. It didn't make any sense.

'Student 1357' was the official University designation for one of his deep cover operatives: Colin Rousseau. He had assigned Colin an undercover role as a driver at a Somali cab outfit in Long Island City, Queens. The owner, a man named Omar Farhan, and several drivers were on the University's terror Watch List, which had a lower threshold than most national watch lists. OMNI had been passively tracking their movements for over a year, and Colin had been working at the cabstand for just over five months. Since Colin's family had originally come from Kenya, he knew enough of the language and customs to blend in without being an obvious plant.

It had been a sleepy assignment and Hicks was thinking of pulling the plug on it. But now, Colin had hit the panic button. When an experienced agent requested an emergency meeting, there had to be a damned good reason.

Hicks wasn't surprised when his handheld showed his Department Chair was calling him. Other professions had the option of allowing unwanted phone calls to go to voicemail. Hicks didn't have that luxury. He knew Jason would only keep calling until Hicks answered because, according to the University's structure, Jason was technically Hicks' boss.

Hicks tapped the icon to allow the call through and brought the handheld up to his ear. "I just got Colin's message."

Jason had never been one for pleasantries or ceremony. "According to your activity log, you had your weekly debriefing with him yesterday."

"I know. I wrote it, remember?"

"And I read it. I didn't see anything there that would suggest a sudden need to meet."

Jason's tone grated on him, until Hicks remembered the Dean of the University had chosen Jason because he wasn't field personnel. Jason was a planner and organizer. If it didn't fall into a cell on a spreadsheet, it held little relevance in Jason's world. Hicks remembered what the Dean had told him when he'd brought Jason on six months before: *Jason is only your superior on paper, James. He's merely your connection to us. Think of him as a link in the protective chain of command. That's all.*

That didn't make working with the son of a bitch any easier. "Field work isn't always predictable. Things like this happen from time to time, but there's no sense in wasting time guessing why he needs to meet. I won't know anything until I actually talk to him."

"I find the sudden urgency of it disturbing. Will you require any assistance?" Jason asked. "Perhaps a Varsity team could be in the area to provide support."

"No thanks." The Varsity was the University's tactical unit, usually reserved for raids or clean up jobs following a hit. Some of them were levelheaded and some were cowboys. He didn't want them anywhere near this kind of meeting. "Colin's my man, my problem. Nothing's going to happen."

"And if it does?"

"Then I'll handle it."

"The Dean is confident that you will. I only wish I shared his confidence. Colin should be sending through the location of the rendezvous in a moment, if he's still following protocol. We'll decide then what precautions are best."

Jason killed the connection and Hicks' screen went dark. Jason always had been a last word freak.

The handheld vibrated again as the location for the meeting had come through. Despite the security of their network, the University had an elaborate, often cumbersome, security protocol for emergency circumstances. Undercover personnel called emergency meetings and could call the location. They could only go through the Switchboard and weren't allowed to contact their handlers directly.

Since most University operatives were usually imbedded with sophisticated, careful terrorist groups, this protocol protected agent and handler alike. The agent called a central number, gave the handler's call sign and message. An operator then transmitted the insisted on often separated key parts of their messages. Locations of meetings were up to the field agent and seldom included in a message requesting a meeting. If the agent was in distress, there were subtle phrases to use that would alert the University that they were being forced to call in. Colin's message had no such warning, so Hicks assumed he was clear.

A map application with the address opened and showed exactly where Colin wanted to meet. Under a footbridge in Central Park at eight o'clock that night.

During the predicted height of the coming blizzard.

Hicks pocketed his handheld and headed down to the subway. There was no sense in questioning the message or looking at the map any more than he already had. He could ask himself all sorts of questions and speculate all he wanted, but he knew it wouldn't do a damned bit of good. He wouldn't know what all of this was about until he spoke to Colin.

Until then, he had plenty of work to do.

CHAPTER 4

20:00 Hrs / 8:00PM

Hicks felt like the artic explorers of old as he trudged through almost a foot of heavy snow toward Central Park. The streets were unplowed and deserted and there wasn't a cab in sight. The MTA had recalled all buses and subways hours ago because of the storm, so walking was the only way he could get uptown. He didn't mind. He'd been in worse weather in worse parts of the world; often with people trying to kill him. Besides, he had short barreled .454 Ruger in the pocket of his parka to keep him warm. He usually preferred the compact feel of a .22 but, given the wind, he went with a higher caliber. Most would've gone for an automatic, but Hicks preferred revolvers. No worries about the damned thing jamming at the wrong time.

Hicks thought a lot about Colin and his phone call as he

trudged through the snow. He'd spent the afternoon and early evening on the University's system analyzing Colin's phone and computer activity. OMNI was tied in to every ISP and mobile service in the world—had been from the beginning—so access to virtually every web-enabled device was only a few mouse clicks away. No other agency had that kind of access. Not even the NSA. The Snowden mess proved that. The Snowden mess also validated the University's obsession with secrecy, even in the intelligence world.

None of Colin's digital activity proved suspicious except for the lack of it in the past day or so. Colin was like most people in the twenty-first century: addicted to his phone. He mostly visited sports sights and online Islamic bulletin boards. He scanned Al Jazeera and the New York Times. When no one was around, he watched SportsCenter clips online and porn sites. Hicks knew Colin had a weakness for Asian chicks and his surfing history proved it.

Since he was undercover, Colin wasn't allowed to have a University device. He went with an independent wireless carrier instead. Just because University devices couldn't be hacked didn't mean the Dean allowed their equipment to be put in harm's way. Operatives were trained, but they were human and humans made mistakes. They lost phones and left them at friends' houses. They got drunk and left them behind. No need to tempt fate. Terrorists got lucky. 9/11 had proven that, too.

Colin had been a rock since Hicks had taken over the University's New York office three years before. Colin had joined the U.S. Army when he was eighteen and had shown a capacity for languages and an immigrant's love for country.

He'd found a home in Intelligence and eventually came to work for the University ten years before.

Hicks had worked with him in other parts of the world and was glad he'd been able to talk him into transferring to the New York Office. Colin was a rare breed who could work deep cover or handle the tactical aspects of the job seamlessly. He could imbed with the bad guys or run a raid on a cell with equal efficiency. And Hicks had every intention of nominating him for Office Head next time an opening came up.

Hicks had fully expected Colin to balk at the cab stand assignment, but he didn't. Hicks had shown him the file and explained the cab stand owner—Omar—was a Somali with some radical tendencies. He mostly hired Somali drivers with equally radical tendencies.

It was the kind of posting some in the University had classified as a cold assignment, but Hicks' gut said different. Too many rotten eggs in one place always raised a stink and he wanted eyes on them for a while. The cab stand vibed amateur, but it only took one strike to bring a cell into the pros. The tacit digital surveillance Hicks had placed on their phones and computers led him to believe Omar and his boys would pull a job if someone gave them a chance—and enough money—to pull it off.

That's why Colin's sudden request for a meeting made Hicks wonder if he'd been right. And he was glad he'd brought the Ruger to keep him company. Trust, but verify.

By the time Hicks finally reached Central Park, the sky glowed purple high above the barren trees. Central Park South was usually filled with tourists and horse-drawn carriages lined up to take said tourists on a ride inside the park. The blizzard had chased them all inside, except for the rare die-hard cabbie looking for a fare.

The weather inside the park was even more severe than out on the street. Snow had been blown into drifts almost shin-high, even on the paths that had once been clear. The wind blew the whole mess in a wild, circular motion.

The park was deserted and Hicks hoped it stayed that way. He hated surprises and a snowbound park wasn't ideal for surprises. Footprints in the snow betrayed early arrivals. Tough going made it hard to sneak up unannounced. Harsh wind fucked with bullet trajectory. Maybe that's why Colin had picked it? He certainly hoped so.

The wind picked up steadily the farther he got into the park; with the snow turning into a driving sleet just as he reached the footbridge. Hicks pulled back the sleeve of his parka and checked his watch. He was ten minutes early. He normally liked to arrive a half hour early, but trudging through shin-deep snowdrifts had fouled up his ETA.

But as he got closer to the footbridge, he saw Colin was already there. University protocol was clear: Operatives were never supposed to be on site until their Faculty Member cleared the site first. Colin knew University protocol better than anyone.

Red flag.

Hicks slowed as he scanned the area as best he could through the sleet and snow. There was no sign of fresh footprints in the snow leading to the site, meaning Colin must've entered through the west side of the park. It looked like he'd come alone, but he wouldn't be able to tell much until he was under the shelter of the footbridge. By then, it would be too late to do anything but react

University protocol was clear on this point, too: if an Operative fails to meet exact protocol, turn around and walk away.

Protocol had its place, but Colin was Hicks' man. He already knew something was off about the whole set up. He gripped the handle of the Ruger in his pocket. Just in case.

The closer Hicks got, the less he liked what he saw. Colin was normally laid back to the point of appearing to be careless. Nothing ever seemed to bother him or upset him or make him happy. Hicks had never known him to betray any emotion other than what his cover required. He was an emotional blank slate, which had made him ideal for the kind of undercover work Hicks assigned him.

But now, Colin was pacing back and forth like a caged animal. He was also constantly blowing into gloved hands. His head was uncovered and his eyes were wide. He appeared nervous and twitchy like a junkie jonesing for a fix. And Colin never drank or used drugs.

Hicks kept his hand on the Ruger in his pocket as he joined Colin under the footbridge. "What's going on?"

"Things, man. Things." Colin kept pacing and muttering to himself. "Things you don't know, man. Things you can't see. Things you don't want to know and don't want to see, see?"

Hicks had only seen Colin two days before, but he looked like he'd aged ten years since then. His eyes were red and his pupils were pinpoints. He looked like he hadn't slept in days and Hicks wondered if he had.

He looked and acted high. Like coke or heroin high, which was a problem. Because Colin didn't do stimulants. He hated needles and alcohol gave him a headache. Even beer.

Red flag number two.

Hicks went to grab his arm, but Colin jumped back; slipping on the icy snow that had drifted under the footbridge. He fell back against the wall of the underpass and stared up at him, eyes wild. "You've gotta pull me out, boss. You gotta pull me out, now. I don't have time to explain, but it's bad, man. Real, real bad. These boys ain't playing and… and, oh, you've gotta pull me out, and you've gotta pull me out right now."

Hicks kept checking both ends of the tunnel. None of this felt right. Colin had always been solid and he never panicked. And he didn't pace back and forth and babble like this. Hicks had seen panic and burnout in Operatives before. Panic was as a part of Intel life as breathing. People did odd things when they panicked. They were late or they were early or they were hiding near by or they ran to him they saw him. But they never stayed in the open, pacing back and forth like Colin was doing now.

Like a goat tied to a stake in the ground.

Hicks didn't try to help him. He pulled the Ruger and kept it flat against his side as he kept an eye on the western approach to the underpass; backing up the way he'd come, glancing over his shoulder as he moved. "Let's get out of here, Colin. Let's go somewhere warm where we can talk. Just you and me."

Colin pawed at the stone wall as he crept away from Hicks. "Don't touch me, man! I don't need you touching me.

I need you to get me out of here, that's all. I need you to get me the hell out of here and away from these people."

Hicks kept backing up; the Magnum flat against his leg. He felt the snow and sleet begin to hit the back of his hood. "Then come with me, and let's get the hell out of here. This way. Right now."

But Colin kept inching along the wall back toward the western entrance to the underpass. "Wait, man. Just... just wait a second, okay? We gotta talk, come up with a plan, you know? Get this straight before we go anywhere so we can..."

Hicks brought up his Ruger when he saw a shadow move at the western end of the underpass. Someone else would've dismissed it as a tree branch moving in front of a streetlight, but not Hicks. He'd spent his life in shadow. He knew the difference.

Colin began to shriek as two men spilled out onto the snowy footpath at the western entrance. The nearest man regained his footing first. Hicks saw a small video camera in his hand. The son of a bitch must've been filming the whole thing.

The other man was farther back, next to a snow-covered bush just off to the side of the path. Colin began to squeal as the man aimed at him. Hicks fired twice just as the gun came around. Both rounds hit him in the middle of the chest. The man's gun fired once as he stumbled back into the blizzard.

The man with the video camera slipped again as he tried to run away; belly-flopping on the walkway but not dropping the camera. He scrambled to his knees, trying to get his feet under him despite the thick snow. Hicks didn't wait for him to get to his balance and shot him in the temple. The cameraman's head flinched at the impact of the bullet before he collapsed dead on the pathway. The video camera was still strapped to his hand.

A sharp wind picked up, blowing snow and sleet into the underpass. Hicks didn't hear a sound, not even the echo of his gunfire.

Not even Colin's screaming.

Hicks found Colin slumped against the wall; a bullet hole in his neck; a red streak tracking the path he had fallen against the wall. The gunman's errant shot had caught him in the throat, and he was steadily bleeding out into the snow.

Hicks knew calling for help was pointless. With that kind of a wound, he'd soon be dead if he wasn't already. Besides, despite everything they'd been through together, the son of a bitch had just set him up.

Hicks crept forward; listening as he swept the area outside the western approach with the Rugerin case anyone else was hiding in the shadows. All he found was a whole lot of snow and the two men he'd just killed. The only footprints he saw showed three men approaching the site and the prints they'd made running away. He lowered his Ruger and listened as the snow and sleet fell around him. Gunshots usually drove everyone away except for cops. And cops were the last thing he needed just then.

Hicks reverted back to his training. He ignored the wind and the sleet and the snow and simply listened for sirens, a police radio, a barking dog, a stifled sneeze. Anything that would tell him if someone was nearby. But all he heard was the wind in his ears and the sleet hitting his skin. A quiet park on a snowy night. The scene would've been postcard perfect if it hadn't been for the three dead men at his feet.

Hicks took a knee and began patting down the dead men's pockets; starting with the gunman. He took in everything at once: the thick, hooded parka, the black ski mask, and the sneakers. He took a closer look at the footwear: cheap Air Jordan knockoffs. The cameraman was in a similar getup, too.

Why the heavy coat and lousy footwear in a blizzard they'd been predicting for days, especially for a hit in a park? It didn't make any sense.

Hicks pulled off the gunman's ski mask so he could get a clear face shot of it with his handheld. The face was unfamiliar but common: thin and black, between twenty and forty and slack in death. He looked too thin to be American and, judging by where Colin had been working undercover, probably Somali. Hicks had never seen either of them in person or in in any of the surveillance images from the cab stand, either. Whoever these men were, they were new players to the game and they wouldn't be playing any longer.

Hicks activated the secure features of his phone and took a picture of the gunman's face. He pulled the ski mask and hood back the way they'd been, then used his phone to scan the dead man's fingerprints. The man hadn't been wearing a glove on his gun hand.

Hicks went through the same procedure on the cameraman—also a black man who Hicks had never seen before. He took a picture of his face and scanned his fingerprints, then uploaded the information to OMNI. If their faces or fingerprints were on record with any government in the world, he'd know about it in less than an hour. If not, the network would automatically begin running image checks on every kind of camera available from that spot to see if it could find a match locating where they'd come from. ATM machines, security cameras, traffic cameras, and even images posted on social media would all be scanned by OMNI; thousands of images per second until they had an idea of who these men were and where they'd come from.

He patted down both men. No wallets. No car keys. Nothing that could help identify either of them. That meant they'd planned this, but if they'd planned it so well, why the lousy footwear? They hadn't just hopped out of a car and shot at him on a whim. They hadn't tried a drive by either. Colin had picked this place, specifically a secluded part of the park. Why do that if he was setting him up for a hit? Was he trying to warn Hicks somehow? If not, why not use one of the distress codes they'd agreed upon?

Hicks took the video camera from the dead man's hand and examined it. It had been on and recording the entire time. He checked to see if it was broadcasting over a wireless hub, but it wasn't. It was recording straight to the camera's SD card.

That was another thing that bothered him. Why a camera? Why not use the camera in a cellphone? The quality was just as good as a stand-alone device. It was just another thing to carry. He'd make a point of examining the camera later. For now, he simply shut it off and put it in one of the deep pockets of his parka.

Hicks searched Colin's body last. No keys, no wallet. No Metrocard, either. No weapon of any kind. Not even a knife. Nothing that explained his betrayal, either. Hicks knew he had a hell of a lot of work to do before he could make sense of any of this.

Hicks stood up and checked the scene one last time to see if he'd missed any clues or relevant evidence. Of course, he hadn't. He looked down at Colin last. *Why did you turn, my friend? How could you...*

Hicks realized 'how' was the answer. Or rather, 'how' was the question.

How did you get here without money or a Metrocard? The subways and buses aren't running due to the blizzard. How the hell did they get all the way to Central Park from Long Island City in the middle of a blizzard?

Colin's initial call to the Switchboard had come in around noon. They'd begun shutting down the subways at two o'clock to beat the storm. Had they sat around the park for eight hours in the middle of blizzard just to set him up?

No. Someone had brought them there. And Hicks bet that same someone was probably still waiting to pick them up. Somewhere close by.

Hicks reloaded the Ruger and began following the footprints of the dead men in the snow. He retraced their steps west, walking into the wind. At this rate, their footsteps would be obliterated in less than an hour, but Hicks wouldn't need that long. He'd tracked men in worse conditions than this.

The sleet and the wind picked up, causing the trees above to sway and creak. He scanned the snowy landscape for any signs of movement, but all he saw was the park's street lamps struggling to provide light. He bet that whoever was waiting for Colin and the others was probably in a car with the engine running. Nice and warm. And easy to spot.

Hicks slowed when he reached the park entrance on Seventy-second Street; ducking his head into the wind more than he had to. It was just enough to hide his face, but not enough to block his view of the street.

He spotted a late model Toyota Corolla on the west corner of Seventy-second and Central Park West. Lights on, motor running. Hicks couldn't see the driver clearly through the sleet, but realized the driver must've seen him. He heard the gear creak as the driver took the car out of park and threw it into drive.

Hicks brought up his handheld and thumbed the camera feature of his handheld alive. He aimed the camera at the car as it pulled away and waited for the handheld to locate the car's black box. Every car made since the mid-nineties had one. It was like waiting for a device to find a wireless network, only this search was much faster. The phone found the black box transmitter and pinged it back to him. He tapped the University's tracking feature on his phone and sent the protocol to the University's OMNI system. Now the system would track the car wherever it went.

Ping, motherfucker. Gottcha.

Hicks put his handheld in one pocket and the Ruger in the other. He saw no reason to go back to the footbridge and decided to turn left; walking south along Central Park West. He typed in a five-digit code on his handheld and waited for someone at the Varsity desk to answer.

Despite the security of the University's closed network, a strict standard protocol was observed every time a field agent contacted the main switchboard. "Switchboard. How may I help you?"

He knew the operator already had his name and location on her screen. "This is Mr. Warren," he said, using the pre-assigned codename that told the operator he was safe and not being forced to talk. "I need to schedule a pickup."

"For when?"

"As soon as possible."

"Understood, sir." He heard a few clicks of a keyboard. "And the pickup would be at your previous location?"

Hicks knew they'd tracked him to the footbridge. His handheld always emitted a tracking signal, but Jason had probably earmarked his signal for priority surveillance. He'd probably already had a Varsity team staged nearby. "That's right. Three items."

"Very well. We'll send someone out for it right away. Thank you for calling."

The line went dead, and Hicks put the phone away. He could've gone back into the park and waited until the Varsity's cleanup squad showed up, but he decided to keep trudging south through the snow on his own. It was best to put as much distance between him and the dead men as possible. The men he'd killed and the friend he'd gotten killed.

He knew the Varsity would take the three bodies back to a University facility where full autopsies would be performed. The purpose wasn't so much for determining cause of death, but charting DNA and other biological statistics that might come in handy later on. Having a dead man's DNA can often prove useful.

Besides, he didn't like the Varsity crowd anyway and the feeling was mutual. There had always been a professional tension between the University's Faculty and Varsity members, not unlike the Marines and the Navy. Each branch worked its side of the street and, on the rare event when the two overlapped, it usually meant something had gone terribly wrong.

And a turned agent qualified as something that had gone terribly wrong.

Despite the thickness of his parka, Hicks felt his handheld buzz again. He expected to see Jason was calling and was sorry to see he was right. A blizzard and a gunfight wasn't enough for one night. Now he had to deal with this terse son of a bitch.

Hicks answered the phone with the standard University all-clear protocol. "This is Warren."

"What the hell happened back there?"

"Weren't you watching the whole thing on OMNI?"

"No," Jason said. "If we'd had you on satellite, I would already know what had happened and I wouldn't be asking you. So, what the hell happened?

Despite the security of the University's closed network, Hicks still kept it vague. "Looks like Colin set me up. He came to the rendezvous point with a two-man backup team. One shooter, one cameraman."

"A cameraman? Was he broadcasting?"

"No. It was a small hand-held number you'd find in any electronics shop. I'll take a closer look at it back at the office. No ID on any of them, including Colin."

"Are they dead?"

"If they weren't, I would be. Which, for the record, I'm not."

Jason was silent for a beat. "Sarcasm is not appreciated,

James."

"Neither are stupid fucking questions. You know goddamned well I just called in a Varsity team for a pick up. I wouldn't have done that if I'd left them making snowmen in the park."

He heard Jason's keyboard clicking. "I see you've uploaded the faces and prints of the dead men to OMNI. I take it you didn't recognize them?"

"No, just Colin. They turned him, Jason. I don't know how the hell they did it, but they did it."

"We'll find out how and why eventually," Jason said. "You know we will. We always do." He managed to sound concerned. "Are you hurt?"

"No." Hicks had more important things to do than worry about himself. "I shot both of the backup team. The gunman fired as he went down and hit Colin in the throat. I think I found their transport vehicle waiting for them at Seventy-second Street..."

"I know. We're tracking it, and it's heading uptown now. I've got someone en route to track him further uptown in case he gets out of the car. Don't worry about him." He heard Jason clicking on his keyboard. "Varsity Team verifies that it's five minutes out. I want you to double back and ride in with them. We can have a secure debrief from our facility. I know how difficult this must be for you. Colin and you were... close."

Hicks kept walking south. "You're wrong. You have no idea how difficult this is. I'm better off on my own."

He knew Jason didn't like to be rebuked. He wasn't in the mood to care. He'd just killed two people and lost an operative he'd known for a decade. If Jason wanted an argument, Hicks would be happy to give him one.

"Have it your way, but I'll expect a full debriefing in person tomorrow."

Hicks stopped trudging through the snow. A sharp wind slammed into him only to be offset by a cross current that kept him on his feet. "You're coming to New York?"

"That's what in person means, doesn't it?" Jason said. "Same time and location as before. Don't be late." The connection went dead.

Once again, Hicks put the handheld back in his pocket and closed his eyes. The sleet had let up, giving way once again to heavy snow. He could feel his temper beginning to build, so he concentrated on being calm and tried to control his breathing.

He'd just lost a good operative. He'd just shot two strangers dead. He'd retrieved good intel and was tracking a suspected transport vehicle. He had material and evidence to examine. The entire idea of the University was built on mobility and digital connectivity. Instant dissemination of information from a variety of positions throughout the globe was what had set it apart from any other intelligence agency. Briefing Jason in person was a waste of valuable time that could be spent tracking Colin's movements and running checks on the backgrounds of the dead men.

But the Dean had told him to work with Jason. To help him become a better Department Chair. So that's what he'd do. Because as much as Hicks hated following orders, he ultimately followed them. Because he had no reason not to.

He pulled his hood a little tighter around his head and leaned into the wind as he headed back to the office he called home.

CHAPTER
5

WHEN HICKS MADE it back to the Office over an hour later, he shut the vault door behind him and fell back against it. The lock mechanism was programmed to engage automatically and the door vibrated as the bolts slid home.

He hadn't felt this exhausted in a long time.

Every day, Hicks undertook a vigorous workout routine. He did extensive cardio work and could lift weights far heavier than someone his size should. Yoga and stretching exercises followed. He didn't look like a strong man and that was the general idea. But after an hour pushing through driving sleet and heavy snow, he barely had the strength to take off his parka. He knew it wasn't just physical exhaustion, but didn't want to dwell on Colin or what had happened in the park. Not yet. He just stood with the back of his head against the door and breathed; grateful for the cold steel of the vault door to dull his growing headache.

The novelty of working in a vault below West Twenty-third Street had lost its effect on Hicks long ago. Three years before—when the Dean had assigned him to run the University's New York office—his directive was clear: make the New York office a model for the University's future.

The first order of business had been to set up a proper base of operations.

The University's New York presence had been little more than a joke since the end of the Cold War in the early nineties. Not even 9/11 had done much to change that. The University's Boston, D.C., and Los Angeles offices had been held in much higher regard and did the lion's share of the University's intelligence work within the United States. Even Miami had a higher standing.

New York had become viewed as a vanity post; little more than window dressing and probably would've been closed altogether if the U.N. hadn't been headquartered there.

The New York office of that time bore little resemblance to the high-tech spaces shown on television shows and movies; with trim, young people in dark suits darting around as they sifted though intelligence data on the latest technological devices. Flat screen televisions, high-speed Internet connections and satellite surveillance.

Until Hicks took over, the University's New York office was simply a part-time operation run out of John Holloway's cluttered York Avenue apartment. Holloway had been the University's point man in the war against Communism once upon a time. But time catches up to all men, spies most of all, and Holloway gradually became a doddering academic more interested in the dusty first editions of his library and attending policy conferences than doing any actual intelligence work. The only information Holloway ever sent back to the Dean was whatever he'd managed to cobble together from the boozy gossip he'd fielded from minor diplomats at U.N. cocktail parties. Holloway had never been fond of technology, and thought his ability to forward Council on Foreign Relations e-newsletters to the Dean was something of an amazing technological accomplishment.

The end came on one drizzly spring morning when the legendary John Holloway when a mailman found him lying dead between two parked cars off First Avenue. His dog—a white Pomeranian he'd named Publius—licking his face.

The University's private autopsy report revealed Old Holloway had died of cardiac arrest due to clogged arteries from years of too much pâté and red wine at too many cocktail parties.

The Dean mourned the death of his mentor, but when he named Hicks as the New York Office Head, it was with a clear mission: make the New York Office relevant again.

The Dean had given him a healthy budget to find a place and advised him to hide in plain sight. Rent an office or buy a large apartment some place and keep a low profile. But regular office buildings were difficult to secure and often more trouble than they were worth. Running the operation out of an apartment or condo was risky, too. Supers with pass keys. Nosey neighbors. Even burglars.

He needed something quiet and not easily found. Something without windows or other tenants. In New York, that was a tall order, but not impossible.

Because Hicks had a plan.

While working in Tel Aviv a few months before coming to New York, he'd learned of a local developer looking to expand his family's fortune by investing in Manhattan real estate. He had just closed on a row of dilapidated townhouses in the west Twenties. This particular developer came from a strong Israeli family who despised the Palestinians. This particular developer had built a fortune of his own by quietly accepting Palestinian investments in his projects back in Israel.

Hicks showed the developer the evidence and made him an offer: give him the ground floor and basement of one of his new buildings and enough space for a sub-basement beneath all three buildings and forget about it. No rent, no lease, no sale. Say no, and the family finds out you've been laundering money for the PLO.

The developer complied.

The result was the University's New York office: a hidden concrete shelter buried beneath the basements of three townhouses on West Twenty-third Street. The University had arranged for secure contractors to build the facility quietly and quickly. Some creative manipulation of the city's building department's records allowed the construction to occur without government interference.

The garden apartment on street level was just for show. It looked benign enough from the outside: curtains on the windows, lights in the windows, even furniture and a full book case if anyone looked inside. People on the upper floors paid a good amount in rent, too.

The stairs down to the basement from the garden

apartment looked normal. The boiler served the two legal apartments above, but the washer and drier had never been used. The basement was merely a stop-gap that led to the subbasement. It was sealed by an ordinary looking wooden door with a large knob and lock. But there was no key to the door and the knob didn't turn. The door could only be opened by reading the biometrics in Hicks' hand when he gripped the doorknob while a camera scanned his facial features at the same time. When the two matched, the hatch opened.

It was an independent structure built with steel reenforced concrete. The facility ran off the city's power grid, but had three backup generators as well as a gas fueled back up. It had its own HVAC unit complete with filters and sensors that could detect radiation and poisonous emissions.

The entire building above him could get obliterated by a nuclear blast and Hicks would still be able to operate for three weeks before he'd have to venture outside.

The computer system, like his handheld, was tied wirelessly to the University's secure network, with a redundant cable line piped directly to the mainframe, which was only activated in an emergency.

But that night, he was just glad the damned place had heat because he was freezing.

Hicks put on a pot of fresh coffee as soon as he shrugged out of his parka and heavy boots. He brought the dead man's camera to the work station and booted up his computer before replacing his guns in the armory. The armory was the size of a walk in closet that was larger than some studio apartments in Manhattan. It was filled with more Kevlar vests, automatic weapons, explosives, and ammunition than most police precincts. The facility was a designated fall back position for the University, meaning that if it ever needed to, Hicks' office could become a forward operations base. He couldn't envision a scenario when that would be necessary, but then again, he hadn't imagined an attack like 9/11 either.

Despite its status as an official University facility, he'd managed to keep its exact location secret from everyone except the Dean. Jason had spent the last six months trying to figure out where it was, but Hicks kept stonewalling him, more out of enjoying Jason's frustration than anything else. The less that bureaucrat knew, the better.

Hicks secured the armory door and went back to his living area to change out of his clothes. His personal living space was in the farthest corner of the room from the work station. Although the bunker was also his home, he viewed it as primarily a workspace. He didn't have any posters or personal photos or personal touches of any kind. He liked it that way. Besides, he had no family worth remembering anyway. Just the computer equipment, a bed, a walk in closet for his clothes and other gear.

Hicks waited for the coffee to finish brewing and tried to keep his thoughts in check. He'd been racking his brain for signs of Colin's betrayal. Little things he could've missed. Hints Colin might've dropped that something was wrong.

But Hicks knew he hadn't missed anything. Colin's debrief had gone smoothly and he had nothing new to report, aside from the general anti-American banter that went on at Omar's cab stand. Big talk and vitriolic rancor meant nothing. Men like Omar ran down America the way Yankees fans ran down the Red Sox. Hicks and Colin had even begun to wonder if they should put Colin on another assignment and return to a more passive surveillance of Omar's cab stand. Tracing cell phone calls and emails as they came through the grid might suffice.

But the Colin he'd seen under the footbridge just over an hour before was not the Colin he'd known. Whatever had terrified him must have occurred within the past forty-eight hours. The question was why. The answer had to be Omar. So that's where Hicks was going to begin.

Hicks logged into the system to see if OMNI had been able to make positive identifications of the two men he'd killed. The system was still running identity checks, but Hicks' instincts told him the two men were Somali. They had that same gaunt, haunted look of the other Somalis that Omar had hired at the cab stand. He knew Omar also thought other Africans were weak and susceptible to corruption from the West which was why he hired mostly his own people. Colin's cover had been feasible since his parents had been from a region of Kenya on the Somalian border, which Omar deemed acceptable.

Colin had told Hicks that most of Omar's drivers were sons of farmers; young men who'd gotten to America more out of desperation than Islamic ideology. If going along with Omar's ranting kept money in their pocket and a roof over their heads, they went along with it. According to Colin, Omar was the only hardcore radical at his stand.

That meant whatever had happened at the cab stand to turn Colin had happened since the debrief. Hicks intended on finding out what.

While OMNI kept searching for identities, Hicks scanned recent email and cell phone intercepts from Omar's cab company and all of its workers. Many of them bought disposable phones—also called burn phones, believing that would make it harder for agencies to eavesdrop. In some cases, they were right, but most agencies didn't have the University's resources. Any phone activated near the garage was immediately tagged and followed for the duration of the phone's life. Every conversation was transcribed, tracked and recorded by OMNI and deciphered by University programs and human analysts. Most of it was just mundane, every day chatter, but every so often, something valuable turned up.

In reviewing the OMNI reports on all emails, text messages, and conversations from phones that had been near the garage in the past forty-eight hours, Hicks didn't find anything suspicious, but that was to be expected. OMNI software translated and deciphered all conversations and emails and texts, listening for key phrases and code words and patterns. Nothing out of the ordinary came up, but Hicks ordered OMNI to re-scrub the conversations to see if he could catch anything new about Colin.

Then Hicks took a look at the camera he'd taken from the dead man in the park. He removed the SD card from the camera and placed it in his computer's drive. After scanning it locally for a virus, he watched the footage from the beginning.

The man had begun filming as soon as Hicks walked into the underpass. The image jerked and went out of focus as the cameraman tried to keep Hicks in frame. Colin looked even more strung out and timid than Hicks had remembered.

The footage jerked wildly as the cameraman lost his footing and slipped from where he'd been standing and lead started flying. The camera was still shooting when the cameraman caught a bullet to the head and died.

The last image on the SD card was of Hicks' face as he pulled the camera from the dead man's hand before shutting it off.

The footage didn't tell him anything he didn't already know, but it told him something. Judging by the way the camera shook, the cameraman had been standing in the cold for a while. It also confirmed that these boys were amateurs. Pros would've had better equipment. They would've outfitted Colin with a small camera somewhere in his clothing. They would've picked a location where they could've seen Hicks without being spotted. They would've dressed warmer and had better clothes than cheap Jordan knockoffs. And they wouldn't have been waiting to shoot him with a gun in their bare hand in a blizzard.

The whole scene vibed desperation. It vibed panic. It vibed intent with no thought given to execution. These men were underfunded and undermanned and inexperienced as hell. Colin must've done something or saw something that scared them and now they were scrambling to protect whatever Colin had threatened.

Hicks ran the serial number stamped on the bottom of the camera and found out it was made in China and bought at a Best Buy in Long Island City, Queens. A cash transaction over two years before. He tried to access the store's surveillance camera footage from the time of the purchase, but it had been long since deleted.

Hicks put his computer to work on the disk to analyze it for other images. Even if a file or image had been deleted or recorded over, the disk might show a trace of what had been on the disk before. And unless the camera had been sitting in a closet some place since it had been bought—or if the SD card was new—chances were good that there'd be something on that card he could use.

While he watched the progress bar of the scan crawl from left to right, Hicks cut, then lit, a cigar: a Nat Sherman Timeless Churchill. It was a long smoke that would keep him focused and grounded while the technology did its job. Even with all of the gadgets and gizmos at the University's disposal, the intelligence game was still a waiting game. A patient man's game. Because intelligence involved human beings and, even in a high tech world, human beings were unpredictable. They moved at their own pace. Technology was a tool, but human beings decided how to use it.

Hicks let out a long plume of bluish smoke and watched it drift up toward the air scrubber in the ceiling. The fan pulled the smoke from the room and the carbon filters scrubbed the air clean. He wondered what Jason would say if he saw him smoking a cigar in a University facility. He'd probably fire off a terse memorandum reminding him that smoking was prohibited in all University facilities.

And Hicks would've politely reminded him this was technically not a University facility. After Holloway's death, Hicks had built the New York office from the ground up through his own means. Extortion, blackmail, and good old fashioned thievery were all fair when assembling a vital intelligence network. He funded his New York Office much the same way. He'd broken an awful lot of laws and even more bones to build the New York office into the flagship of the modern University's network. And although the Dean had given his approval, he'd given little else beside the hardware and remote access to OMNI to make it happen.

Hicks wanted it that way. He'd never wanted to be just a clock watcher, some asshole who scribbled down bits of information he overheard and entered them into a database while he calculated his pension every month. He'd been trained to take the fight directly to the enemy and he couldn't do that from behind a computer screen. He'd crafted his office to be the tip of the spear and he kept it very sharp. Sharp enough to cut anyone who got in front of it. Including people like Jason.

To Hicks, the only thing more important than the University's overall goal was protecting the New York Office. Whoever had turned Colin had also threatened Hicks' operation. His natural impulse was to order a Varsity squad to hit Omar's garage as soon as possible. But he also knew a raid would only confirm Omar's idea that he was being watched.

Hicks didn't know what Omar knew or what Omar suspected. Colin had been trained to lie under interrogation, but he'd died before Hicks could've questioned him. Ordering a Varsity raid on Omar's garage would only confirm Omar's suspicions that he was being watched. Hicks decided to investigate him in other, more subtle ways.

Hicks took another long pull on his cigar and looked at the status bar of the SD card's scan. He willed the scan to go faster, but knew it would take as long as it took. He took another pull on his cigar instead. He just hoped there would be something on that disk he could show Jason because he didn't want to get dressed down by that goddamned bean counter first thing in the morning.

He'd just flicked his cigar ash for the first time when the search program pinged that it was finished. He clicked on the results and saw three ghost images that had been recorded over on the card. The first two were blurred shots of something that looked like a ceiling and maybe the top of a woman's head. It was as though someone had turned on the camera by accident.

But the third shot was solid gold.

It would've made great blackmail material had he recognized anyone in the shot worth blackmailing. Pure party time action.

Instead, it showed a black woman in a hotel room, looking to be in the middle of a striptease. The street ink above her left breast was a crude image of a dollar sign. Her blonde dreadlocks covered her face.

But in the background, there was a black man in the bathroom, stark naked as he serviced a woman from behind who was bent over the sink. His face was obscured, but the reflection in the mirror was clear. It took a couple of seconds for the program to clear up the image, but when it did, the man's face was as clear as a passport photo. He was also black, but lighter skinned than any of Omar's Somalis. He was otherwise clean shaven except for a pencil thin moustache. Hicks had never seen him before, but knew the image would be clear enough for OMNI to identify him. If he was in any database in the world, they'd find him.

Hicks selected the man's face, pasted it into the OMNI facial recognition software, linked it to the two previous searches of the dead men and let the system go to work. He took another long drag on his cigar and let the technology do its thing.

He had no idea who the man was or if he had anything to do with what had happened in the park. He could've just been a guy who'd gotten his picture taken during a drunken night out with the boys. He could've been the reason why Colin was dead. That was the problem with intelligence work. A definite maybe was often the best one could hope for. But wars had been started over less.

Hicks' had no intention of just sitting around waiting for the searches to run their course. He brought up the OMNI tactical screen for New York City and selected the trace he'd put on the car that sped away from him outside Central Park. OMNI had tracked the Toyota as far north as an indoor parking garage just off Broadway up in Washington Heights. The program showed the car had driven straight there after leaving Central Park West and got there in about thirty minutes. Pretty good time considering the streets hadn't been plowed yet.

There was no proof linking the driver to the Somalis in the park, but someone going that fast in that kind of weather must've had a reason. Hicks clicked on the icon showing last location where the satellite had tracked the car. According to the car's black box, the car was registered to Mr. Jacfar Abrar at an address in Long Island City, Queens.

The same part of Queens where Colin had been working undercover. According to immigration records, Abrar was also Somali. Just like Omar.

Hicks clicked on Abrar's file, which opened a window showing Abrar's Somali passport photo, age, height, and resident alien status. He didn't look like either of the men Hicks had killed in the park. Abrar didn't look familiar from any of the surveillance photos Colin had taken of cab company regulars, either. Hicks wouldn't know for sure until the system had identified the other the two dead men and the man from the camera, but it looked like three new players were in Omar's operation. The question was why them and why now.

He had OMNI scan Abrar's cell phone records, ATM, and credit card accounts. His cellphone hadn't been on since noon the day before and had last been located at the cab stand. He sent out a ping to turn it on, but the battery had either been removed or was dead. There'd been no cell signal coming from the vehicle while OMNI was tracking it, so chances were, he didn't have a cellphone on him either. And there'd been no sign of him anywhere since the car had been parked in Washington Heights.

Hicks flicked his cigar ash in the ashtray and thought about going to bed. It was only going on eleven, but he was tired and knew Jason would be ruthless during the meeting in the morning. He loved finding inconsistencies between written reports and verbal summaries even in the best of times. Now that an Asset had been killed, he'd be relentless.

Hicks decided he'd better write up a summary of what had happened in the park and make sure he went through his last report to Jason for anything he could use to hang him. Sleep suddenly dropped way down the priority list.

Then the search icon on his monitor blinked, showing OMNI had identified all three men he'd searched for. But when he clicked on the icon to retrieve the results, he saw the following message:

PLEASE CONTACT YOUR DEPARTMENT CHAIR FOR
MORE INFORMATION.

Son of a bitch. Jason had blocked him from seeing the results.

Hicks felt his temper beginning to spiral again, so he sat back in his chair and took a long drag on his cigar instead. An agent in the morgue, two dead hostiles and a third on the loose and Jason was playing parlor games with information.

Hicks knew he'd better review every one of Colin's status reports for the last six months before his debrief with Jason. He poured himself another cup of coffee. He knew there was a damned good chance he'd need to make another pot.

CHAPTER 6

THE NEXT MORNING was like most New York mornings following a bad storm: brisk with blue skies almost too bright to look at. It was as if the city was trying to make up for the miserable weather. The snow was still mostly white because the pollution and dogs hadn't gotten to it yet. Large chunks of the sidewalk still hadn't been shoveled and wouldn't be for some time, but there'd been enough foot traffic along Bleecker Street by then to have beaten down something of a path.

Hicks navigated through the snow; avoiding the stumbling pedestrians coming from both directions while balancing the two cups in the Styrofoam coffee carrier. One cup was a large black coffee for himself and a soy vanilla chai latte for Jason. Because Jason was a soy vanilla chai latte kind of guy.

Most of the cars on the street had been parked in the same spaces since before the storm began and were buried under several inches of drifted snow. Hicks didn't know how Jason had managed to park his black Ranger Rover in the same spot where it always was, midblock close to Sullivan Street. Maryland plates.

Hicks hadn't expected Jason to get out of his warm SUV to help him with the coffee and Jason didn't let him down. He simply watched Hicks go all the way to the corner and walk back in the street as cars crawled through the thickening slush. But he was kind enough to unlock the doors and take his latte from the carrier as Hicks climbed into the SUV.

"Thanks for the help." Hicks pulled the door closed. The inside of the SUV was warm and spotless. He took special joy in grinding the snow and rock salt from his boot treads into the passenger side carpet.

"Thanks for making me drive up here in this shit." Jason took the lid off the cup and blew on it, even though Hicks knew it wasn't that hot. "Traffic into the city was a nightmare."

Hicks drank his coffee the way it was. He liked it hot. "You're the one who decided to come up here, ace. We could've had this discussion over the phone and saved a lot of trouble."

"That's not how I work and you know it. You lost an agent yesterday and University protocol says that requires a field visit from your Department Chair. And, as much as you might hate that fact, I am your Department Chair."

"And I already told you it's being handled."

"I find your definition of 'being handled' troubling to say the least. Do you call three dead men in Central Park 'handled?' Do you think allowing a suspected accomplice to escape 'handled?' Do you call having to bring in the Varsity to clean up your mess 'handled?' Looks like a Grade-A catastrophe to me."

Hicks looked at Jason for the first time since getting in the car. He was as equally nondescript as Hicks, though his coloring was much fairer and his features more delicate. His penchant for J. Crew sweaters and Lindberg frames led people to believe he was a computer programmer or a high school swimming coach or an accountant. Anything but what he was. The Dean liked his people to appear innocuous and Jason succeeded. In Hicks' opinion, it was the only thing he was good at. "I don't think blocking me from seeing the identities of the men I killed being 'handled' either."

"Do you honestly expect me to allow you to see sensitive information less then an hour after what happened in Central Park? Without even being able to survey the situation or your status first hand? You must be out of your fucking mind."

Hicks smiled as he sipped his coffee. "Don't curse. It doesn't go well with the latte."

"You really think this is just one big joke, don't you? That you can handle everything with just a few keystrokes and a few emails?"

"I think one of us has almost twenty years of field experience, ace, and it sure as hell ain't you. You've been on the job six months, and I don't know what you were doing before that, so forgive me if I don't take rebuke from a rookie."

"The Dean gave me this assignment for a reason."

"Yes he did," Hicks said, "just like he put me in charge of the New York Office for a reason, too. Field operations aren't easy. They go to shit all the time and almost never go according to plan. Surprise is part of the job, even when a good man like Colin is involved. People snap. They make mistakes. Things go south and, when they do, it's professionals like me who know how to handle it. And you holding back information from me makes all the bad shit that went down that much worse."

"I don't see how three dead men in the park could get any worse."

"Which is exactly why you're riding a desk," Hicks said. "You see three dead bodies. I see two threats neutralized and a suspect pinged by OMNI as he escaped, not to mention the images we were able to pull off the SD card."

Jason looked like he wanted to say more. He looked out the window instead. "Sounds like a man who fucked up and is doing his best to put a positive spin on a bad situation."

"This job isn't about spin. It's about taking effective action on the information we gather. It's about getting as much information as you can when you can get it. You'd know that if you had any idea about how to do your job."

Jason slowly slid his latte in the beverage holder near the gear shift. Hicks knew he'd already pulled the chain of command as tight as he dared. He just didn't care. He half hoped Jason took a swing at him. He'd like a legitimate reason to break Jason's arm.

Instead, Jason said, "You don't know the first thing about me or what I've done, and I'll be damned if I'm going to justify my credentials to you. I'll release the identities of the men you killed when I'm convinced you're capable of running this operation according to University protocol. And right now, you haven't convinced me."

"Let me try to enlighten your thinking, then. I've got a hot investigation that's getting colder each second I waste sitting here kissing your ass. Who gives a shit? All I care about is finding out why my agent is dead."

"You were there when he was killed," Jason said. "You already know *why* he's dead. You need to know what caused them to catch on to Colin."

"And it's exactly because of that semantic bullshit that I need you to stay out of my way and let me do my job."

Hicks watched Jason trace the inside of his mouth with his tongue. "And if I don't, you'll call the Dean directly, won't you? Go right over my head."

"No," Hicks admitted, "because he probably already knows what you're doing. You wouldn't have the balls to hold back those identities without his support. So you've got his blessing for now, but how long until I start leaning on him about you?"

Jason looked at the steering wheel; then back out the window. "The Dean not only knows I embargoed your searches, he also knows why I did it. I told him I think you were too close to Colin and have lost all of your objectivity in this case. I think there's a good chance you missed something in your recent debriefing session and I'm not comfortable with your ability to see things clearly."

Hicks figured that's how he saw things. He didn't agree with it, but it still stung. "You've probably been through every report I've filed from Colin. I spent half the night going through them myself. Twice. And I know I didn't miss a damned anything, I know you know it, too."

"We both know a report is only as thorough as the person who wrote it. I'd think a man with your extensive amount of field experience would know that. I think your objectivity here is clouded by your long friendship and working relationship with Colin. And I'm afraid that lack of objectivity will pose a serious hindrance in your ongoing pursuit of Omar. Revenge has no place in our line of work, James. You've said so many times, according to your file."

"You read it in my file, but do you have any idea what it actually means?" Hicks realized he was grabbing the paper coffee cup tight enough to buckle it and placed it in the beverage holder instead. "When the Dean assigned me here, this office was one step above a glass-to-the-wall operation. Now it's the best network in the entire University system."

"No one's interested in listening to you narrate your own highlight reel, James. That was then. This is now."

"Then let's talk about now. Now, I've got an office with over a hundred sources and field personnel who turn over solid, actionable intelligence to me every single week. No other office in the System has that kind of output."

"Not every week," Jason said. "Let's not get ahead of ourselves."

"Then let's talk money. I've got a revenue stream that not only keeps the New York Office off the University's grid, but it keeps the University's bursar account fat and happy. That same money keeps your candy ass in Ranger Rovers and lattes and Izod shirts. You don't trust me?" Hicks laughed. "Junior, I don't give a shit because the Dean knows that if I go, the whole operation goes with me."

"Pride goes before the fall," Jason said. "We know more

about what you do here than you think."

"You only know what I share with you. So, either you release the identities of the three men or this thing gets a lot nastier than it has to be."

Jason slowly lifted his latte out of the cup holder. "I could be forgiven for taking that as a threat."

"I don't make threats. I just tell it like it is."

Jason sipped his latte as he watched New Yorkers of all ages toddling through the heavy snow. The city had closed the schools thanks to the blizzard and it seemed like every kid in the world was out on the street; letting themselves fall into the snow banks while their fathers or mothers or nannies told them to stop.

Hicks noticed the manicured nails on Jason's right hand and the wedding ring on his left. He wondered if the ring was real or just cover. He wondered if Jason had children and what kind of father he'd be. Was he an asshole in every aspect of his life or only with him?

Jason took another sip of his latte and licked his lips clean. "You're right. We don't have to like each other. We don't even have to respect each other, but we do have to work together. Under other circumstances, I'd probably ask the Dean for another posting because I don't enjoy working with people I despise and, believe it or not, I despise you."

Hicks toasted him with his coffee. "Feeling's mutual, Ace."

"I despise you so much, that I'm not going to give you the satisfaction of transferring to another office. And I'm staying not just because I enjoy making your life miserable, but because I think you've lost your objectivity. I think you're putting the University—and the Dean—at risk and I owe him too much to let that happen."

"So making my life miserable is just a bonus for you?"

"Yes," Jason admitted. "Yes it is."

"Marvelous. Are you going to release the search results on the three men or not?"

"I'll agree to give you the identities of the two men you killed, but not the image you retrieved from the camera."

Hicks knew he'd given in too easily. "Why not?"

"Because that image was embargoed by another government when OMNI ran the search."

"Embargoed?" Hicks hadn't heard that term in years. "By who?"

"We're working to figure that out," Jason said. "It looks like one of our European cousins did it when OMNI searched Interpol's database. We still have the image, but Interpol shut down the search and embargoed the information. The Dean is going to look into it personally, and we hope to know much more later today. Needless to say, that image is of someone who's being protected for a good reason."

Hicks knew this was how it was in the Life. Two steps up and one step back. "Fine. Any word on Colin's autopsy?"

Jason referred to his handheld. "It came in a few minutes before you got here. Our doctors say his system was pumped full of a combination of heroin and cocaine. Chances are he probably would've died from cardiac arrest if Omar's man hadn't shot him. Given his known fear of needles and avoidance of alcohol and drugs, we surmise that he was drugged in an attempt to get him to talk. So, for all intents and purposes, he was already dead by the time you got there." Jason looked away. "I'm sorry about that. I didn't mean to be so... clinical about it. I know he was your friend. For what it's worth, the injection site on his arm was bruised, implying that he didn't let them stick him easily."

That was the Colin that Hicks had known. "What about the two men who were with him?"

"I'll see to it that the identities of the two men you killed are sent to your handheld as soon as we're done here. I'm afraid you'll find it pedestrian reading. No red flags and no known ties to extremists except that they're both Somali."

Hicks had figured as much. "I checked our passive surveillance of the cab stand and the whole place has been dark since yesterday. No sign of Omar, the drivers, or any of the cars, either. It's seems they all scattered just before Colin went to meet me at the park."

Hicks didn't like where any of this was leading, but it only seemed to be leading one place. He had no choice but to state the obvious. "I think Omar's network was a hell of a lot bigger than we thought."

"Which makes Omar far more dangerous than we thought," Jason said. "Which means we're going to have to work closely on this from here on in. Our personal animosity aside, we need to help each other to keep a bad situation from getting even worse."

"That means I need to be apprised of every new development in this case, and you need to wait for my approval before you act on any intelligence. The I.D. on this man from the camera should've come back with the two men you killed. It didn't. Colin's assignment should've been wrapping up and, instead, he's dead. There's more at play here than our animosity for each other. And perhaps more than we know."

Hicks decided to quit while he was ahead. "Agreed. I'll keep you posted."

As Hicks opened the car door, Jason said, "Stay in touch. And stay safe."

Hicks smiled before he closed the door. "Gee, Honey. I didn't know you cared."

CHAPTER
7

HICKS WAITED UNTIL he got back to Twenty-third Street to download the files Jason had sent him. And just as Jason had warned him, the background on the two Somalis he'd killed had been a dead end. All of Jason's posturing about his goddamned information embargo had been just that: posturing.

According to the file, the two men he'd killed were a couple of twenty-year old orphans raised in a Christian missionary in Somalia. That same orphanage sponsored them for student visas so they could come to the Land of Opportunity and bring their knowledge back home with them. Their passports had been stamped at JFK four months before and they'd fallen off the radar since then until the moment Hicks had killed them.

They'd entered the country legally with legitimate passports and sponsors. That meant they'd probably gotten involved with Omar after they'd gotten into the country. And since OMNI had never tracked either of them to the cab stand or any of the drivers, it confirmed that Omar's operation was much bigger than he'd previously thought.

Somehow, Omar had managed to build up a network while being under the watchful eye of OMNI and Colin. Sending a couple of rookies with Colin to the rendezvous probably meant Colin hadn't told Omar much about the University. If he had, Omar would've sent pros or just flat out killed Colin and cut his losses. Hicks figured Omar had drugged Colin to get him to talk. The bigger question was why. What had Colin seen?

It must've been something that Omar had wanted kept secret. Something that hadn't shown up in six months of passive and active surveillance from the finest intelligence array in the world.

All Hicks had to do was find out what it was. And to do that, he'd have to start from square one.

He toggled his screen to see Colin's autopsy report. The autopsy photo of Colin's corpse on a slab came up first. A white sheet draped over his body with gaps and sags where none would be if he had still been alive. Places where the doctor had cut into him. He stared at the picture until he thought he could see each pixel of the image. *Why are you dead, my old friend? Why did you set me up?*

Omar had disappeared and the dead men were dead ends. The only lead Hicks had left was the image of the man on the camera's memory card. An image a foreign government was protecting. And two dead men from an organization far larger than Hicks knew existed.

He was beginning to think this was far above the skill set of an untrained Somali cab driver with bad intentions. This felt like it was something more.

Hicks almost jumped when his phone began to buzz. It was the Dean himself.

Hicks had worked for the man for almost twenty years, but had never met him. He had no idea where the Dean lived or where he worked or what his name might be or even what he looked like. They'd always communicated over the OMNI network by phone and via email, but never in person.

The University prided itself on 'dynamic diversity.' There was no central office or campus, but hundreds of offices each hiding in plain sight, all remotely connected through OMNI.

Hicks had spoken to the man hundreds of times and, based on the conversations they'd had and the decisions he'd made, Hicks pegged him for an old field man. A good one at that. The kind who knew when to step in, when to give advice and when to back out of the way. Skills Jason didn't have and probably never would.

When Hicks answered the phone, the Dean said, "You're brooding, aren't you?"

The man's ability to read people had always impressed him. "How do you know?"

"Because you've been staring at the same screen for ten minutes after a night of furious activity. You've been staring at those pictures from Colin's autopsy for so long that I can practically feel it burning a hole right through you."

Hicks should've remembered that OMNI kept track of its

user's keystrokes. No one else had access to all of that except for the Dean. "I could've been in the bathroom."

"Not you. Not that long. Besides, I owed you a call to express my condolences over what happened to Colin. He was a good man. I hope you don't blame yourself for his death."

"I don't," Hicks said, almost believing it. "I just don't like how this seems to be much bigger than we know."

"All that means is that your instincts were right from the beginning," the Dean said. "You knew Omar was up to something and you stayed with it, despite all evidence to the contrary. That's the human element I'm always talking about, James. OMNI is an invaluable tool, but it still takes a human's instinct and training to wield her properly. This business with Omar proves me right."

"Speaking of humans," Hicks said, "did Jason debrief you on our meeting today?"

"He's promised me a full report by close of business today. All he said was that it was far more productive better than he expected it would. I know that working with him isn't always easy, but he really is quite brilliant in certain aspects of the job."

Hicks had never pulled punches with the Dean before and he wouldn't start now. "He's nowhere near as smart as he thinks he is."

"I can't argue with you there," the Dean said, "and I know better than to waste time trying to change your mind. Jason is valuable if only because he's young and youth can always be exploited by more experienced men. Men like you and me."

Hicks heard the tinkle of ice and the sound of the Dean sipping something. Hicks always envisioned the Dean as a scotch man, sitting behind a large oak desk, sipping Laphroig or Johnnie Walker Blue Label. Neat, of course. He just as easily could've been sipping lemonade on a porch in Savannah for all Hicks knew, but he preferred his vision of the man better to whatever the reality might be.

The Dean went on. "Besides, we should table the discussion of Jason's shortcomings as a Department Chair for another time. We have more important business to discuss. Your friend who drove the getaway vehicle is dead."

"Dead?" Hicks sat up straight. "How do you know?"

"There's a reason why we couldn't track him from the garage," the Dean explained. "I thought we'd simply lost him due to the angle of the satellite or the snow storm, so I took the liberty of having a varsity member check the garage for the car. He found our friend shot and dumped in the trunk of his own car. Whoever did it just walked away. I've had techs reviewing the footage of every camera in the area, but none of it bore fruit."

Hicks wasn't as surprised as he was troubled. "Sir, the speed with which this situation is getting complicated is troubling, to say the least."

"I'm more troubled about something else," the Dean said. "I was able to determine that the image you found was embargoed by the British."

"Are you sure? Not the French?"

"Their system did it automatically, which means the facial recognition matched someone they're looking to protect for some reason. I've made some calls to find out who the man is and why they're hiding him. But answers will take time, if we get them at all. In the meantime, tell me your next course of action regarding Omar?"

Hicks hated what he was about to say, but didn't see that he had any choice. "We should probably grab Omar as soon as possible." He toggled over to Omar's OMNI screen, which showed zero hits in activity on any of his phones or emails or vehicles since the day before. "The system shows he's been quiet since before the incident in the park, but that's to be expected since he probably knows he's being watched. Taking out Omar is our best chance of stalling whatever Colin uncovered. At least for a little while."

"Do you think you can get him to talk?"

"No, but Roger will. He could get a mute to recite Shakespeare."

"Agreed," the Dean said. "Our friend's peccadillos certainly make me glad he's on our side."

Roger Cobb's interrogation technique was brutally intricate and incredibly efficient. He wasn't afraid of gore, but gore wasn't the sole purpose of what he did. "He's a gifted interrogator, sir."

"Normally, I'd agree that picking up Omar and handing him over to Roger is the best course of action," the Dean said. "But what if I told you there might be another way to go about it? What if I told you there's a cleaner way we can get this bastard to give us everything we want without tipping him off and interrupting his plans?"

Hicks knew the Dean wasn't a deliberate man. He never came at something head on. He also never simply thought out loud. Everything he said or wrote had a purpose, even when it was in the form of a question.

"You know I never deal in hypothetical questions, sir, but if that was the case with Omar, I'd be very interested in what you had to say."

"Good, because it's the real reason for my call. It appears Omar is in quite a panic. He's been on the phone since midnight calling every fundamentalist financier in the book, begging them to send him money."

Hicks had learned long ago to never doubt the Dean, but he still found it difficult to believe. "How could Omar even get their numbers, much less get them on the phone?"

"An excellent question, and one we need to answer quickly. Omar has called several well-known patrons to ask them to finance an imminent, major offensive he's prepared to launch against the West. Part of his pitch is that time is of the essence and he needs financing to pull it off. Unfortunately, he's not giving out with any details unless they agree to fund him."

Hicks quickly re-clicked through Omar's OMNI profile and the profiles of all the drivers. None of them had used any of their known cellphones or email accounts in over a day. "Where the hell is he calling them from? OMNI is tracking every number Omar's been near in the past six months, and I'm coming up with zero."

"That's because he's in flight," the Dean explained. "He's been making the phone calls I just mentioned from throwaway phones while parked in a series of strip mall parking lots all over central New Jersey. Never more than one call from the same number and never two calls from the same lot. It's primitive but effective so far."

That only raised more questions for Hicks. He kept clicking through Omar's OMNI file. In the year since he'd been tracking Omar's movements, both passively and actively via Colin, Omar had never gone anywhere near New Jersey. Not even as a driver in one of his own cabs.

Omar had secrets.

And so did the Dean.

"How do you know all of this, sir?"

"Because Omar contacted a man in the Middle East who has been a friend of the University in the past. Two men, in fact, though one is more of a friend than the other. There have been times when this man has informed us of radical actions that would damage his interests so he was more than happy to let us know about Omar's call. As you know, these men pride themselves on anonymity and discretion. A stranger calling them out of the blue begging for money for a mysterious attack has caused them to circle the wagons. They're wondering how an unknown like Omar was able to reach them and they're very unhappy."

Hicks didn't mind that. The longer these old bastards kept their checkbooks in the drawer, the fewer people got killed. "Has Omar gotten anyone to finance him yet?"

"Everyone's turned him down except our friend, who has agreed to string Omar along until we tell him how we want to proceed."

"Who's our friend?"

"Compartmentalization, James. I'll tell you at the right time," the Dean said, "but now's not the time."

Hicks hated working blind, but he knew the Dean wasn't the kind of man you pushed. If he was holding something back, then it was for a reason. "Did this source tell you why Omar needs funds?"

"No. For a beggar, he's being very cagey about details. Omar isn't being greedy, though. He's only asking for a pledge before he agreed to tell them more, especially over the phone. Omar implied that he's being hunted by the Great Satan and in dire need of assistance quickly. He's telling people that he's working on a sacred plan that will strike deep into the heart of the infidels and leave a scar that will take generations to heal. His very words, according to our source."

It sounded like a lot of desperate bluster to Hicks. He knew Omar wasn't a trained terrorist, just a very enthusiastic amateur looking to make it into the big time. Colin must've discovered whatever Omar was working on, but Colin hadn't told him who he worked for. If he had, Omar wouldn't have sent rookies with him to Central Park. The phone calls Omar was making proved that whatever he was working on required an infusion of cash.

Hicks didn't waste time wondering what Omar was planning. He focused on the opportunity he had to find out for certain rather than speculating.

"We can either grab him and turn him over to Roger and hope he can break him," Hicks said, "or we can put someone close to him and pull the information out of him that way."

"Of course, I know the path I would choose, but since New York is your office, it's your call."

Hicks admired the Old Man's sensibilities. By allowing Hicks to make the choice, the Dean had plausible deniability if things went to shit. Even the Dean ultimately answered to someone, namely the University's Board of Directors. Hicks' decision made it Hicks' mess if things went sideways.

"Interrogations can always be tricky," Hicks said, "so I think we need your source to help us get close to Omar."

"I'm happy to hear you say that," the Dean said, "because I've got an idea on how we can do it as safely and quickly as possible."

Hicks thought he would. The Dean probably didn't get out of bed in the morning without knowing what he'd dream about that night.

"I want to use Omar's zeal and inexperience to draw him out and trip him up," the Dean explained. "He's obviously very desperate, and he doesn't have the slightest idea of how these kinds of operations are funded. We're going to use his naivety to our advantage by sending in someone to play savior for him. We're going to make sure an emissary from our Middle Eastern friend will arrive at just the right time with a bag of cash and the promise of more to follow; as soon as Omar reveals everything about his plan, of course."

Hicks liked the plan, in theory. But there was nothing theoretical about field work. A solid op took weeks, often months, to plan properly, and they didn't have that kind of time. If Omar really was ready to hatch some kind of an attack, they'd need to move fast.

"Unfortunately" the Dean went on, "I don't think you have anyone On Staff who could serve as a convincing bag man on such short notice, do you?"

Hicks didn't, and the Dean knew it. He had trained Faculty Assets from nearly every ethnic group at his disposal. Dozens of men and women of all races, colors, creeds, and backgrounds who could pass for damned near any nationality in the world if they had enough time to back away from their current assignments. As big as Omar's plot may be, the University still had dozens of important deep cover operations underway throughout the city.

Hicks wouldn't throw one of his own people into this without proper prep time. Hurry and haste usually got the wrong people killed. "I've got Enrollees and Assets who could do the job, but none are in New York right now. No men, anyway, and I know Omar will not accept a woman as an emissary."

"I know," the Dean said. "Which is why I've already got someone in mind."

Hicks figured he did. But he didn't like outsiders coming in on one of his operations, even one as flawed and rushed as this one was shaping up to be. Hicks' New York team was diverse, and they'd all been handpicked by him. He knew all their strengths and weaknesses. He knew how to use them and when. A new player in the mix, even just one man, could throw all that off. "I'm still confident one of your people can handle it, sir. I've got a man who was in deep cover in Tehran and another who..."

"Who has been working in J.P. Morgan for the past ten years and hasn't been undercover for almost fifteen years," the Dean said. "I'm familiar with all of your Faculty Members, Assets, and Enrollees, James, but I'm afraid this decision isn't up for debate. Omar has already surprised us with his ability to evade surveillance and discover Colin's identity, at least in part. Besides, we don't know what Colin may have told Omar about our operations in New York, so we can't risk one of your men going in. We need to embed someone who is trained in this sort of operation very quickly before Omar gets desperate and does something wild. Amateurs are at their most dangerous when frightened."

Hicks knew he was right. The Dean was always right. That didn't mean he had to like it. "Of course, sir."

"I need you to alert all of your people about what happened to Colin and let them know they need to be on guard just in case Colin talked about them," the Dean said. "Send the alert via the liquor store spam email so they know it's a critical message."

Hicks didn't need to be reminded of protocol. "I'll send it out as soon as possible, but I'd like to talk more about the man you have in mind for the Omar mission, sir."

"I've already got our people vetting several candidates I've deemed suitable. In the meantime, I need you to take an educated guess on how much money we should offer Omar to satisfy his immediate needs. If we give him too much, he's liable to think he's being set up by the CIA or one of our brother agencies. We give him too little, he'll only waste time bartering for more. You've been studying him for months, so your input is vital."

Hicks had seen this scenario play out in other parts of the University before. An Office Head would let their superior run an operation and, gradually, the Dean's office pushes the Office Head out of the entire op. Hicks wasn't about to allow that to happen to him.

"Where is the money coming from, sir? I take it that our Middle Eastern friend won't agree to finance it."

"Not a chance," the Dean said. "He's an ally, but an irregular one at best. We can't compel him to pay for anything like this."

That was music to Hicks' ears because now he knew how he'd be able to control the entire operation. The oldest form of control there was. "An op like this will take at least a hundred grand for Omar to take our decoy seriously."

The Dean skipped a beat. "Did you say a hundred thousand dollars?"

"I did, sir. Omar probably doesn't know how much to ask for, so a hundred grand is a good way to buy our decoy a seat at the table. We don't offer it all to him at once, of course. Maybe half to start with as a good faith effort to get the conversation started."

Hicks could practically hear the calculations going on in the Dean's mind. The University bureaucracy was far more streamlined than the bureaucracy of any intelligence agency in the world, but it was still very much a bureaucracy. A hundred grand was more than he could approve through petty cash. And Hicks knew that.

"Are you sure you're not being too generous? That's an awful lot of money to offer a small time operator like Omar. Maybe we offer ..."

"Omar has shown enough sophistication to detect Colin was spying on him. He's proven that he has enough resources to get the contact information of some very influential financiers in the Middle East. And he's confident enough in whatever he's planning to have risked getting himself killed by calling them out of the blue. A hundred grand is a nice round number. I'd rather have it and not need it than need it and not have it." He moved in for the kill. "Besides, I have a way to get the money outside the University system."

"I'm sure that won't be necessary. The University has more than enough in the Bursar's account to finance it."

"I know, but it'll take a couple of days for you to get all the approvals to release that kind of money. We don't have that kind of time. Luckily, I've just closed a new Asset; a finance man who's cash heavy at the moment and is looking to stay in my good graces. Why finance it ourselves when we can use other people's money? Risk free, too."

"That's the Russo man, isn't it?" the Dean asked. "I still don't see why we need another finance man. We've almost got as many money men as lawyers enrolled as Assets these days."

"This one is better than most at moving large amounts of money very quietly," Hicks explained, "and we're going to need a lot of cash on hand to get Omar to trust us. If he checks and sees our man only has fifteen thousand, he might clam up and that defeats the purpose of what we're trying to do here. My man's got a hundred grand just sitting in his safe right now."

This time, the Dean skipped two beats. "A hundred thousand? Are you sure?"

"Positive, sir."

"I suppose you have a point, but are you sure you're that liquid?"

Between his dozens of extortion operations and other legitimate investments, Hicks' New York office brought in over three hundred grand a month to the University's Bursar's office. That didn't count for the operating capital he held back to independently finance the New York office, which was close to that. "I'm plenty liquid, sir. And I know for a fact that Russo has that much cash on hand. He'll be happy to get it to us quickly and quietly."

"Not to mention that providing the money will give you a certain level of operational control." He heard the smile in the Dean's voice. "Well played, James. Well played indeed."

Hicks lied. "I'm only thinking about the success of the mission, sir."

The Dean laughed. "You've never thought of only one thing in your life. I think a hundred thousand is more than generous, but as they say, it's your money. How long would it take you to have that much on hand?"

"Within a matter of hours at most," Hicks said. He hoped Russo hadn't moved it from his home safe. "When do you think your operative will be here in New York?"

"The process is already underway. I'll be in touch with the particulars." The line went dead.

Hicks tossed the handheld on the desk and slowly pushed himself away from the computer. Away from the phone and OMNI and anything to do with the University. Just for a little while, he needed quiet.

There was no other sound in the bunker, not even the pop and creak of his chair as he moved. Just the antiseptic hum of the florescent lights and the computer's drive.

Conversations with the Dean were often closer to sparing matches than knife fights, but still took their toll. The Dean never came straight out and said what he wanted and he always held something back, even when he didn't have to. Secrecy was the hallmark of their business and details were a way of keeping score. In the University System, the truth was an arduous process and something to be avoided at all costs.

At least the Dean had allowed him to finance the operation. Hicks knew he hadn't talked him into anything or pulled the wool over his eyes.

Now all Hicks had to do was get the money.

Given the events of Central Park, Hicks was fairly certain that Colin hadn't told Omar's men much about the University or Hicks' New York network. But Omar still had the good sense to run after his men went missing. That meant Colin may have told him something about the University, but there was no way to know exactly how much. Since Colin had known about many of the ways Hicks financed operations, so he couldn't risk using the usual funding channels. But Colin hadn't known about Russo, which made him the best option.

Hicks checked the time on his computer monitor. It was going on six o'clock, so Russo should still be in his office.

The money man had a lot of bad qualities, but being a clock watcher had never been one of them. Hicks' months of surveillance on Russo had shown the money man was a creature of habit who went straight home most nights after work. Tuesdays and Thursdays were for his girlfriend. He always stopped off at the Bull and Bear and ordered a Laphroig on the rocks while he waited for his mistress to show up. He liked red wine with dinner. Usually Pinot Noir or Chateau du Pape. Desert was usually an all-night event back at her place. The wife chose to believe he stayed over at their studio apartment in Murray Hill. She'd never bothered to check up on his story. Besides, with Vinny out of the house, it allowed her to have her girlfriend over to spend the night.

Yes, the Russos led complicated lives.

Hicks called Russo's private line, but it went straight to

voicemail. Then he called the main office number, but the receptionist said he was gone for the evening.

Hicks didn't like that. Russo going home early was a derivation from his schedule. And Hicks didn't like derivations.

He went back into OMNI and tried to track Russo's cellphone. The phone had been turned off, but the last GPS ping was fifteen minutes old and showed the phone was at Russo's house on Long Island.

He could've had OMNI send out a signal to turn Russo's phone back on, but Russo wasn't used to the yoke just yet. Turning on his phone might spook him into doing something stupid and Hicks needed him calm. He needed Russo alive; at least until he got the hundred grand he needed to finance the Dean's undercover operation.

Hicks directed OMNI to focus the University satellite on the two-story Tudor house that the Russo family called home in Suffolk County. He selected the 'full scan' option and the image on Hicks' screen began to change.

The OMNI lens focused on a typical suburban home on a cul-de-sac, a bit larger than any of the others in the area. The Russo property's normally-manicured lawns were now covered in a thick layer of snow, as was the separate two-car garage in the back. The whole scene appeared far more wholesome than it actually was.

Hicks selected the Thermal option as the satellite began reading heat signatures in and around the property. It revealed two cars in the garage; one engine slowly cooling from red to orange in the brisk November night. Vinny's car. Judging by the heat signature of the engine, he'd just gotten home.

Hicks scanned over to the house. He saw a single heat signature in the living room; the size of the shape and its location on the couch read like Russo's wife, Marie. Another shape was in the den on the west wing of the house read it was Russo himself, sitting at his desk.

There were no other heat signatures in the rest of the house, except for the heat signature of a cat in the upstairs bathroom. And, from what Hicks could see, Tabby had gotten into the laundry.

Hicks could've called Russo or emailed him, but chose not to. Because some conversations were better face-to-face.

He pulled his coat from the hook and went outside.

CHAPTER 8

THE DRIVE OUT to Russo's place took just over an hour, which wasn't bad considering it was seven o'clock at night. A lot of companies had closed because of the blizzard, so rush hour traffic was much lighter than normal.

Russo's street house looked like something out of a Norman Rockwell painting. The colors of the Christmas lights along the eaves and roofs gave the snow a multicolored glow. Someone had even made a snowman complete with a carrot nose and raisins for the eyes and mouth.

Hicks would've thought the scene was damned near wholesome if it hadn't been all so contrived. Because in the course of his research on Russo, he'd also done research on the people in his immediate circle. Neighbors, friends from church, and people in the contacts folder of his phone. It paid to be thorough. After all, blackmailing a guy whose brother-in-law was an FBI agent could make things more difficult than they needed to be without proper preparation.

That's why he resented the Rockwellian facade of Russo's street because it was just a facade. Russo's neighbors were tax cheats and embezzlers, adulterers, and prescription pill addicts. Two had done time for vehicular manslaughter and one of them had been a coke dealer in college before she changed her name and moved to New York. Some of them voted Republican but paid illegal aliens to shovel their driveways and mow their lawns. Some of them were vocal Democrats who drove Mercedes and gave nothing to charity. They celebrated holidays, but left their religion at the front door of whatever church or synagogue they attended, if they attended at all.

Russo's street wasn't all that different than any of the other streets in the rest of the neighborhood or in the rest of the country for that matter. Human frailty was everywhere. Human frailty was Hicks' stock and trade. Frailty was the grease that made the wheels of the University turn. Frailty justified its existence and kept its coffers filled.

There was a part of Hicks that knew his choice of professions should make him regret what he'd done with his life; for living off other people's misery. But he didn't feel an ounce of regret for anything he'd done because what he did served a higher purpose.

Hicks parked his Buick on the street a few houses away from Russo's house. He pulled up the OMNI feed on his car's dashboard screen and saw that Russo hadn't moved from the den. In fact, it looked like he was more slumped at his desk than before. He looked well on his way to getting quietly drunk. Alone.

Hicks figured this was a result of their conversation. He'd seen this happen to new Assets before. Russo was no longer the head of the pack; the master of his own universe. None of his many secrets were his alone anymore. A stranger now had a knife to his throat and access into every unsavory aspect of his life.

Normally, Hicks could work up some sympathy for an Asset while he or she adjusted to the yoke, but he couldn't work up a lot of sympathy for Russo. Not since the Madoff mess. Russo had gotten greedy and careless with the wrong people and would've gotten himself killed if Hicks hadn't stepped in when he did. Men like Vladic always found out when someone was stealing from them, and when they did, the thief and his family took a long time to die badly.

Hicks didn't have the time to accommodate Russo's acceptance of his new reality. He needed the hundred grand Russo had in his safe and he needed it fast.

Hicks walked up the shoveled brick path to the front door. He knew the Russos always entered the house through the garage, but he wasn't supposed to know that. He could've easily popped the lock and gone in that way, but with Mrs. Russo around, there was no need to cause a scene. He rang the front doorbell instead.

A string of gentle chimes rang somewhere deep within the house. The sound had just died away when Marie Russo answered the door.

According to Hicks' surveillance of her husband, Vinny complained to his mistress that his wife had begun to lose her looks. Hicks' file on her showed she'd certainly been prettier when she was younger—the years and children and a marriage to Vinny had certainly taken their toll—but she still looked pretty despite everything. Her eyes were sunken and harder than they'd been in their wedding photos. Her face thinner, but surprisingly free of wrinkles.

Judging by the emails Hicks knew she'd sent and the websites he knew she'd visited, Hicks knew she was overly conscious of the weight she'd been unable to lose after giving birth to her daughter twenty three years before, but she carried it much better than most.

"May I help you?" she asked.

Hicks flashed his best weary smile and used a name he knew she'd heard—one of Vinny's employees—but had never met. "I'm Jerry Parsons from the office. Vince asked me to drop off something for him on my way home."

"Oh, of course," she said, remembering his name. She opened the door a bit more as she stepped back. "He's in the study just down the hall."

Hicks thanked her, but he already knew where it was. He'd already been in the house twice before when no one was home. Tapping into security cameras and reading emails and phone calls could only tell so much of the story. Technology couldn't completely replace seeing something with his own two eyes.

That's why he knew the door to the den didn't have a lock, so he walked right in without knocking.

He found Russo sitting in the same position that Hicks had seen from the thermal image—at the desk with a glass of scotch in a rock glass in front of him. The TV was off and so was the radio. Even the computer screen on the desk was dark. Vincent Russo was just a man in a wood-paneled man cave, with only his trouble and his booze to keep him company.

Russo didn't even bother to look up when he heard the door close. "Marie, how many times have I told you not to bother me when…"

And when he did look up, he saw Hicks standing on the other side of the desk. "Hello, Vince."

Russo's eyes went wide. "You? How did you… how did…"

"Marie let me in," Hicks explained. "She's not as run down as you tell people she is. You should do yourself a favor and compliment her more often. I know you've got Inez on the side, but you still live here, so…"

"What the hell do you think you're doing here?" He made a move for his desk drawer—the same drawer where Hicks knew he kept a nine millimeter Glock.

That's why Hicks had his gun out first. He pointed the .454 Ruger at Russo's head more for effect than intent. "Leave the nine where it is, Vinny. No need to get killed over an empty gun."

Russo looked down at the drawer, then at Hicks. "How do you know it's not loaded?"

"Because I unloaded it when I did a final sweep last week and you haven't touched the drawer since. If you do now, I'll shoot you in the knee just to prove a point."

Russo sank back into his chair and dropped his head in his hand. It was a similar pose to the one he had in his office, but much more resigned. "Yesterday, you punch me in the face and hit me in the balls with a stapler in my office. Today, you just stroll into my house and pull a gun on me. What'll you do to me tomorrow?"

"Nothing I don't have to." Hicks could see he already had Russo cowed, so he lowered the gun. "It's time to start being part of the team, Vinny. I need you to do something for me, and I need you to do it tonight."

"So this is how it's going to be, isn't it? Never knowing when you're going to call or show up with some fucking request? From now until the day I die, I'll always have to worry about you buzzing in my ear like a fucking gnat?"

"I already told you that you'll hardly even know I'm around so long as you do exactly what I tell you to do. I won't ask much, and I won't ask often, and I'll never ask you to deliver the impossible. And that's why I'm here now."

"I don't care why you're here now," Russo said. "I don't care what you do to me or to Vladic or to my family, because I don't give a shit about anything anymore. Go ahead and shoot me. You'll be doing me a favor."

Hicks didn't like his tone. "What's wrong? What happened?"

"You're so fucking plugged into my life, so why don't you tell me?" Russo pounded the desktop with the heel of his hand. "Do you honestly think I'm worried about some fucking lunatic four thousand miles away who *might* get around to killing me in a couple of days on the off chance him or any of the other fucking illiterate peasants who work for him can figure out that I skimmed from him? Why do you think they hired me in the first place? Because I'm their money guy. I'm the one who handles all the financials for them so they don't have to worry about it. He even said he expects me to steal, so long as I don't get crazy about it."

Hicks smiled. "A psychopath's sense of crazy changes from day to day."

"It would still take you a week to teach that ignorant fuck how to open his email and another week to explain what the spreadsheets mean. You want to send it? Be my guest. Because by the time he does get someone on a plane to come over here and wack me, I won't give a shit anymore."

Hicks realized there was more behind this than just bravado. "What happened?"

Russo rubbed the sore hand he'd just pounded on the desk. "What do you care?"

"When we were in your office, I told you that your problems are my problems, so if something's bothering you, I want to know what it is."

"My junkie son is what's bothering me. That's what you called him yesterday, isn't it?"

Hicks didn't bother apologizing because he knew it wouldn't do him any good. "What about him?"

"He's back to putting shit in his arm again. Or smoking it. Whatever the hell he's decided to do, the effects are still the same."

Hicks had been afraid of that. His son was Russo's one weakness. "What is it this time? Heroin?"

Russo nodded. "For the amount of money I've spent trying to get that kid clean, I could've bought a small island in the Caribbean. I came home last night after making your miserable fucking acquaintance and he flat out hits me up for money. No explanation, just sticks out his hand and demands it. I was in no mood for his bullshit, so I told him to leave me alone. What does he do? He goes up to my room, steals a handful of my gold cufflinks and my Rolex before he tears ass out of here. I didn't know he'd taken anything until later that night, and I haven't seen him since. He won't pick up his phone, and he's not with any of the scum he usually hangs out with. None of the ones I know, anyway."

Hicks didn't want the answer to the next question but he had to ask. "How do you know?"

"You're not the only one with connections here. I have my ways."

Hicks didn't pretend to be impressed. "You've got an uncle who's retired NYPD and a few friends who are lieutenants on the Nassau PD. Which one did you call?"

Russo shook his head. "Jesus, you really do know everything, don't you?"

Hicks didn't like Russo going outside the circle. He didn't like him asking people to look into his family problems. He might get the idea to tell them about Hicks and, if that happened, it could become a problem. Not an unsolvable problem, but messier than Hicks wanted. "Answer the fucking question."

"My uncle worked narcotics and still has some friends who work the streets. He called around but no one knows of anyone trading Rolexes for dope. Not in the last few days, anyway."

"You tell your uncle anything about me?"

"No, darling. No one knows about us."

"Keep it that way." In all of his surveillance of the Russo's family, Hicks hadn't really focused on the son, Vincent Russo, Junior. But with a little research, Hicks figured he could find him if he had to. Junkies were like rats, often taking the same paths to the same places to get their fix. He hoped he wouldn't have to look too hard.

"I'll make a deal with you. I know you keep a hundred grand in cash in your safe. Don't bother lying about it because I know it's there. You hand it over and I'll see what I can do about finding your kid."

"No."

"That's not a word you say to me. Give me the money, and I promise I'll help you find Junior."

"I said no. Want me to spell it out for you? N-O and here's why: I don't care what you do to me or how you've screwed over people like me in the past. Because you're not the only one here who can put things together. If you're coming in here unannounced like this, I'll bet it's because you need that money pretty damned quick. That's good, because I need my son back pretty damned quick, too."

"We can talk about that after you hand me the money."

"No, we'll talk about it now because he doesn't have that kind of time. This is the third time he's come out of rehab and if it doesn't take now, I don't know if it ever will. I don't even know if he'll survive the treatment and if he doesn't survive it, neither will I."

Talk like that was a bad thing for an Asset. "Don't say that."

"It's the truth. As God is my witness. You want to threaten my wife and daughter? Knock yourself out. They're two of the most ungrateful, greedy little bitches in the world. Neither of them has had any use for me for years and the second I die, I don't know who'd be the first to call the lawyer. Vladic can gut both of them as far as I'm concerned, if it would bring my son back."

Russo paled and sagged back in his chair. He looked at the bottle of scotch and his empty glass, but made no attempt to reach either. "He's a sweet kid when he's clean. Nice. Respectful. Creative as hell." His eyes began to water. "I know he can make something of himself if he can just kick this shit once and for all. He's only twenty years old, for Christ's sake. But he's my whole world and everything I've built is to give him some kind of chance, so if he's dead, I might as well be, too because I've got no reason to live."

When Russo looked up at him, Hicks saw no trace of hate or anger, just flat resentment in his eyes. "I got home early this afternoon and moved the money. I put it in one of the safe deposit boxes I've got all over the island. You say you know everything there is about me, so you know I'm right. I split the money up so none of it is all in one place, and you don't know which banks I put it in because I stopped at all of them for exactly the same amount of time."

Hicks felt his temper beginning to spiral again. The Ruger was beginning to become a viable option. "Don't do this, Vinny. You're playing a dangerous game."

"You'll probably be able to pull whatever computer voodoo bullshit you do to get your way into some of the boxes," Russo went on, "but probably not all of them in time before you need the money. So here's what's going to happen. You're going to take the same resources you used to dig up shit on me and you're going to use them to find my son and bring him back home where he belongs. Dead or alive, I don't care. I just need him here with me so I know where he is, not lying dead in some crack den with the rats..." He choked off his words and looked away. "And don't bother telling me you can't do it because I know goddamned well you can. People like you can do anything they want when the price is right, and it's right now. I've worked with people like you before."

Hicks gripped the Ruger tighter. "You've never met anyone like me. So how about you open the safe, so I know you're not bullshitting me."

"You know so damned much, how about you open it yourself?"

He snatched Russo by the hair and pulled him up out of the chair. He had good balance for a man so drunk and Hicks pushed him over to the picture that hid the wall safe. "Open it yourself and show me it's really empty."

Hicks stepped back as Russo slid the picture aside, revealing the gun-metal wall safe behind it. He spun the dial and pulled the safe door open. It was as empty as he'd said it was, except for the safe deposit keys.

"You don't bullshit me, and I don't bullshit you," Russo said as he stumbled back to the chair behind his desk. "Get me back my son, and you get all hundred grand. You don't, I don't care what happens next."

Hicks stood there, staring into the gaping maw of the empty safe as if it was mocking him. Emptying the Ruger into it would've made him feel better, but it wouldn't have accomplished a damned thing.

Only getting Junior back would get him the hundred grand he needed.

Hicks turned away from the safe. "Do you have any idea where I can find him?"

"No," Russo admitted. "I already told you he's not where he normally goes, and I don't know where he could be. You've got fingers in so many pies, you can figure it out for yourself."

"You're about to cross a dangerous line here, Vinny," Hicks said. "You're sure you want to do this?"

"Fuck you and your line. Just get my boy back."

Russo reached for the bottle of scotch, but Hicks snatched it from him before he reached it. "I'll find your son, but you I need you sober. As soon as the banks open tomorrow, you get into those boxes and gather up the money. You'd better have it stacked and ready for me by noon when I pull in the driveway because, if you don't, I put a bullet in Junior's head before I put one in your belly."

"I'll have the money, don't worry about that," Russo sneered. "Let's just hope you're as good as you say you are."

Hicks tucked the Ruger back in his waistband before he decided to shoot this son of a bitch. He pulled Russo's glass toward him and poured himself three fingers of scotch. A drink before the war.

"Tell me where your son usually goes to get high."

CHAPTER 9

O N THE DRIVE back to Manhattan, Hicks brought up Junior's file on his dashboard screen, then had OMNI check Junior's police record. The file read like a requiem for an addict. The kid had been in and out of the system a few times already in his young life. All of them drug charges. Junkie beefs and juvie bounces. Nothing too violent or heavy.

According to his rap sheet, Junior had seemed to bounce back and forth between heroin and crack since he'd been fifteen years old. No coke or meth, at least not in enough of an amount to get him busted. It was spoiled brat syndrome, plain and simple; a disease caused by too much money and not enough supervision. It happened in every neighborhood in every country all over the world.

Junior's latest relapse played into the reason why Hicks

had thought Russo would make a good target in the first place. Hicks figured his kid's struggles would make him easier prey and more willing to become an Asset. Hicks hadn't counted on Russo using it as leverage against him.

Getting Junior back wasn't impossible. It was a pain in the ass, especially since he'd painted himself into a corner with the Dean about funding the covert op against Omar. If he didn't come up with that money in time, Jason would make sure he got pushed out of the op altogether. Hicks wasn't going to let that happen.

According to his record, Junior tended to go on the nod in one area in Brooklyn. As junkies were creatures of habit, he decided known associates in that part of the city would be a good place to start.

If Hicks had the time, he would've farmed out the request to one of his NYPD assets to track down Junior for him. It would cost him a couple of bucks, but it would've been worth it. Unfortunately, Hicks didn't have that kind of time, so he had to do it the hard way. Hicks had OMNI open the folder he had on the tacit surveillance on the Russos. The system tracked all the phone calls, text messages, web browsing, and online activity of all four members of the Russo family.

Hicks opened Junior's phone records and looked up the last time the phone had been used and where it was located. The phone's last recorded position was heading west toward Manhattan from the Russo's house in Suffolk. It wasn't much to go on. There was an entire junkie wonderland between Suffolk County and Manhattan alone. That didn't count the places he could've gone in the Bronx, Queens, and Brooklyn.

He checked the numbers Junior had called in the last

day or so and found several calls to numbers that came up as either disposable phones or to young women he'd called before. Hicks tapped on each of their numbers and accessed their records. Social media pages came up as part of the search. It looked like Junior had a thing for brunettes. Hicks smiled. Maybe Junior was worth saving after all.

The only common thing about the phone calls was that they only lasted thirty seconds. That meant voicemails. None of the calls had been returned. Hicks knew why. It was junkie desperation; pleas either for cash or a place to crash. Daddy's cuff links and watch might help him get well for a while, but not for as long as he needed. No amount of money in the world would help him to get well for as long as he needed.

Hicks struck gold when he checked Junior's text messages. He'd texted a number registered to yet another burn phone, only this one had been used more than once and paid for by a credit card belonging to one Devron Jackson. According to his record, Devron was a twenty-six-year-old African American from Bensonhurst. Five-feet-eight- inches tall and weighed a buck-forty soaking wet. Several convictions for possession and dealing and intent to distribute. An assault with a deadly weapon charge had been dropped. Devron dealt heroin, Junior's poison of choice. Devron was a good place for Hicks to start looking for Junior.

He brought up the location of Devron's phone, backtracking to where it had been answered when he and Junior traded texts. Only one location popped up for that number all day long: an abandoned railroad substation in the middle of Queens.

In the old days, Hicks would've had to drive over to the

place to get a good look at it. Today, someone would've just pulled up the street view of a search engine map. But Hicks activated the OMNI satellite parked over Manhattan to give him a live image from a satellite two hundred and twenty miles above the earth.

He typed the address into the interface and the satellite zoomed in on the exact building. Given that it was night, there wasn't much he could see under normal view, so he switched to the thermal view of the building. It revealed about a dozen or more shapes milling around the ground floor of the substation. Most of the heat signatures came up as dull red blobs on the floor. They were alive, but unconscious. Probably junkies on the nod.

He spotted the two red shapes walking in between the people on the floor and Hicks pegged them to be watching over the customers, making sure none of them tripped too hard and choked to death on their own spit. Like the old saying goes: Dead men don't buy smack. The satellite also picked up two more skels posted at the entrance and one in the back. Probably keeping watch to make sure no one robs the customers. Safety was priority one to these fuckers.

Judging by what he could see via the OMNI feed, the place looked like a shooting gallery. The protection looked minimal, but present. Hicks would respect it, but didn't fear it. And it wasn't going to keep Hicks from bringing Junior home quickly. People were going to have to die before that happened. But everyone in the substation had already signed their own death warrant a long time ago.

Hicks tried to access Junior's phone. It was off, but there was still signal. He pinged it to turn it on remotely, but it came up dead. That meant the phone wasn't just off. The battery was completely drained. The junkie bastard must've forgotten to charge it before he grabbed daddy's jewelry and bolt out of the house. So much for heroin junkie reliability.

So Hicks had the satellite sweep the building for smartphones or tablets; anything that might have a wireless connection and a camera. He got hits on several phones belonging to some of the junkies passed out on the floor.

Hicks accessed each one in turn, but all phones were either in pockets or bags. None of them gave him any idea of what the room looked like. All he heard was muffled farts and snores while their owners tripped the light fantastic. Hicks closed his eyes. His was a charmed life.

But Hicks scored a hit on the second to last number he tried. The signal corresponded with a red thermal signature of a man who was walking among the images of junkies on the floor. Hicks activated the phone's camera and got a clear, but jerky, picture of the inside of the place. It looked like the man was talking while he was moving through the people scattered on the floor.

Hicks had OMNI record the images that came over the feed; dark images of shapes lying prone on the floor. The cavernous old substation was only lit by weak candlelight and whatever streetlight filtered in through the boarded windows. The images didn't look clear to the naked eye, but Hicks knew OMNI's image enhancement programs would pick Junior out of the crowd, if he was there at all.

The man's phone conversation appeared to have ended because the camera panned down to a view of his shoes. White sneakers. Laces pressed. Blue jeans cuffed just so.

Hicks bet that was Devron. He was patrolling the gallery like a boss.

Hicks didn't care about Devron's conversation, so he didn't bother listening to it. But he kept the camera feed active as he uploaded Junior's Facebook profile picture to OMNI and asked it to match the image to anyone in the substation. Hicks watched the system go to work as tiny hexagons flashing on faces Hicks couldn't see with the naked eye as the drug dealer threaded his way among his customers.

The system quickly seized on one image of a figure slumped against the wall. OMNI froze the image and automatically enhanced it. The program lightened it and compared it to the confirmed image of Junior's face. A green status bar crawled across the screen from left to right as the program went to work. The original image was nothing but a blurry profile shot of a kid passed out against the wall. OMNI cleaned it up, brightened it, and matched the profile with Junior's known facial characteristics. It came back with an eighty percent match. Not perfect, but close enough for him to make a decision.

Hicks had found Junior. Now he'd have to go in and get him.

Hicks checked his watch. It was already going on ten o'clock and he figured Junior would be on the nod for hours; probably well after sunrise. Plenty of time for him to pull together a quick raid of the place. He selected Junior's heat signature on the thermal feed and had OMNI keep an eye on him. If Junior so much as scratched his balls, OMNI would notify him.

He activated another of the satellite's lenses to scan the

perimeter again. It looked like there were at least three guards at the place, probably more. All of them probably armed. Hicks knew he could probably shoot his way in there alone if he had to, he didn't need to risk it. New York was his town and, Colin's betrayal aside, he still had plenty of resources.

Because Colin hadn't known everything about the New York Office. He didn't know all of the assets and he certainly didn't know all of their skills. It was Hicks' first rule of intelligence work: never tell everyone everything. Always hold something back. He still had a few people he could call for help. A job like hitting a drug den would require a special kind of backup.

And he knew just the right man for the job. Except in this instance, the right man just happened to be a woman.

CHAPTER 10

IT WAS ALMOST eleven by the time Hicks got to the The Mark
Hotel on Seventy-seventh and Madison. He'd stopped by his
place first so he could change into a shirt and blazer before
heading uptown. The Mark Bar wasn't the type of place you
trudged into in a parka and gloves, not even when the weather
called for it. Not for the kind of role he'd be playing, anyway.

He had no problem spotting Tali as soon as he entered
the bar. She was exactly where she'd texted she'd be; alone,
nursing the same cocktail she always ordered, but rarely
finished: Hendricks martini straight up with a twist of lemon.

She was wearing a classic black cocktail dress that could
be found in almost any dress shop or department store in the
world, but she somehow managed to make it look *couture*.
She had dark hair, light olive skin and high cheekbones and

green eyes one might not expect an Israeli girl to have. She was more striking than beautiful, but exotic enough to draw quick glances—both desirous and envious—from most of the men and women in the place.

Yet, despite the empty stool next to her, no one sat near her. Despite her beauty, there was something about Tali that didn't invite company.

Despite appearances, Hicks knew Tali wasn't one of the pros who cruised the Cocktail Circuit of Upper East Side bars looking for a sugar daddy on a Thursday night. She wasn't looking for someone to buy her drinks or help with the rent or listen to her sob story about her sick kid at home.

Hicks knew Tali for who and what she really was—a highly trained operative from Israeli Military Intelligence on an extended liaison mission to the University. And Hicks knew she was killing time while she waited for her latest assignment to meet her at the bar for a nightcap before heading back to her place for the evening. Her current assignment happened to be a Texas real estate investor looking to buy his way into a couple of development projects in the Middle East. The man was long on cash, but short on discretion, which made him a good source of information. Hicks doubted that Tali shared every bit of information the man told her—she was an Israeli agent first and foremost—but she passed along more than enough intel to keep Hicks funding her stay in New York.

Hicks and Tali had slept together once in London six years before. It was before he'd been named the head of the New York Office and before Tali had been loaned out to the University. They'd both been working on a related project and wound up stuck at a romantic hotel on a rainy London evening. It hadn't been casual, but it hadn't been serious, either. Neither of them had mentioned it since she'd arrived in New York, though Hicks often wondered if she'd ever given it any thought. He didn't want to know the answer, so he never asked the question.

Tali didn't pay Hicks any mind when he sat one stool away from her, but he knew she'd been trained to see everything. He'd always admired her focus and discretion. There was no telling who might be watching either of them or why. And, in Hicks' experience, someone was always watching.

He caught the bartender's eye and ordered a scotch on the rocks. Since that's what he'd had at Russo's house, he decided it was safer to stick with it. The bartender served it to him with a glass of water on the side, then took his credit card and kept the tab open for him.

Knowing the bartender was probably listening; Hicks looked Tali's glass and said, "That looks awfully dangerous."

Tali looked at his scotch and exaggerated her accent. "That doesn't look like buttermilk, either."

Hicks cued her by asking, "Your accent is familiar. What is that? Russian?"

She answered in Russian in a pleasant tone that didn't reflect what she said. "What the fuck are you doing here? I told you I'm working."

Hicks responded in Russian. "I wouldn't be here if it wasn't important."

She cocked an eyebrow as she looked back at her martini. "Why are we speaking Russian anyway? Your accent is dreadful. Your French is better."

"But we're in a French hotel, my love. Why take chances

on someone understanding us?"

"I'm not your 'love' and if you're so worried about taking chances, you're taking a big one by coming here tonight. That redneck pig will be here any minute, and he won't like you being here when he walks in."

Hicks knew her assignment was six-and-a-half feet, two-hundred-sixty pounds of pure Dallas bluster. He had a particularly mean, protective streak where Tali was involved; which Hicks knew was more about his pride than her honor. "Don't worry about me. I can handle myself."

"I'm not worried about you. I'm worried about you putting him in the hospital if he swings at you. He won't be much use to me if he's in a coma. I'm too close to getting him to tell us who he's working with, and I can't risk you blowing that in a lousy bar brawl. Now, for the last time, why are you risking my cover like this?"

Hicks winced as he sipped at his scotch. "Because I need a favor. A big one that utilizes your particular set of skills."

He watched her stir the lemon rind in her martini with her pinky nail and found it surprisingly erotic. "I've told you before I'm not a whore. I do what I do for my country and that is all."

"I never said you were, and I'm not asking you to be one now. I'm talking about your skills with a rifle."

She broke character and looked at him quicker than she should have. "Is this about the alert you sent out earlier?"

Since Hicks was asking for her help, he decided to tell her the truth. He only had a certain level of authority over her anyway and asking him to serve as a sniper was outside the mission parameters the University had agreed upon with her superiors in Tel Aviv.

"Colin got turned by the people I'd assigned him to watch. He set me up to take a bullet last night in Central Park, and I don't know why."

It was the first time he'd ever seen Tali betray any kind of sincere emotion. "Are you hurt? Is Colin okay?"

"I'm fine, but Colin didn't make it. Neither are the two men he'd brought with him to kill me." Hicks took a sip of scotch to take a little of the sting out of the memory. "I don't know how much he told them about any of us before he died, but since he didn't know much about your assignment, you're one of the few people I can trust in New York right now."

Tali went back to looking at her drink. "I still can't believe Colin turned. Do you know why he did it?"

"I don't know, but that's what I'm trying to find out. It's too complicated to explain before your Texas friend gets here, but I just need you to help me with a little housekeeping tomorrow morning."

'Housekeeping' was the University's code for an assassination. Even though they were speaking in Russian, certain protocols still had to be observed.

"What kind of housekeeping?" she asked.

"A little high dusting." It was code for a sniper assignment. "Nothing you haven't done before and in worse conditions. And with minimal risk to you."

Hicks would've been disappointed if she'd agreed to do it right away. "Tell me more about what happened with Colin. Did he compromise any of us? Are the rest of us in danger? I'm not just talking about me. I'm talking about the others working for you in New York."

"Have you noticed anyone watching you?"

"Don't answer a question with a question." She stabbed at the lemon peel with her pinky nail. "I hate it when you do that."

Hicks didn't dare annoy her any further. She wasn't the only sniper he had On Staff in New York, but she was certainly the best shot. "My gut tells me he didn't tell them much but, then again, I never thought Colin could be turned, either. I know you're working on a big assignment now, and I know this is beyond our agreement, but I could use your backup tomorrow morning."

Tali inched her cocktail glass away from her. "Is this against the people who hurt Colin?"

Hicks didn't see a reason why he should lie to her. "No, but it'll help me get closer to the people who did. It's difficult to explain in the time we have."

"Of course," Tali smirked. "There is never a straight line between Point A and Point B. Where and when do you need me there?"

"The job is in Queens across from an old railroad building. I'll send you a detailed mission package as soon as I get back to the office. I assume you still have your handheld."

"No, I pawned it to pay for the drinks. Of course I still have it, I just don't carry it all the time. I check it several times a day. How many targets are we looking at?"

Hicks shrugged. "Maybe four. The railroad building has become a shooting gallery for junkies."

She looked him up and down and surprised him by actually smiling for once. "You need backup for only four? You must be slipping in your old age."

Hicks felt himself smiling, too. "I'm not slipping. I'm just old enough to not push my luck when I don't have to. The layout's tricky and I'm going to have to extract one of the junkies. I'll feel a lot better with you watching my back on the way out."

Tali looked at her glass again. "High dusting, just like you said."

"With minimal risk to you," he reminded her. "Standard equipment should suffice."

"Of course," she said. "Just send me the details and I'll be in position before you get there."

"Thank you," he said. "It'll mean an early start, though. Your Texan won't like that."

Tali shrugged her slender shoulders. "I'll do what I always do. Give him his little blue pill; he passes out and I tell him he was wonderful."

"Good girl." Hicks drained most of his scotch. The smoky burn felt good at the back of his throat. "Now, how do you want me to get out of here? If I just pay for my drink and leave, especially since we've been speaking Russian, the bartender might get suspicious. So you should act like I just..."

She quickly turned away from him as if slapped and sat ramrod straight. She snapped her fingers at the bartender and said, "This man is bothering me. He is a rude and common pig. I want him removed immediately." The act drew enough attention from the other patrons to be convincing, but not enough to be unbelievable.

Hicks feigned drunkenness and threw up his hands. "I'm going, I'm going." He drained his scotch and signaled for the check, which the bartender quickly printed up and gave to him.

As he reviewed his bill, he said to the bartender, "Christ, this new crop of Russian broads sure are touchy, aren't they? There was a time when speaking Russian got a guy special treatment from a Russian girl. Now? Nothing. Fucking Berlin Wall came down and now they all…" He made like his mind drifted as he tipped the bartender thirty percent. He'd always had a soft spot for bartenders and wanted to make sure he could come back to the bar again if he had to. A generous tip was a good way of staying on a bartender's good side.

Tali didn't look at him as he walked out of the bar either, trailed by the murmurs of the well-heeled clientele of the Mark Bar.

CHAPTER
11

HICKS HAD ALREADY been in position for over an hour by the time sunrise rolled around. He was less than ten miles away from the stylish décor of the Mark Bar but, given his current surroundings, he might as well have been on the other side of the world.

The convoluted absurdity of the entire situation wasn't lost on Hicks. He'd just arranged for an Israeli sniper to watch his back as he raided a drug den to retrieve the junkie son of a money manager who would give him a hundred grand to finance an operation against a suspected Somali terrorist who may or may not be planning some kind of attack on U.S. soil. One thing led to another and none of it might lead anywhere except smack into a brick wall.

Hicks felt the enormity of all the possibilities and

intricacies begin to build up inside him again, so he closed his eyes and focused on his breathing until he cleared his mind and calmed down. Nothing was ever a straight line in the intelligence game. When it was, it was too good to be true and couldn't be trusted. Every single thing was just one fucking serpentine path from one point to the next with the serpent frequently swallowing its own tail.

Hicks had known all of that before he'd gotten into the intelligence game, but it still bothered him at times. He decided to push his doubts and frustrations aside and compartmentalize like the Dean had said; focusing on the immediate task at hand. He had to get Junior out of the shooting gallery and home to daddy so Hicks could get that hundred grand.

When Hicks opened his eyes, the streetscape before him was still as bleak as it had been before. Rusting corrugated metal gates and dirty windows and sagging power lines stretched between termite ridden wooden poles. An old drunk adjusted his balls as he shambled across the street.

"Christ," Hicks thought, *"maybe I should've gone into insurance after all."*

In the light of a cold autumn dawn, the abandoned substation building looked even more rundown than it had on the OMNI feed. Its red brick façade had been faded by time, scorched by fire and tagged with layers of graffiti. Every pane of glass that could be broken had long since been broken and hastily boarded up in many places, but not all. The roof had long since gone to seed and bore the remnants of dead shrubs and weeds that sprouted up through the snow.

The building had once been part of a mighty transportation

network that took goods and people out to and back from Long Island. Now it was a forgotten ruin from the near-past; a haven for junkies looking for a quiet place to shoot poison into their veins for temporary peace.

Hicks had parked more than a block away from the building to avoid being spotted by any of Devron's lookouts. He didn't want to be mistaken for a cop—or worse—a rival drug dealer. Although he could see the building from where he'd parked, he got a bird's eye view of the entire facility via the OMNI feed on his handheld and dashboard screen.

The substation was set up in an ideal spot for a small incursion with minimal collateral damage. And, in clandestine work, minimal collateral damage meant minimal attention from any police patrols that happened to be rolling by.

The old substation was located in a seemingly forgotten industrial area that didn't see much traffic until later in the morning when workers showed up for their shifts. Across the street from the substation: an overgrown embankment lead up to the deserted railway; overgrown with trees and weeds. It afforded no cover whatsoever for anyone, including Devron's men.

If Hicks had been given enough time to plan, he could sweep in there with three guys; take out the guards and pull Junior out in a minute flat. Unfortunately, time and resources were not on his side. He felt his temper spike again. Fucking Colin.

An apartment building across the street from the near side of the substation offered a perfect sniper's perch for Tali, assuming shooting would be necessary. And Hicks fully expected shooting to be necessary.

The OMNI viewpoint high overhead showed two men guarding the front door. One appeared to be a black man, the other appeared to be Latin. Both of them were wearing polar fleece with the sleeves cut off despite the temperature being just above freezing. The fashion statement revealed veined arms and bulging biceps. The Latin man was sporting some impressive ink: a tattoo of a grinning skeleton showing five playing cards over his bony shoulder: a red queen, two black aces, and two black eights. Commonly known as 'A Dead Man's Hand.' The name 'Death Dealer' was written in calligraphy beneath it.

Hicks knew Tali would nail Death Dealer first. She hated tattoos. His partner would die next, probably from the same bullet if she could get the angle right. Hicks smiled. That woman was nothing if not efficient.

The OMNI feed didn't reveal anyone else outside the building, so he flipped it back to thermal feed. He picked up the heat signatures of about a dozen people still inside. Junior hadn't moved from the spot where he'd been sprawled out for the past few hours. Only three other people appeared to be ambulatory, strolling around the prone figures on the floor.

Hicks didn't bother adjusting the satellite's camera to check if Tali was in position. It was easer just to ping her handheld directly. "You in position?"

Her answer was immediate. A red dot appeared on his chest over his heart.

"I'll take that as a 'yes,'" he said.

The red dot disappeared.

Hicks put his Ruger in his lap and slipped the Buick into gear. "Look sharp because here we go."

A S SOON AS Hicks pulled up in front of the substation, Death Dealer and his friend puffed out their chests as they swaggered toward the car.

Death Dealer was the taller of the two and made a big show of bending to look into the car. Hicks didn't roll down the window.

Death Dealer yelled, "You best be moving that car, asshole, if you don't want to get hurt."

The .308 round from Tali's M24 rifle punched a hole in Death Dealer's chest. His partner was sprayed with a red mist, but had less than a second to react before a round slammed into his skull. Both men were dead on the sidewalk before the last echo of Tali's shots died away.

Hicks put the car in park and kept the motor running as he got out of the car. He kept his Ruger flat against his leg as he quickly walked toward the substation. He could see the doors were locked and was thinking about going back to pat down the corpses for a key when Tali fired and blew the lock to pieces. Hicks kicked the doors in the rest of the way and walked inside.

Hicks recognized Devron from his mug shot. He was walking toward him; his phone still pressed to his ear. He lowered the phone when he heard the door bang open. "What the fuck is goin' on out there, G-Dog. I already told you about keeping that..."

At the same moment that Devron realized Hicks wasn't

G-Dog; Hicks leveled him with a headshot at near point blank range.

The Ruger was designed for impact, not stealth, and the shot boomed like a thunderclap in the cavernous substation. Every junkie anywhere near consciousness jumped to their feet and bolted for the door. The huge windows on the street side of the building had only been boarded up halfway to the top. Hicks knew that, from her vantage point across the street, Tali would be able to provide some cover if he needed it.

Hicks did his best to dodge the herd of staggering junkies as he tried to locate the two other men he'd seen on the thermal OMNI feed. They may have been guards. They may have already run away when they heard the gunfire. Either way, they were unaccounted for and most likely armed. Hicks kept an eye out for them as he made his way to where he thought Junior was passed out.

Hicks found the young man lying in the same position where he'd been for the past few hours, still unconscious; a backpack as a pillow and a river of drool running from the corner of his mouth. His arm was draped over a woman next to him, but there was nothing romantic about the gesture. The woman's eyes were open and vacant. Hicks figured she was either dead from opiate shock or was well on her way. Too far along for Hicks to try saving.

He saw Junior's chest rise and fall in ragged, shallow breaths and knew the little bastard was still alive. And Hicks was that much closer to a hundred grand.

He was about to pull Junior up off the floor when he caught movement near an old piece of machinery to his right.

It wasn't the panicked movement of fleeing junkies, but the deliberate movement of someone moving into position.

Hicks managed to hit the deck just as the man opened fire from behind an old turbine. The rounds sailed high above his head, striking the brickwork of the wall behind him. He rolled clear and came up ready to fire just as the gunman's weapon clicked dry.

Hicks had a clear shot on the gunman and was about to fire when Tali's bullet punched a hole through the center of the gunman's chest; spinning him away from the machinery. Hicks held fire. No sense in wasting a bullet on a dead man.

In his ear, Tali said, "Get the boy and move. I'll cover you from here."

Hicks scrambled to his feet and went back to Junior. The young man was still too out of it to move on his own, so Hicks snatched him by the collar, jerked him to his feet, and threw him onto his left shoulder. The effort was easier than it should've been for a kid his size. Junior was only about a hundred pounds; heroin scrawny.

Anyone aware enough to get out of the building had already taken off by then. There were still a fair amount of people still on the substation floor; completely oblivious to what was going on around them.

Just as Hicks carried Junior back to the entrance; a shot rang out before he reached the door. Hicks doubled back and laid Junior down behind an old turbine. He crouched low while he talked to Tali.

"You got an angle on this asshole?"

"Negative," she said. "He ducked for cover just as you fell back. I don't have a shot. Your best bet is to leave the kid where he is and search for the gunman on your own. I'll take him if I get the shot."

Hicks knew he could wait out the gunman, but that would take time and time wasn't on his side. Despite the early hour, someone had either heard the shots or seen the horde of crackheads that had just hit the street and called the cops. He wanted to put as much space as possible between him and that substation as soon as possible, but turning his back on a man with a gun would be suicide, especially with Junior weighing him down.

To Tali, he said, "I need you to fire a round at his last position. See if that makes him jump."

Tali began firing into the old machinery at the far end of the building, Hicks broke cover and ran at a crouch toward the row where he'd last seen the gunman. He found the man lying flat on the ground, hands covering his head. As soon as Tali stopped firing, the man began to get to his feet, but turned when he saw Hicks walking toward him.

The man slowly raised his hands, but didn't make an effort to drop the gun. It wouldn't have mattered anyway. He wasn't one of the strung out junkies. He'd gotten a good look at Hicks' face. Hicks put him down with a single headshot.

"All clear," he said to Tali as he tucked away the Ruger and went back to grab Junior, "Just keep an eye out. There may be one or two more hiding in here someplace."

He threw Junior over his shoulder again and humped it outside; dumping him in the back seat of the Buick before climbing in behind the wheel. He was glad he'd kept the motor running. He did a tight U-turn and headed back down the street toward Manhattan.

As he sped off down the street, he asked Tali: "We are clear. Any sign of survivors?"

"OMNI shows no active threats," Talia reported. "Just sleeping junkies and dead bad guys. You didn't need me at all."

"Couldn't have done it without you, Ace." Hicks saw the street ahead of him was clear, so he floored it. "That was some real Oswald shit you pulled back there, young lady. I owe you one."

"Oswald was a pussy," she said, "and you don't owe me anything. Colin was a friend. So are you. Stay safe."

Hicks didn't bother asking if she needed a ride. She'd probably just give him another smartass response and that would kill his growing good mood. Tali had gotten out of much worse places than an industrial site in Queens. He knew she'd be long gone before the cops even got there.

Hicks already had a good idea of how the cops would play it, too. They'd roll up on the scene and work it like the place had been hit by a rival drug gang. The ballistics from Tali's rifle would probably throw them off a bit, but the ordinance was the same that American and European forces were using in Iraq and Afghanistan. The cops would figure a vet must be working with one of the gangs. They'd waste time running down all snipers with priors who'd just rotated back into the world. The cops would be extra cautious for a while until they began to forget all about the substation and think the sniper thing was just a fluke.

He doubted the NYPD would look too hard for whoever shot up the shooting gallery anyway. No citizens had been killed and no one would be calling out a manhunt to find the guys who'd killed half a dozen drug dealers. The event itself might make the eleven o'clock news, but it would be forgotten by the weekend. The cops might even forget it before then.

Hicks turned off the main avenue and hit the highway to take Junior back home. He stole a glance back at Junior and saw he was still passed out cold; coasting from the shit he'd pumped into his veins.

Now that he could see Junior in the growing daylight, he noticed all the junkie signs clearly: the sunken eyes and pockmarked yellowed skin and thinning hair that came from years of dedicated abuse. Junior was only twenty years old but looked like a hard fifty. His demons had him by the throat and whatever treatment his father had gotten for him hadn't done him much good so far.

All of that was going to change. Hicks was going to see to that. For Junior's sake. But more importantly, for the University's sake, as well.

A FTER TELLING RUSSO he'd rescued Junior, Hicks drove around killing time until the money man texted him he'd gathered the hundred grand.

It was just before ten in the morning by the time Hicks rolled into Russo's street. The cul-de-sac was buzzing with people going about their post rush hour routine. People getting a late start into work and parents coming back from morning errands. Just a regular day in suburbia; a humdrum morning gradually blending into a humdrum lunchtime. Ham and Swiss on white, no crust, and a glass of soy milk. Carrot sticks for desert. Gotta stay healthy. Life is so boring.

Nothing ever happens in the suburbs. Woe is fucking me.

It was all part of a sleepy, privileged existence they took for granted because they didn't understand what true lawlessness was like. They didn't know how easily their comfortable lives could be thrown into turmoil by just a few people with bad intentions at the right place and time.

The people on Russo's street complained about boredom, but didn't have the slightest idea of how much work went into keeping life that way. But Hicks knew because he'd made a career of doling out controlled doses of order and anarchy in order to keep everything in balance.

Hicks pulled up in front of Russo's house and got the money man on the phone. He wasn't surprised that he answered on the first ring. "Is that your car out front just now? Do you have him? Is he okay?"

"First things first, Vinny," Hicks said. "Do you have the hundred grand?"

"Yes, I gathered it quickly. I lied about having it in several banks. I only had it in one box. I went and got it as soon as they opened this morning. You can check if you want to. How is my boy?"

Hicks only cared about his own questions, not Russo's. "And you have all one hundred grand?"

"Yes, goddamn you. All of it in cash just like we agreed. Now tell me how he is and you tell me now!"

"You'll see for yourself in about thirty seconds," Hicks said. "You're going to bring the money out to the car, nice and slow, open the passenger's side door and get inside. You fuck around or waste my time, I drive away, and you don't see your son again."

Hicks killed the connection before Russo could argue or waste more time asking a lot of damned fool questions.

Russo was out on his walkway less than ten seconds later. He was still wearing the same clothes from the night before and hadn't shaved, either. Hicks unlocked the doors and let Russo inside.

Russo dropped the bag on the seat and forgot to close the passenger door as he kneeled on the passenger seat and reached for his son. "Junior," he wept as tears ran from his eyes. "Junior, it's daddy. It's me. I'm here."

Hicks grabbed Russo by the collar and pulled him down into the seat. "Close the door and keep your mouth shut."

Tears streaked down Russo's face as he did as he was told. He pulled the door closed and craned his neck to look back at his son. "I'm grateful to you for this. So grateful. You'll see. I'll…"

"Open the bag and let me see the money."

Russo's hands trembled as he got hold of the bag—a regular laundry bag—and opened it. He pawed through it and, via a quick count; it looked like all hundred thousand was there.

"You see? It's all right there, just like I told you it would be. Every penny. A hundred grand just like you wanted. And I promise, now that I have him back, I'll never let him do anything like this again. You've brought him back to me, and I'm so grateful that…"

Hicks scanned the street for anyone who was looking at the car. But as busy as the street was with mommies and daddies and nannies, no one was at this end of the cul-du-sac. That was good. "Put the bag in the back seat and take a good look at your boy."

Russo did as he was told. He reached back and put a hand on his son's shoulder. "Wake up, son. Wake up and let's get well. Let's get you inside where you belong."

"The only one who's going home is you," Hicks said. "Because he's coming with me."

This time, Hicks didn't have to push Russo into the seat. He fell back on his own. "What… what are you talking about? You said… you promised that…"

Hicks drew the Ruger and jammed it into the side of Russo's neck; pushing him against the passenger side window at an awkward angle. "I told you I'd get your boy back and that's exactly what I did. But I'm not going to let you have him because you don't know how to handle him. You don't have the balls to make sure he gets clean and I mean all the way clean. So I'm putting him in a facility where he won't have any choice but to straighten out. After ninety days, your boy will come back clean, sober, and refocused."

"But you can't do this to me," Russo wept. "Why are you doing this?"

"Because this isn't some after school special, asshole. I need you focused on the shit I need done and I can't have you worrying about this spoiled little bastard falling off the wagon in another three weeks." He pressed the barrel a little harder against Russo's neck. "So if you have any objection, tell me now, and I'll kill you both right here because you're no good to me if you're worrying about him. Understand?"

Russo nodded slowly that he did, just as the tears began to fall again. "I do. I guess it's the right…"

Then, Hicks jammed the barrel of the Ruger against

Russo's neck until the money man gagged. "And if you ever try to strong-arm me or hold out on me again, I'm going to be really disappointed. So disappointed, in fact, I'm going to take it out on him. I'll even make you watch before I hurt you even worse. Do you understand me?"

Russo nodded as best he could before Hicks pushed him out of the car. He almost tumbled out into his driveway, but he somehow managed to keep his footing.

Hicks pulled the door shut and pulled away from the curb. As he drove away, he saw Russo in his rearview mirror; looking lost in front of his own house while he watched a total stranger drive away with his son.

The same stranger he'd asked to rescue his son only a few hours before.

The same stranger who'd barged into his life and taken it over only a day before that.

The same stranger he'd allowed into his life by playing games with other people's money.

Hicks adjusted his mirror so he wouldn't have to see Russo standing there like a lost kid at a carnival. Fuck him anyway.

He knew there was a chance Russo might be so distraught that he might go into his den and blow his brains out. The gun was empty and Hicks had already taken all the ammo from the house, but he could've bought more. Or he could OD on his wife's sleeping pills. Hicks didn't care if he did. He had the money and that's what counted. If he got the kid straightened out, then it was a bonus.

He was halfway back to Manhattan when the dashboard screen showed an incoming call from Jason. He would've loved to ignore the call, but knew Jason was already tracking him on GPS. Ignoring him would only make a bad situation worse. He pushed the button on the steering wheel that allowed the call come through.

"This is Wallace," he said, using was the standard code that he was safe, but not alone.

"You've been very busy," Jason said. "Using our assets for your own vendetta."

"No vendetta, Ace." Out of habit, he checked to see if he was being followed. He wasn't. "Just doing what I've got to do to get shit done."

"Admirable," Jason said. "Who's that in the back seat anyway? OMNI can barely read his vitals."

Hicks didn't see the point in getting into the details. "He's nothing for you to worry about. I had to get Junior here out of some trouble in order to get his old man to help me finance your undercover operation against Omar. It turned out okay."

"That's what you think. Do you have any idea how much you put us at risk? What if you'd been killed? What if the police grabbed you on your way out of the place? What if they grab you still?"

Hicks smiled. "I didn't know you cared."

"I couldn't care less about what happens to you," Jason admitted, "but the Dean does, and he's who counts here. And there was no reason for you to risk exposure over a hundred thousand dollars. The money could've easily come from the Bursar's office."

"Which would've taken time we don't have," Hicks said. "Let's talk about something important, like my new operative. Have you narrowed down the search yet or are you still making up your mind?"

"You really are a condescending, despicable son of a bitch when you want to be."

Hicks switched into the passing lane and fed the Buick some gas. "Daylight's wasting, sunshine. I need details, not character assessments. What beauty are you sending me?"

"Our colleagues in Army Intelligence are bringing someone who should fit your requirements nicely. I'll send you a detailed profile on him in a few moments."

Hicks figured it could wait until after he dropped off Junior. "And what if I don't think he's qualified?"

"There's no doubt as to his qualifications," Jason said. "As for whether or not you like him, well, that's a risk we'll have to take. If you don't like him, the deal is off and we hit Omar as soon as we can. I don't have to remind you that there are risks in taking that course of action, too. Those are our options, none of them pretty."

Jason wasn't exactly a glass-half-full kind of guy, even in the best of times. "When does he get to New York?"

"I'll send you his file in a minute. In fact, he's being brought up to the city as we speak from Virginia. I believe he should be there some time this afternoon just before rush hour."

Hicks didn't like the sound of that. "Did you say he's being *brought* up from Virginia?"

"Yes. He was transferred him from Kansas just last night."

"Kansas?" He hadn't known Jason long, but he knew the way his mind worked and if there was a way he could make this op difficult for him, he would. "Kansas as in Fort Leavenworth, Kansas."

Jason said nothing.

Hicks grabbed the wheel tighter. "You're sending me a fucking jailbird from a federal penitentiary?"

"You're the one who stressed how quickly this operation had to come together, James," Jason reminded him. "If we had enough time to put together a proper op, we probably would've been able to find some squeaky clean, well-trained agent for you. But, as it is, this is the best we can do under the circumstances. If you can't make it work, then perhaps the Varsity should step in and run this entire operation for you?"

Hicks knew Jason would like nothing better than be able to take credit for bringing Omar in. Justice for Colin and stopping whatever Omar was planning didn't matter to him. He only cared about scoring points with the Dean. And Hicks would be damned before he let that happen. "Just have them bring the jailbird to the regular rendezvous spot on the west side and give me an call when they're an hour out. I'll be back in the city by then."

"What about your friend in the back seat?" Jason asked. "What's to become of him?"

"Not your problem."

Hicks decided he'd be the first one to kill the connection for once. He fully expected the little bastard to call right back, angry that he'd been dismissed. Instead, the dashboard screen showed that Jason had sent the information package on the operative as he'd promised.

Hicks didn't waste time wondering about what beauty they were sending him from Leavenworth. Probably some pissed off Ranger with a bad attitude and a hatred of superior officers. Hicks wasn't worried. He'd handled bad asses before.

Besides, before he worried about that, he still had one more item to check off his list.

Hicks adjusted the rearview to get a better look at Junior. Still passed out cold. He hadn't moved since they'd left the substation. He probably didn't even know where he was.

In a way, Hicks envied him.

CHAPTER
12

THERE WERE FEW things in the world that looked more ridiculous than a nightclub at ten o'clock in the morning. And despite all of its oddities, Roger Cobb's nightclub was no different.

After parking the Buick in the fenced in lot next door, Hicks let himself into the club through service entrance. He didn't bother bringing Junior inside with him. The boy still had a couple of hours of flying time before he climbed down from the dragon's back. Might as well let him keep sleeping.

The Jolly Roger Club was one of the more popular underground venues in the city. It had become a haven for the various types of vice that weren't always legal and, therefore, the club was not open to the general public. To call it a nightclub would've been vague. To call it a sex club would've been limiting its customers to the definable. It drew people from every level and strata of society and rarely actually closed.

Anything beyond the pale was the norm at the Jolly Roger; 'a dish for every taste' as Roger himself liked to say, as long as they could pay. The bar served top shelf booze and genuine absinthe, as well as liquid cocaine and other exotic opiates. All the usual drugs of choice were also on the menu.

The basement had a dungeon that would've make the Marquis De Sade blush. The subbasement was an opium den. Private sex chambers and corners were hidden throughout the darkened club. The Jolly Roger catered to every fetish and passion and proclivity on the Kinsey Scale and then some.

Hicks had worked with Roger all over the world. Those who knew him in the intelligence community regarded Roger as the best interrogator in the University system; a man who had mastered the delicate craft of using pain and fear to get the most out of a target without killing them. Despite the premise of primetime TV cop shows stressing forensics; dead men couldn't tell you much.

When Roger told him he wanted to leave the rigors of fieldwork behind, Hicks jumped at the chance to bring him to New York. Hicks gave him the money to start The Jolly Roger and it had been one of the best investments he had ever made. It not only provided a source of steady revenue for the New York Office, but had proven to be an invaluable way to blackmail some very powerful people as they did some very lowbrow things deep in the darkened rooms of Roger's club.

Hicks walked up the narrow stairway and through a maze of narrow hallways to get to Roger's apartment. He knew the door would be unlocked and didn't bother to knock before going inside. Of Roger's many faults, modesty wasn't one of them.

Roger's residence was more of a chamber than an apartment. Hicks wasn't surprised to see a naked young man passed out in a sex sling suspended from a hook in the ceiling. Hicks didn't know when or how Roger had managed to rig the hook that high and didn't plan on finding out, either.

Other men and women were in various states of undress and unconsciousness were lounging in candlelight on couches and duvets and pillows throughout the large, windowless room. Roger's chamber had the sprawling grandeur of Genesis sans the majesty.

Roger was propped up in the middle of an oversized bed that was twice the size of a normal king-sized bed. His glasses perched on the end of his nose as he tapped through his iPad. He would've looked like an aging college professor glancing over the New York Times on a sleepy Sunday morning if it wasn't for the naked men on either side of him; chained by their hands to the headboard. Their leather masks were the only allusion to modesty.

Roger looked up from his tablet when he heard Hicks clear his throat. "Ah, James," he smiled. "How good of you to drop by."

"Hope I'm not interrupting anything." Hicks motioned to the two nude men flanking Roger. "Looks like you had a hell of a night."

"This?" He waived it off. "Just another Tuesday." He set the tablet on the bare chest of the man to his left. "You look tired. Want some coffee? A client just sent me an entire sack of new coffee I think you're going to just love."

The idea of something as wholesome and commonplace as morning coffee in a place with a man in a sex swing struck Hicks as odd. But he remembered he was dealing with Roger Cobb and in Roger's world, odd was a term that had no meaning. "Sure, but I'll make it if you're… busy."

"Nonsense!" Roger threw aside the sheets as he swung out of bed. Hicks managed to look away before seeing more of his friend than he wanted to.

Roger ignored the bathrobe on the edge of the bed and walked naked to a small pantry in an alcove set into the side of the room. "What brings you here so early, my friend? It isn't like you to just drop by like a next door neighbor borrowing a cup of sugar."

Hicks didn't like talking around strangers, especially when they were dozing on pillows or handcuffed to bedposts. "It's important, and it's private. And, speaking of private, I'd appreciate it if you'd cover up."

Roger turned and smiled ever so slightly. He was a pale man of fifty with a runner's body, even though he didn't believe in exercise. His fair blond hair was almost white and he was lean and wiry and shorter than Hicks by an inch or two. When clothed, Roger gave the impression of being slight; almost to the point of being gaunt. But, like Hicks, he was far stronger than he looked.

"You jealous, old chum, or just embarrassed?" Roger looked him up and down. "Aroused, perhaps?"

Hicks tossed him the robe. "Just dangerously decaffeinated. It's already been a long day and it's not even noon yet. I need at least a cup of coffee in me before I see your Jolly Roger flapping in the breeze."

"You're no fun." Roger shrugged into his robe. "A wise man once told me that variety is the spice of life."

"If that's true, then your life is all peppers and hot sauce."

Roger grinned. "You have no idea." He hit the grind button on the coffee machine. Many of the people lounging around the room reacted to the whirring of the coffee grinder, but none of them seemed to wake up enough to leave.

"And don't be afraid to speak freely around my friends here," Roger said over the sound of the machine. "Last night was my Sensory Depravation Workshop. Beneath their masks, their eyes are taped shut and their ears have been plugged. I allowed them to speak but I'm afraid their voices went hoarse a few hours ago."

Hicks tried not to think about exactly why they'd lost their voices and hoped like hell Roger wouldn't tell him. Hicks' mind was already crowded enough without Roger's fetishes clamoring for space. "I'm sure everyone had fun, but I'll still wait until we're alone."

"Fun has very little to do with any of this," Roger said as the coffee machine stopped grinding and began to heat the water. "Neither does sex, really, though it's got more to do with it than fun. It's about embracing one's true nature. One's entire *being*, not just the façade we present to the world. The light as well as the dark. The accepted as well as the taboo and everything in between. The pain and the pleasure and all that comes with it." He wrinkled his nose. "It's a real mind fuck when you start to really think about it."

Hicks just watched the coffee machine gurgle as the coffee began to filter into the carafe. He hoped the smell of fresh ground coffee would deaden the stench of sweat and stale sex that filled Roger's bed chamber.

"I think you'll like this particular type of coffee," Roger went on. "It's a civet bean; which is produced in a manner that men like you and I can appreciate."

Since Roger's asides always had a point, he decided to play along with it. He was too tired to argue and still had a couple of minutes to kill while the coffee brewed. "Why?"

"Because civet beans come from Indonesia. The beans are first consumed by a mongoose; a creature that can easily be mistaken for a rodent both in appearance and action, but is actually—biologically—a feline. The mongoose first ingests the bean, then digests it and excretes it."

Hicks hadn't gotten much sleep and knew his mind might begin to drift, but thought he heard Roger correctly. "You're serving me cat shit coffee?"

"Don't be so crass, James. Yes, the bean is later collected from the dung of the mongoose, cleansed and roasted, thus giving it its unique flavor." Roger's smile returned. "Not unlike us. It's a process we can appreciate given all the shit we've been through and come out the other side better for it. I find the irony of the whole thing so fucking... rich."

The idea of drinking coffee plucked from cat shit would've turned off most people, but Hicks had eaten worse things and would probably do so again before he was through.

They stood in silence while the coffee brewed.

After the carafe was filled, Roger led Hicks through a panel of sliding Chinese doors at the other end of the room and into a small parlor with furniture that looked more suitable to Versailles than a sex club on the west side of

Manhattan. Roger took two coffee cups and saucers down from a cupboard and set them on the table between them. He poured Hicks a cup, then himself. The aroma was enough to give Hicks a jolt, but the taste even more so.

"That is good," Hicks remarked.

Roger agreed. "At over one-hundred-fifty dollars a pound, it should be."

Hicks set his cup down on the saucer. "I know we make good money from this place, but we're not making enough for you to be pissing away one-hundred-fifty dollars on coffee."

"Don't be such a Republican. I get it as a gift from a client in Jakarta who has his own civet plantation. His tastes are a tad on the eccentric side whenever he comes to New York, so he always makes it a point to send me a couple of pounds when he can as an expression of gratitude."

Hicks didn't want to think about the kind of sexual eccentricity warranted free samples of one-hundred-fifty dollar a pound coffee.

Roger sat on a velvet-covered Ottoman and set his cup and saucer on the glass coffee table in front of him. "I got your email alert yesterday and it was disturbingly vague. What happened?"

He gave Roger a quick rundown on Colin and Omar and everything that had happened in the park.

"But Colin didn't use," Roger said. "He didn't even drink."

"I know," Hicks said. "I think they shot him up full of heroin to get him to talk. I don't know if he told them about anything other than me, so it's best that everyone in the Office be on their guard."

"A wise policy." Roger looked at him, but not like he'd

looked at him before. "I know you two were close. How are you dealing with it?"

Emotions were an expense Hicks couldn't afford yet. "By trying to find out Omar's game. Until a couple of days ago, I thought he was nothing more than an amateur, but he's a hell of a lot more organized than I thought."

"If he caught on to Colin, then I'd say you must've underestimated this Omar by quite a bit. What does our beloved Dean have to say about all this?"

Hicks gave him another quick rundown on how everything had unfolded with Russo, Jason, and the Dean.

"Ah, the serpentine path we tread to protect our great nation," Roger said when Hicks was finished. "Crafty move about the hundred-thousand-dollar buy in, though. You knew the Dean would rear up at the expense."

"He let me have my way," Hicks admitted. "I'm sure Jason lobbied hard to run the whole op himself, but all the trouble I went through to get the money was worth it to keep Jason out of our backyard. I'll be damned if I'll let that asshole run an op in my own city."

"Our Jason does love his palace intrigue, doesn't he? The little shit." Roger sipped his coffee. "Is he married? Straight?"

"He'd have to be a human being first. I don't think they programmed him with a personality before they sent him to our planet."

"Interesting." Roger smiled over his coffee cup. "A week here might do him some good, then. Help him get in touch with the more intimate aspects of his nature. By the way, any idea about who they're sending up to work Omar? A familiar face, I trust."

"No. Jason just sent me the guy's profile while I was driving down here." Hicks saved the best for last. "I think he's a jailbird from Army Intelligence."

Roger laughed. "Doesn't Jason know the ones who stay out of jail are much better than the ones who get caught?"

"Either way, I'm stuck with him. Omar is panicked, and I don't have anyone On Staff right now who can serve as a convincing emissary in such a short amount of time. And there's no guarantees that you'd be able to get Omar to talk in time if we grab him."

"Oh, honey, I always get them to talk," Roger said. "But the open-ended time element is troubling. Trapping him with money is a wise tactic. Flush him out. Lower his guard and nail him."

Hicks began to grow aggravated again, so he took another sip of coffee. He'd spent the morning killing people. He wanted a drink. He wanted a cigar. But he wouldn't allow himself anything until the Asset was in place. He needed to stay pure if this was going to turn out the way it needed to.

"I need you to stay frosty until further notice, Roger. That means no booze, no nose candy. None of that shit until this is settled. If I call, I'll need you to right away."

Roger threw open his hands. "Have I ever refused you anything?" When he saw the joke fell flat, he added, "Anything at any time. You know that."

Hicks had known Roger long enough to know what he could do when he put his mind to it. And it was a comfort to have him around. "In the meantime, I've got Russo's kid in my back seat and I need him to get the Treatment."

"Getting people sober isn't my forte, but we have all the

necessary accoutrements to get the job done. What's the boy's poison?"

"Heroin. I need him straight because, with all my other money men possibly being compromised, I need his father's head in the game and I can't afford to have him worrying about his son. I'd appreciate you taking a look at him while I review the package Jason sent me on our new jailbird."

Roger drained the rest of his coffee and placed it on the saucer on the table. "Then I'd best see what I can do for him. How old is he, by the way?"

"Twenty, I think."

Roger's eyebrows rose. "He cute? Corruptible?"

Hicks took out his handheld. "Goodbye, Roger."

CHAPTER
13

THE MILITARY COPS who were transporting his new asset told Hicks they'd be at the rendezvous point by two o'clock. Hicks was there by one-thirty.

The meeting point was a small parking area near Chelsea Piers at Twenty-third Street and the Hudson River off the West Side Highway. Hicks chose it because it was a public area, outdoors and popular with joggers and dog walkers, even on a cold November afternoon with piles of snow still on the ground. It was the last place a spy book or movie would pick for such a meeting, which made it the perfect place for exactly that kind of meeting. People were easy to spot in abandoned or industrial places. They stood out in deserted buildings, but not standing around a busy parking lot along the West Side Highway in the middle of the day.

SYMPATHY FOR THE DEVIL

Besides, after reading the Asset's personnel file, Hicks knew he had a hell of a lot more to worry about than being spotted by Omar's men. His new operative's name was Hasim Kamal, who'd changed his name to Hank Kimmel before enlisting in the Army ten years before.

Now he was an ex-Army Intelligence operative; a Green Beret with a long rap sheet and a rotten attitude. According to his record, Kamal had breezed through the demanding Special Forces training regimen, but chaffed against the restraints of command. His personality tests showed that he had a natural resentment of authority but possessed a high level of self-motivation. That quality served him well running black bag operations in Afghanistan, but it had also landed him in prison.

Men like Kamal had been trained to do much more than the Rambo guns and guts stuff they showed in the movies. Kamal's high level of intelligence led his superiors to send him to Wharton to learn how business worked. He breezed through the courses as easily as he had the Special Forces program. Then Army Intel tasked him with setting up his own shop in Afghanistan to run guns and information to and from America's allies. He'd proven exceptionally good at espionage and living a double life.

He was so good that he'd managed to prevent his superiors from learning about the lucrative opium business he'd set up on the side. And the string of whorehouses for GIs in Karachi. The fact that Kamal had branched out into the drug and flesh business didn't bother the brass as much as the fact that he'd kept all of the profits for himself.

During his court martial, he changed his name from

Hank Kimmel back to his birth name of Hasan Kamal and claimed to be a pious Muslim persecuted in an infidel army. His sudden Islamic epiphany did little to endear him to the military tribunal and he was sentenced to twenty years hard labor.

This was the man Jason believed was the best chance at reaching Omar.

And Hicks had to admit that he was probably right.

Hicks needed a man who Omar would believe was representing a wealthy financier who might support whatever he was planning. The operative had to be able to finesse Omar into believing the financier would fund it if it sufficiently glorified Allah. Hicks needed a man who could project enough authority to command respect from Omar and his people, but not enough to kill Omar's confidence altogether. He needed to get Omar to spill his guts about whatever he was planning. Hicks knew the trick would be to get Kamal to tell him everything that he saw.

When the black Explorer with Virginia plates, pulled up into the parking lot, Hicks knew he'd have the chance to ask Kamal in person.

He watched the two plain-clothed MPs get out; one providing cover while the other opened the rear passenger door to let Kamal out. He was in federal prison blue pants and a threadbare green Army parka that was too small for him. His hands and feet were shackled and the MP discreetly unhooked him and let him loose. They pointed out Hicks to Kamal and watched their prisoner walk away. Both had their hands near their weapons. One deviation from the path and they'd probably put Kamal down.

Kamal was about a head taller than Hicks—about six-two—and much broader. His official service picture showed he'd had a lean, trim physique once upon a time, but a year's worth of prison chow had given him more of a sunken, fallow look. His eyes didn't look as confident as they once did. They were wider now and far more intense. That was good. Hicks knew Kamal's dark complexion and Islamic upbringing would help him fit in with Omar's crowd. It was human nature for people to be more inclined to trust people to whom they could relate. It would just help convince Omar that Kamal was the real deal; the man with the cash to make all his dreams of death and destruction come true.

In the latest pictures Hicks had seen of Kamal at trial, Kamal had a bald head and was clean shaven. The man who walked toward him now was still bald, but had a ragged beard streaked with gray. That was very good indeed, Hicks thought. That level of commitment would put him in solid with Omar's crowd. They liked their lunatics scruffy.

Hicks leaned back against the Buick as he watched Kamal approach. He didn't move to welcome his new charge or shake his hand. But given the drastic size difference between the two of them, he was glad he had the .454 Ruger on his hip.

When Kamal got close enough, Hicks let his coat fall open so he could see the grip of the gun on his hip. "You Hank Kimmel?"

"That was only the name I took to blend in with my oppressors. My given name is Hassam Kamal." He offered a hint of a bow. "As-salaam-Alaikum."

Hicks wasn't impressed. "Save the ceremony for the

150

shitbirds in the prison yard, ace. Last time I checked, pious Muslims don't run drug rings and whore houses. That shit didn't cut you any slack with the tribunal, and it cuts even less with me. Anybody tell you why you're here?"

"Broad strokes, but I guess you'll tell me more, right?" Kamal blew into his hands and rubbed them together. "Shit, man. Couldn't we have met inside where there's heat and shit?"

"Answer the question."

"All I know is that when I landed in Kansas, a white man in a black suit met me on the tarmac and told me there'd been a change of plans. He handed me off to two more white men who brought me here in chains."

Hicks looked back at the two MPs by the suburban. One looked Asian and the other was black. Neither of them had taken their eyes off Kamal. "Funny. They don't look white to me."

"White isn't just a matter of skin pigmentation. It's a mindset of oppression."

"Well now you've got another white oppressor whose presenting you with two choices. The first choice is that you do a job for me and, if you follow orders and live, maybe earn yourself some good will from your Uncle Sam."

"I already got that part on the tarmac," Kamal said. "How about you tell me what's behind Door Number Two?"

"I let those two nice MPs back there take you back to Kansas. No Dorothy and no yellow brick road for you, Toto. Just twenty years of hard time in a military stockade. I don't give a shit about which one you chose so long as you chose right here and right now. What's it going to be?"

"I need to know more before I make up my mind."

Hicks shook his head. "You know that's not how this works. You come on board, you're in, and then you get briefed. You say no, your oppressors back there take your ass to jail for the next twenty years."

Kamal smiled. "Is it dangerous?"

"We didn't bring you here to sell Girl Scout cookies. Last chance."

Kamal looked around him. There wasn't much of a view of the Hudson from where they were standing, but the sky was high and blue overhead. Cars sped by them in both directions on the West Side Highway. It wasn't ideal, but it was life, and it was more of life than Kamal had seen since being in jail. It was a beautiful day to make a choice between bad and worse decisions.

"What about when it's all over?" Kamal asked. "Do I have to go back to jail?"

"That depends entirely on you," Hicks said. "You get results, you go free. Maybe even have a chance at a better life for yourself. But if you fail or lie to me or defy me at any time, even once, you go straight back and do every minute of your sentence."

Kamal shook his head. "Sounds like some real Dirty Dozen shit if you ask me."

"Oh, but I am asking you, asshole." He made a show of checking his watch. "What's it going to be?"

Kamal looked up to the cloudless sky and closed his eyes. "I choose freedom."

Hicks gave a thumbs-up to the MPs and watched them climb back in the Explorer.

Kamal turned and watched the men drive away. "Just like that, huh? You got that kind of pull?"

Hicks opened the back door of the Buick. "Get in. We've got a hell of a lot of work to do and not a lot of time to do it."

Kamal clapped his hands and let out a whoop as he began to get in the back seat. "Free at last, free at last. Thank God almighty, I'm free at last."

Hicks knife-edged his left hand hard into Kamal's throat. The move caught the bigger man off guard and at a bad angle. He dropped to the asphalt, dead weight, gagging. All of the advanced training in the world couldn't prepare you for a quick punch in the throat.

Hicks dropped and put a knee hard into Kamal's gut and his .454 Ruger Alaskan under his chin. "Get this straight right here and now, asshole. This isn't a fucking vacation, and you're not free. Those men were the last chance you had to back out and stay alive. From here on in, I own your miserable ass. One false move, one fuck up, or step out of line..." Hicks pressed the barrel of the gun against Kamal's left ear. "You catch two taps right there and dumped in the river. Understand me?"

Hicks didn't know what he expected Kamal to do once he got his breath, but he sure as hell didn't expect him to laugh. And that's just what Kamal did. A deep belly laugh from the soul. "You crack me up. You think this is the first time I've had gun at my throat, motherfucker?"

"No." Hicks thumbed back the hammer. "But it'll sure as hell be the last unless you start taking this shit seriously. The second you think you're indispensable, I'll show you just how wrong you are."

"Killing me in a parking lot ain't very subtle for the CIA."

"A dead black man in a parking lot ain't exactly breaking news. And I'm not CIA." He moved the Ruger back under Kamal's chin. "We good?"

Kamal winced as he tried to get up, but couldn't. "Can't get any work done by lying here, now can we?"

HICKS DROVE, TAKING intermittent glances in the rearview mirror to watch Kamal rubbing his throat.

"You slammed my head good when you took me down, man. Got me all fucked up. Might have a concussion."

Hicks focused on the thickening crosstown traffic. "I thought you Green Berets were supposed to be tough?"

"Fool me once shame on you," Kamal said. "Fool me twice, it's your ass."

Hicks smiled. "Yeah, I'll have to keep that in mind."

"Hey, what's that gun you pulled on me anyhow? Looks like a .38 but felt a whole lot heavier."

"That's because it's not a .38. It's a .454 Ruger Alaskan. Range isn't great, but up close, it'll core a charging grizzly bear."

"Fuck you mean 'core a grizzly bear?'"

"You ever core an apple? Same thing. Except it could do that to a charging grizzly. Put a hole in him from crown to culo and stopped him cold, even at a dead charge."

Kamal blinked his eyes clear. He looked out the window at the growing lunchtime traffic and Hicks saw him mouth the words 'core a grizzly bear.' Hicks knew he'd made his point.

Given the traffic, the drive out to the apartment in Queens could take a long time, so Hicks decided to strike up some conversation. Maybe get to know him a bit before he started briefing him. "I read your file and it looks like you were a pretty good soldier. How'd you go from being G.I. Joe to being the Birdman of Alcatraz?"

"You don't know how it is, man," Kamal said. "They train you to serve and they train you to kill, but they don't train you how to live with it afterward. To handle all the shit you see and keep it from eating you up inside. It's hard to maintain, man. It's damned hard."

Hicks took a sip of the civet coffee Roger had fixed him for the road. It was an hour cold but still flavorful. "Wow. Sounds rough."

"Man, you don't know the half of the shit I've seen."

"So, let me get this straight. You volunteered for the army, then volunteered again to become a Green Beret, then volunteered yet again for Army Intelligence. You knew all of these things you were volunteering for were forward units bound to see action. You see said action, and then decide to use that as an excuse to break the law?" Hicks laughed. "Don't bullshit a bullshitter, ace. Least of all me."

"Alright, white man. Let's follow your lead and cut the bullshit. If you're not CIA, what are you? NSA? FBI? Some other black bag bullshit outfit?"

Hicks wouldn't tell him any more than he had to, but he had to tell him something. He needed him focused on Omar's men, not who Hicks worked for. "I'm not part of the alphabet soup you're used to dealing with, so don't waste time guessing. All you need to know is that we had the juice to get you out of jail and we've got enough juice to stick you right back there if we have to."

Kamal threw up his hands. "No problems here, boss man. I've always been more of an entrepreneur than a detective, so it doesn't make a damned bit of difference to me who's signing the checks. Just tell me who to salute and who to kill."

"If everything works out the way it's supposed to," Hicks said, "you won't be doing much of either. You're going to be playing the money man for a financier from Afghanistan. The man you're supposed to be fronting for doesn't know you but will vouch for you if it comes to that."

"What's this money man paying for?"

"We don't know, and that's the problem," Hicks told him. "We need you to give this clown Omar the money, get him talking, and then tell us whatever you learn. He's supposed to be planning something big, but those are all the details we have. The money you give him will help us find out a hell of a lot more. I'll give you a complete file on Omar when we get to where we're going."

"What kind of player is this Omar trying to be?"

"That's what we're trying to find out, which is why I put my man inside his cab stand. Omar's travel pattern tipped us off. Trips to Yemen, Pakistan, Egypt, and Syria but never back home to Somalia. That was strange. He also made some large cash transfers while he was over there; the last one for thirty grand to an electronics store in Aleppo, Syria."

"I know where Aleppo is, man," Kamal said.

"Good for you," Hicks said. "We've never been able to get to the bottom of where Omar's donations went or what they paid for, but it was large enough to catch our attention. My man was one of the few non-Somali drivers in the place but was still able to blend in with the rest of them.

"So if he's so good, why am I here?"

"Because he got turned a couple of days ago, which caused Omar to run. He also somehow got the numbers for a bunch of Middle Eastern types who like funding actions against the West." He looked at him in the rearview mirror. "You're the guy who works for a financier who's sympathetic to his cause."

"We'll get to that part in a minute," Kamal said. "What about your man? He dead?"

Hicks kept his eyes on the traffic. "Yeah."

"Any of the others live?"

Hicks looked at him in the rear view mirror until Kamal looked away.

"Stupid question, I guess. Sorry I asked."

"Omar's gone off the grid," Hicks went on. "The only way we can flush him out is through you. You'll be playing the role of the financier's emissary. You'll give him some money and make him pitch you on what he's planning. Then you report back to me and we move on from there. A day's work, maybe a day-and-a-half and you're home free. All you have to do is follow your training and you get your freedom."

"If it was that easy," Kamal said, "I'd still be in a goddamned jail cell. How the hell did a cab driver from Queens get contacts like that? And all that money?"

"That's something I hope you'll ask Omar," Hicks said. "You're the man with the money he needs, so you're entitled to ask all the questions you want. I've already put a list of questions I want you to ask. You'll have plenty of time to memorize it before I put you with Omar."

"Whole goddamned thing sounds a little too simple for my taste."

"And simple's the way it's going to stay, unless you complicate it. If I had someone On Staff with your combination of skills and background, I'd be briefing them right now instead of you. But you know Omar's religion and you understand his customs. You literally speak their language. We've even worked out a cover that's close to the one you had in Afghanistan. Your cover's still good as far as the locals are concerned. Everyone thinks you ripped some people off and ran back to the states. No one knows you were Army Intelligence."

"How much of a bankroll will I be working with?"

"A hundred thousand. You'll give them ten at the initial meet. More later after you and I debrief. You'll have the entire hundred in your room at all times in case they demand to see the money."

Kamal let out a long, low whistle. "That's an awful lot of money to place in the hands of a convicted felon like me."

"I'm not crazy about it," Hicks admitted, "but you're a stranger to them, and they have no reason to trust you right off the bat. We never told them how much the financier would send them, but a hundred grand in cash should make them believe you're serious. Tell them you can get more if that's what it takes."

"A man like me could have a lot of fun in this town with a hundred grand."

"A man like you will catch a bullet in the eye if you take that bag from your room without my say so."

"Are you really always this uptight or is this just for my benefit?"

"These sons of bitches just turned one of the best operatives I ever worked with," Hicks said, "so I'm not exactly in a joking mood. You take these guys lightly, you're liable to wind up dead just like him."

Kamal threw up his hands. "Fine. Jesus. How many people are we working with?"

"I don't know how many Omar will have with him."

"No, I mean our team. Us. You and me. How many others working with us?"

Hicks never shared operational detail with an unknown operative. He talked about the setup instead. "I've set you up at a small apartment in Astoria. It's simple and plain because Omar and his people like simple and plain."

"How plain?"

"You'll have a bed, a laptop, and a throw-away phone at your disposal. You'll be able to read all about your cover story on the laptop once I give you the password, but you won't be able to email any friends or reach out to anyone while you're under. Our mission files are encrypted, so even if they do look at your computer, all they'll see is spreadsheets and travel itineraries. Your file says you're good with computers, but you're not better than me. If you try to email anyone, I'll know, and there will be consequences."

"I figured that," Kamal said. "Now how about answering my question about backup."

Hicks was encouraged. At least he was paying attention. "You'll be under constant surveillance," was all Hicks said. "Anything happens, we'll know about it. Keep your phone on you at all times, even if they make you take out the battery."

"What good is it if it doesn't have the battery?"

"More good than you know," was all Hicks told him. He checked the rear and side view mirrors to see if they were being followed, but didn't see anything. "Just keep the phone on you if you can."

"You got it, chief," Kamal said. "By the way, I'm going to need a gun."

Hicks had been wondering when that would come up. "No way."

"Then you might as well turn this thing around and take me back to the Penn, because there ain't no way I'm going in there unarmed."

"You're not muscle," Hicks explained. "You're the money man and money men don't need to carry guns. You're a boss. You're Santa Claus, the Easter Bunny, and whatever Muslim equivalent there is all rolled up in one package for these guys."

"I ain't bulletproof neither," Kamal said. "If these assholes throw down, I'll need to be able to defend myself."

"You're a fucking Green Beret," Hicks said. "You are a weapon. Besides, if they pat you down and find a weapon, they'll get suspicious. We need them calm and talkative. No one's going to throw down anything but information. All you have to do is pump them for details, pass it along to me, and you're a free man. And I'll be there to back you up the entire time."

Hicks took another look at him in the rearview mirror. He watched Kamal pulled at his prison shirt. "I'm gonna need some walking around money. Get me some new clothes, at least. The shit I've got on are stockade threads. I can't roll up on them dressed like this. I need to make an impression."

"I've got the kind of clothes Omar will expect you to wear at the apartment. The place is already stocked with food, too. After I drop you off, you're not allowed to leave the apartment until you meet Omar. No walking around money. No getting beers or getting drunk because pious Muslims don't drink beer or get drunk, remember? After we get you settled in and debriefed, you'll call Omar and set up a meeting for tomorrow. Everything you need to know about your cover is already on that laptop. We won't call them until you're comfortable with your cover."

"As long as I'm comfortable with it by tomorrow, right?"

"Like I said before, you're a Green Beret. You can handle it."

"I'm glad one of us thinks so," Kamal said. "So what do I call you, anyway?"

"Whatever you want, Ace. It makes no difference to me."

"How does Power-Tripping Cracker Motherfucker sound to you?"

"I've been called worse." He looked at Kamal in the rearview. "Don't be nervous, honey. This isn't your first dance. You'll do fine, and all the boys will love you. Just stick to the plan, and you'll come out of this better than you were going in."

Kamal folded his arms across his chest and went back to staring out the window. "I don't like you."

Hicks steered the Buick into the passing lane. "Then you're in good company."

CHAPTER 14

HICKS DROVE BACK to Manhattan after getting Kamal set up in the apartment—the top floor of a four-story walk up in Astoria.

Kamal had spent most of the time complaining about everything. The décor wasn't right. The clothes were uncomfortable and bland. The food in the fridge was lousy. Hicks reminded him he was supposed to be a pious Muslim on a mission, not some drug dealer in a Miami Vice episode. He even complained about the large Islamic wall calendar Hicks had tacked to the wall next to the door. Said it was depressing as hell.

Kamal was complaining about the television being too small even as Hicks walked out the door.

Hicks didn't tell Kamal that the apartment was under

surveillance via the cellphone he'd given him as well as the TV. Both items were plugged into the OMNI network and monitored everything that went on in the apartment without Kamal's knowledge. Kamal didn't know the phone was designed to transmit even when it was off or even when the battery was removed. He certainly didn't know the TV had been optimized to monitor his every move. OMNI would send him an alert if Kamal left the apartment or so much as touched the hundred grand.

But Hicks didn't expect to get any alerts. He figured Kamal would take a couple of hours and get himself acclimated to his newfound freedom. Maybe take a shower or grab some sleep in the first real bed he'd seen in over a year. He was a free man now and, one way or the other, he wouldn't be going back to prison. If he did what he was told, Hicks would give him a chance at getting a job within the University system. If he failed, Hicks would put a bullet in his brain.

That's why Hicks was surprised when the Buick's dashboard screen showed an OMNI alert for a call being made from the burn phone he'd given Kamal. A call to the number Omar had given the Middle Eastern financier so his emissary could reach him.

Hicks didn't know whether to be pleased by Kamal's enthusiasm or disturbed by it. He couldn't have properly reviewed Omar's file in such a short amount of time. Hicks had given it to him only twenty minutes before.

He listened to the phone ring as the traffic approaching the Fifty-ninth Street Bridge slowed to a crawl. It was a bad time to be taking the bridge; just after six o'clock and rush hour was in full swing. But for once, Hicks didn't mind the traffic. He could concentrate on Kamal's conversation with Omar.

When someone answered in Arabic, Kamal responded in kind. The banter ended there as Kamal didn't speak Somali and wasn't expected to. His cover was from Nigeria—the same place where his parents had been born—so there was no expectation of a common language.

But Hicks still recognized the voice on the other end of the line. It was the same voice he'd heard on hundreds of hours of surveillance audio. It was the voice of Omar.

Kamal wisely switched to English with a heavy Nigerian accent. "I am afraid, my brother, we have the same faith but different languages. I suggest we meet and discuss our brotherhood in person where our privacy can be assured."

Hicks couldn't see Omar, but he could hear the excitement in his voice. "Yes, of course, my brother. We have much to discuss and much to make our uncle happy. We thank Allah that he has told him to send you to us. Your faith will be well rewarded."

Hicks hoped Kamal would play it aloof and he did. After all, he was the one with the money Omar needed. "Then I suggest you have someone meet me tomorrow morning at ten o'clock so we can discuss the matter in greater detail. I despise tardiness, so be sure not to be late."

Kamal gave them an intersection near the Astoria apartment and killed the connection.

Hicks hadn't told Kamal the cellphone was designed to transmit even when it appeared to be off. Since it operated on the OMNI system, the screen could be dark and the battery could be removed, but it was still powered wirelessly by the network. The computer and television worked the same way.

Hicks expected Kamal to call him and ask him how he thought it went, just as they'd discussed. He expected Kamal to be like most field agents and need some kind of reassurance that he'd done well.

But Kamal didn't call. He didn't say a word or make another sound. Not even a whistle. Instead, he heard what sounded like a light switch click off, followed quickly by a light snoring.

Hicks killed the connection. He knew OMNI would monitor the scene and automatically alert him if Kamal went on the move or if he made or received another call.

Kamal was obviously one cool customer. Hicks was beginning to think that maybe Jason had sent him the right man for the job after all.

A text message from Jason appeared on his dash board screen:

> AN ENCOURAGING BEGINNING. WHERE
> ARE YOU GOING NOW?

Hicks decided not to respond. A little bit of Jason went a long way and he'd been dealing with the insufferable bastard all day long.

He needed a drink.

CHAPTER
15

Hicks had always preferred the lobby bars of New York's grand hotels as opposed to the Irish bars, cocktail lounges, and other types of watering holes throughout the city. He liked the mix of locals and visitors and how the crowd was almost different every single night. Change made patterns harder to form and patterns lead to predictability. Predictability meant death for people in his line of work, so the fewer people who knew his habits, the better.

The Bull and Bear Bar on the corner of Forty-ninth and Lexington at the Waldorf Astoria was his favorite bar in the city. He liked the circular wooden bar and the way the light hit the bottles just so, especially after sunset. He liked how the bartenders were always efficient and friendly, but never got too chatty. The bar drew a nice mix of well-heeled travelers and jaded New Yorkers who sometimes dropped in for a couple of drinks before catching the train back to Suburbia. Occasionally, some wide-eyed tourist might wander in and nurse a beer, shocked at how much it cost while they gawked at the drapes and the bronze bull and bear above the bar. They went there so they could tell the folks back home that they had drinks one night at the Waldorf Astoria as if paying more than ten dollars for a glass of alcohol made them cosmopolitan.

Ambiance was a state of mind. Liquor dulled the pain no matter where you drank it or how much it cost. The romance of booze was a glass of bullshit, but he ordered it anyway.

Hicks lucked out and found a parking space on the street a block away. He left the events of the day and the chilly New York evening behind him as he pushed through the revolving doors of the Bull and Bear. It was after seven o'clock by then and the after-work crowd had thinned out a bit. The pre-dinner folks had already gone to eat and the restaurant was still busy.

That left the die-hards at the bar; the people who had good reason to drink and no reason to be anywhere else. Hotel guests, mostly. Business travelers and tourists too tired to go anywhere else. And people like Hicks, who just needed to be somewhere other than where they were supposed to be.

Hicks never walked into a bar with an agenda. He never went in looking for company or conversation or to meet a woman. He never had an agenda because he hated being disappointed and New York was a city built on a bedrock of disappointment. But he never allowed himself to bring alcohol into the Twenty-third Street office. The life of an

Office Head was a lonely enough and drinking alone only made it more so. He'd seen many a good Office Head devolve into self-pity and drunkenness, and he'd be damned before he let the same thing happen to him.

Besides, his job afforded many more pleasant ways of getting himself killed.

That made it a bit easier for Hicks to spot the woman who was sitting alone at the right side of the bar, near the stairs that led back up to the rest of the hotel. She was tapping away furiously on her BlackBerry and didn't look happy about it.

He decided she was probably north of forty, but not by as much as she looked. She wore a gray business suit that revealed a thin, but not skinny, frame. Her short blonde hair might've looked severe on another woman, but she managed to wear it well. Her pearl earrings were just feminine enough to soften her overall look without going overboard. She the hands of a pianist—long and elegant—that busily pecked out that email on her Blackberry with great urgency.

There was something about her that he liked more than just her solitude or possible availability. He sensed a strength in her or maybe, or maybe an intent sense of purpose, simply by the way she looked. Either consciously or subconsciously, women always put thought into how they looked. If that was the case, and Hicks believed it was, then he liked the way her mind worked.

The half-drunk glass of white wine at her elbow didn't look like it had been touched it in a while and whatever the email was about, it was demanding all of her concentration. Judging by the look on her face, he was glad it wouldn't appear in his inbox.

SYMPATHY FOR THE DEVIL

Hicks noted the absence of a ring on her left hand, not that he'd ever let a few ounces of gold and rock get between him and a good time. It was all just innocent chatting and flirting until it became more than that. And if it did, he let nature take its course.

He sat down two stools to her right on the other side of the curve. It gave him a good view of most of the bar and restaurant. He could see who came in off Lexington Avenue and who walked down the stairs from the hotel. He wasn't expecting any trouble in a place like The Bull and Bear, but in Hicks' world, trouble was never that far away.

The bartender, a brunette he remembered called Gayle, recognized him from the last time he'd been there about a month before. She knew him enough to be polite but not enough to be overly friendly and certainly not enough to remember his name.

"Long time, no see." She laid a paper napkin on the bar. "What can I get for you?"

"I'll have a Laphroig, double and neat. Water on the side, please."

He'd hoped ordering the Laphroig might get the businesswoman's attention, but if it did, she didn't show it. He'd found the name of the scotch was always a good icebreaker. And if that didn't work, the smoky odor of the stuff usually did the trick.

She kept thumbing away at her keypad, paying no attention to him at all. Just like Tali. But he saw her expression soften just a bit as Gayle placed the double Laphroig on the napkin and the bartender took his card. He told her to keep the tab open.

The woman finally lowered her Blackberry and looked at his drink. "Which scotch is that?"

He noticed her eyes were an unpleasant shade of blue. "It's called Laphroig. It's got a real smoky flavor."

She went back to reading her Blackberry. "Never heard of it before. Smells like an ashtray."

"Beauty is in the palate of the drinker. On a cold night like this, there's nothing better."

"No thanks." She began tapping away at her device. "I'll stick with my wine."

Hicks knew he had to strike the right balance. He needed to be charming without being too suave. Suave tended to put women on the defensive so early in the dialogue and he was far too intrigued by her to let her pull up the drawbridge just yet.

"In vino veritas," he quoted. "And judging by the way you're pounding away at that Blackberry, someone's about to get a hell of a lot of truth from you."

"That's one way of putting it." Her eyebrows flicked up as she kept typing. "Don't you just hate it when people tell you how to do your job?"

"It's an occupational hazard with me. What kind of work do you do?"

"I'm a consultant," she said; the response coming a little too quickly. "Organizational Psychology. Sounds like a lot of nonsense unless you're familiar with what it is, but it's important, believe me."

"I'm sure it is." Hicks sipped his scotch and felt warm as the smoky booze hit home. The temporary relief alcohol gave him was the only real emotion he allowed himself to feel. It was a safe emotion because it was easy to control. It came out of a bottle, and it could be kept there until he decided to have it. He liked it that way. "You don't strike me as the kind of woman who enjoys wasting her time."

"Now I'm curious," she said. "Just what kind of an impression does a woman who enjoys wasting her time give? In your opinion."

Hicks gave it some thought. "Someone who kills a buzz by responding to emails in a place like this. And all appearances to the contrary, I think you'd prefer to be enjoying your wine right now."

"You've got a point," she said as she turned the Blackberry off and tucked it in her suit jacket pocket. He noticed she didn't put it on the bar or in her bag, which was on the bar next to her. Instead, she put it in the right hand pocket of her suit jacket, even though he was sure she was a lefty. Her wine was on her left side, but Hicks was sitting to her right.

She said, "What did we do before these damned things anyway?"

"We had conversations," Hicks offered. "Real relationships and real lives, not all the virtual reality of tablets and smartphones. I remember when you had to go to the store if you wanted to chat on line."

"I think we've gotten dumber as the phones have gotten smarter." He watched her reach for her wine with her left hand. "What about you? What do you do for a living?"

Hicks was in a playful mood. "Take a guess."

Her eyes narrowed as she gave him an appraising look as though he was a work of art or an antique. "Given what you've said so far, I'd say you're probably a philosopher. Or a professor of some kind."

"Let's just split the difference and say I'm a philosophy professor," Hicks laughed. "I wish I had it so good. Unfortunately, I don't. I'm in sales."

"Sales can be interesting, depending on what you sell."

He gave his standard answer. "I sell technology solutions to businesses. My clients tell me what they need and I help them find a solution that makes sense." It wasn't a total lie, and it was close enough to the truth so it was easy to remember after a couple of drinks. "It's not as sexy as Organizational Psychology," he flicked his finger against his glass, "but it pays well enough to keep me in Laphroig."

"Sounds like you help people solve problems they didn't know they had."

"That's the general idea, in theory. When everything works out the way it's supposed to, which it almost never does."

"If things always worked out the way they were supposed to, most people would be out of jobs," she said. "All day long, all I hear are problems and that's after everything has fallen apart. I just sift through the pieces, make recommendations and they pay me for my time. I'm never around long enough to see the good I've done, if any. There's always another contract to fill and another company that needs help." She seemed to have caught herself and rolled her eyes. "Listen to me grumbling. I can't really complain, though." She picked up her glass, again in her left hand. "Keeps me in white wine."

Hicks drank as she sipped. He decided to let the silence between them grow. He knew they'd reached a critical moment. The conversation had either run its natural course and they'd go their separate ways or she'd find a way to keep the conversation going. He had a feeling she'd find a way to keep it going.

He took a casual look around the bar. A few new people had drifted in and out since he'd sat down, but no one had come in alone. No one was paying much attention to anything other than the glass in front of them or the person sitting next to them.

She asked, "You're very observant, aren't you?"

"People watching is my favorite hobby," he admitted. "Everyone has a story and everyone has a reason for being here, even if it's no reason at all."

"You really *are* a philosopher, aren't you? And what's your reason for being here?"

"Good conversation and good company. Yours?"

"Work," she allowed, "and maybe some good conversation as well."

Just the kind of answer Hicks had been expecting. "Where's home?"

She hesitated for an instant before saying, "Virginia. Alexandria, actually. Nice place, but it's not New York."

"Well, if it was, it wouldn't be Alexandria. Where'd you go to University?"

This time, the hitch wasn't as subtle, but she rebounded better. "I never had the grades for a university. It was Dallas Community College for me and proud of it. First in my family to ever get that far in school, by the way. Communications major. Never thought I'd wind up in organizational psychology, but here I am."

Hicks smiled. "Life is like that. Who would've thought a

philosophy major would end up selling computer solutions? So, how long have you been working in education?"

This time, there was no hitch. No pause at all, just correction. "Well, it's not really education. It's organizational psychology, which is kind of related, but not really."

"It's all psychology, I guess." Hicks took a drink and put his glass back on the napkin. "After all, if you weren't really a psychologist, you wouldn't have been sent here to analyze me. Would you?"

She tilted her head just enough to show confusion. "I'm sorry?"

"This is a new one for Jason. They used to only send men to analyze men and women to analyze women. The whole opposite gender thing risks skewing the results."

She appeared flustered. "I'm not sure what you're talking about, and I don't even know anyone named Jason."

"Maybe not," Hicks said, "but you definitely work for the University. I'm just surprised they didn't send a trained field agent to look me over. I'm curious. Why did they send you?"

He watched her take her Blackberry out of her suit pocket and put it in her bag as if she was getting ready to leave. "I don't know how much you had to drink before you got here, but I think you're past your limit already. You're not making much sense at all."

Hicks looked at his glass of scotch and focused on the facts. "The first mistake you made was asking what kind of scotch I was drinking. I asked for Laphroig, which could be bourbon or rye or even whiskey. But you already knew from reading my file that I only drink scotch. Then you put the Blackberry in your pocket instead of your bag. Most women put their Blackberry on the bar or in their bag if it's near by. You didn't. You put it in your right hand pocket even though you're left handed."

"No, I'm not."

"Your bag and your wine are on the left side of you and you drink with your left hand. That's not much to go on normally, but remember, I'm trained to see those things. You put it in the pocket closer to me because you thought your handheld could record our conversation better. That's why I know you're not a field hand because a field hand would know the damned things pick up sound anywhere. But you're not familiar with the device, are you? I could tell by the way you were pounding the damned thing when I got here."

"I don't know what…"

"Your other mistake was that you hesitated when I asked you wear you lived. You were going to say something else, probably Maryland, but forced yourself to say Alexandria. Nice place, but I'd wager you live in Maryland. Virginia's close enough, though, but I wondered why would you lie about where you're from? That's why I asked where you went to University. You paused for just a second and said Dallas. But you don't have a Texas accent and you would've had one if you'd spent enough time in Dallas to go to a community college. And you wouldn't have lost it by living in Virginia. Softened it, maybe, but you'd still have it."

She folded her arms. "Are you a writer? Because this is some good material you're coming up with."

Hicks went on. "You're obviously not used to field work because you're a little rough around the edges. You didn't put your phone in your bag because they don't allow bags in the

University's Behavioral Analytics Department in Maryland. You put your Blackberry in your pocket because you didn't want me to get a look at it because I might recognize it. You put it in your right pocket because you thought it would make it easier for OMNI to hear us. And most damning of all, you never asked my name because you already knew it."

She blinked. Twice.

"Now, if I'm wrong, I'll pay for your drink and walk out the door. But if you leave, I'm going to give the Dean a full report on just how you screwed up and, my guess is, your equipment will be terminated before you reach the corner and Jason will be in a hell of a lot of trouble for wasting University resources like this." Hicks finally looked at her. "How'd I do?"

She didn't react. She didn't even blink. She simply sat still with her arms still folded across her chest. She looked around at various people at the bar and then back at her glass. "This... this isn't..." Her hand quivered as she reached for her wine.

Hicks subtly slid it away from her. "Calm down. You're not in trouble, and I'm not going to hurt you. I'm not going to burn you with the Department, either, so long as you do exactly what I tell you. I already scanned the room and no one is shadowing us so it's just you and me."

She looked at her hands. "But the hotel cameras?"

"I checked them a long time ago. They face the street and the cash registers, not the patrons." He had another question on his mind. "Now you're going to tell me who sent you."

"But they're still tracking our phones." She struggled to keep her voice a whisper. "They'll know we were here. And my handheld is on."

"Let me see it."

She dug it out of her bag and handed it to him. "It's not my normal device. They gave it to me today before they sent me up here. There's an icon I had to select to start recording, but…"

Hicks found it and togged it off. "That's what you were banging away at it when I got in here, wasn't it?"

She nodded. "It didn't seem to be working."

He handed it back to her. "That's because it isn't. These old concrete buildings make it tough for OMNI to get a signal." He smiled. "Even the University technology has some limits, which I find refreshing, in a way."

She dumped her handheld back in her bag like it was on fire. "But they'll know we met, right?"

"They'll know we were in the same bar together, but they don't necessarily know we spoke. The security cameras don't point to the patrons, remember, so there's no immediate danger. But you'd better tell me who you work for and who sent you so we can figure this out together."

She reached for her glass of wine again and, this time, Hicks let her take it. "You were wrong about one thing. I don't work in Behavioral Analysis. I work in the Field Analysis Department in Maryland." She took a sip and shook her head. "Christ, you picked up on that fast. Your file said you were highly observant, but I didn't know you were that good."

"Skip the flattery and tell me who sent you."

"I don't know who ordered you to be observed and that's the truth," she said. "The order came in through the system yesterday morning with an information package on you and an assessment date starting today. I only got off the train a little more than an hour ago."

Hicks knew she wasn't lying. Her supervisor would've known who'd ordered the observation, but not necessarily her. "What did they want you to find out about me?"

"General appearances and impressions," she told him. "Your state of mind. Your mood. How you conduct yourself in social situations. Are you chatty in situations where alcohol is involved? Do you say too much or too little? Your superiors seem to be concerned that you might be showing signs of field rust and are in need of a sabbatical. I've read your record and god knows you could use it. Moscow. Tehran. Guatemala."

Hicks wasn't interested in going down memory lane with a total stranger. "How did you know I'd be here? Not just where I was, but where I'd go. Hell, I didn't even know where I was going until I got over the bridge."

She set her glass of wine on the bar. "I don't think I can tell you that."

Hicks pulled out his handheld. "Then update your resume, sweetheart, because you're going to need a new job."

"Okay, okay." She slumped, ruining her perfect posture for the first time since he'd gotten there. "I didn't know you'd be here, but I had an educated guess."

"How?"

"It's part of a new system the University is putting in place. It's called Coherent Speculative Analysis. It measures metrics of faculty personnel based on their actions in the field. It takes all the data of where they go, what they do, and when they do it, adds in factors like stress and mood, and uses it to predict what a subject might do next. It takes time to build up a composite, but after a while, it can be a fairly good predictor of movements."

Hicks had heard rumblings about that kind of program within the University for a while, but had never heard anything concrete about it until now. It wasn't enough that the University was already plugged into almost every network device on the planet. They were spying on their own people, too. "Go on."

"Your metrics predicted a strong likelihood that you'd come here after what you'd done today and where you were driving from," she explained. "It also took your past actions into account and, since you hadn't been here for a while, I took a gamble you'd stop at a bar in midtown. When I saw you had begun to look for a parking spot in this area, I took a gamble and came here."

Hicks hated being predictable, even when a supercomputer was doing the predicting. "Jesus. They don't even trust their own people anymore."

"They never have. This program has been in development for over a decade and it's finally starting to become reliable." She took her glass of wine. "You're right about me reading your file. I know about what happened to your agent and, believe it or not, I have helped field personnel deal with that kind of loss in the past. That kind of thing is never easy, and I can only imagine what you're going through."

"No you can't, so don't even try." He took a long pull from his glass and signaled the bartender for another round. "And another wine for the lady. She's earned it."

"No," she said. "I'll have what he's having. Exactly the same way."

Hicks looked at her. "You sure? You said it smelled like an ashtray."

"It does, but I really hate wine. I'm a tequila girl, actually. Your file said you preferred elegant blondes and, since I don't like cocktails either, so white wine was the best I could come up with."

Hicks smiled. "Is that really in my profile? That I like elegant blondes?"

"It is, along with a lot of other things. But your real name has been redacted. It's the only file I've ever seen where an Office Head's entire background was missing. All it lists is your current identity and your safe identity as Warren."

"Adds to the mystery," he said. "You haven't told me your real name, either."

She took the glass of scotch the bartender placed on the napkin in front of her. "Do we really need names at this point? It'd kill the mystery, right?"

Hicks clinked glasses with her. "Touché, madam. Speaking of mysteries, are you really a blonde."

She drank the scotch and didn't even flinch at the taste. Maybe she really was a tequila girl after all. "That's smoother than I thought it would be."

Hicks drank too. "The booze or my line?"

"Both," she smiled. "And just like with the Laphroig, there's only one way to find out. By sampling it for yourself."

HICKS FOUND OUT for himself after the third round of drinks.

The University had allowed her to book a room in the Waldorf for the rest of the week, so the mystery was solved after a short elevator ride to her room on the eleventh floor.

She was different than Hicks had expected her to be, even after she'd lowered her guard. Her body was lean and toned, yet soft in all the right places. Their lovemaking was more sexual than sensual and kissing hadn't entered much into the equation. She squeezed his neck when she climaxed, but no nails across the back or moans of ecstasy.

When he climbed off her, he thought she'd be distant and avoid being close. She surprised him by laying her head on his chest.

"Well, I would've lost that bet," he admitted.

"What? That I'm not the stuck-up bitch you thought I was?"

"No. That you really are a natural blonde after all."

She ran her hand over his chest. "That's one mystery solved." He felt her tense. "You know none of this was part of the assignment. This was about you and me, not work."

Hicks had run honey trap operations for a good portion of his life and knew this wasn't one of them. "I know that, but I thank you for telling me anyway."

"Yes, of course you would." She settled back down. "Stupid me."

Hicks held her closer. "You're married, aren't you?"

"Was it that obvious?"

"No, just a feeling I got."

"I suppose you have to live off your feelings, don't you?

Your impressions?"

"I do. They're usually right for the most part, the way my impression of you was right about you working for the University."

"And the way your impression of Colin was wrong?"

He wanted a cigar or a cigarette, but could tell she didn't smoke. "It's not the same thing. He died because of outside circumstances that were beyond my control. With you, everything was right there. I was just smart enough to see it."

"That's why I know you would've seen it with Colin if there'd been anything to see. Deep down, you have to know that."

Now he really wanted a cigarette. "It doesn't help much. He's still dead."

"And you're alive and doing something about it. That's what's important. Your work is important and you're very good at what you do. Your reputation in the University is very impressive, though a bit..."

"A bit what?"

"Troubling, I guess. Your file is full of professional accomplishments, all of them impressive, but nothing personal. Nothing about your real name or where you're from or what you did before the University. The only hobby they have listed for you is that you like blondes and drink scotch."

Hicks smiled. "There are worse pursuits. Some might call them virtues."

"But other members have many hobbies listed. Painting or art or travel. Things like that. Nothing like that is listed for you, and I have a feeling I know why." She picked her head off his chest and looked at him. "You don't have anything else besides this, do you? All of you have is this job, this life. And you don't want anything else."

Hicks liked the way she looked now. Not as hard as she had looked downstairs, but her eyes were still just as cold. He'd never been big on self analysis, mostly because the subject bored him. And a one night stand wouldn't change that. "I can see why they sent you to make a field analysis of me. Says a lot about your skill set, too."

"I'm obviously not much of a field agent." She ran her hand down his chest to beneath the sheet. "But I've got my talents."

"Is that so?" He felt himself begin to harden again. "Prove it."

And that's exactly what she did.

CHAPTER 16

HICKS LEFT HER early the next morning and stopped by the Office to change clothes and gear up. He knew he'd be spending a lot of time in the car, so he wouldn't need the parka. Instead, he wore a lighter winter coat complete with Kevlar lining. He wasn't expecting things to get hot, but he took extra speed loaders for the Ruger and six extra clips for the Glock backup.

According to the tracker in Kamal's phone, he had been picked up by Omar's men in Astoria and driven out to the Midwood section of Brooklyn.

Judging by the audio Hicks could hear from the phone, the drive to Brooklyn was a quiet one. Hicks wasn't surprised. Over the past several months of surveillance, he knew Omar had run a very tight ship. He never told any one person more than they needed to know; either at work or in his personal life. Omar was a confirmed bachelor with few habits and none of them bad. He read the Koran, prayed every day at exactly the same time, and went to bed before nine.

Most likely, he'd sent two of his stooges to go pick up Kamal rather than risk the exposure of going himself. They probably weren't like the rookies he'd sent to the park. Omar wouldn't make the same mistake twice. These boys probably weren't hired guns, but Hicks bet they'd be sharp enough to spot a tail. Omar had always been careful and he'd be even more careful now.

Hicks knew he didn't have to drive out to Brooklyn. He could've easily monitored everything via OMNI from Twenty-third Street. Kamal could handle himself if things got dicey and didn't need backup, even if he was unarmed.

But Hicks drove out there anyway because nothing about this operation felt like a regular op. It wasn't just because of Colin's death. He'd lost men in the field before and probably would again. Death was part of the job.

It was because of something the woman had said to him last night in bed. 'If there'd been something to see, you would've seen it.' He knew she was right, but it helped to hear it from someone else.

There was desperation to Omar's actions that felt like something was about to happen and happen soon. Something big and permanent. Omar had led a quiet and deliberate life up until this point. If he was getting worked up now, it must be for a very good reason.

Hicks had just gotten to the Brooklyn Bridge when his dashboard monitor showed that Kamal's cellphone had stopped moving. Judging by the audio feed he caught via the phone, the men had gotten out of the car and were walking inside. He selected the GPS on the touch screen of his dashboard and started in that direction.

The audio quickly became muddled as several men began speaking in Arabic at once. Hicks was hardly fluent in Arabic, but he'd picked up enough of the language to know it was just the customary exchanges of blessings and platitudes.

Hicks was encouraged by the sound of a familiar voice in the mix. Omar's. If he was there, then they'd learn more about his operation and fast.

The other voices dissolved into mumbles as Hicks heard Omar beckon Kamal to come with him. That was followed by the creak of a door and the sound of metal chair legs scraping on hardwood. A private conversation between Omar and his patron's emissary.

Good.

Hicks let another car cut in front of him as he concentrated on hearing what was going on in that room. If he'd been in the command center, he could've pulled up the video from Kamal's camera phone, but he knew the system was already doing that. He'd check it later. For now, he concentrated on hearing what was going on there while not crashing his car.

He heard Omar begin speaking in Somali, but Kamal tactfully shut him down.

"My apologies, my brother." The Nigerian accent on his English was perfect. "I am from Nigeria and am not familiar with your language. We can speak in English or even French if you prefer."

Omar chose French. "Then let us speak in the language of

the somewhat lesser white devil."

Kamal laughed and responded in kind. "A wise choice, my brother. Now, our wise uncle who shall go unnamed has asked me to come visit you to help you with some difficulty you are having."

"You are wise to avoid mentioning him by name, but before we speak of him, your wounds trouble me. The cuts and swelling on your face."

Hicks gripped the wheel tighter. He knew he shouldn't have hit him yesterday in the parking lot, but he'd needed to make a point. He only hoped Kamal's bruises didn't throw him off their game plan. *Stick to the script, you son of a bitch. Stick to the script.*

"These are the marks of the martyr I wear proudly, for they are ccourtesy of the Nigerian Special Police," Kamal said. "I don't think of them as wounds. I think of them as honors won in our ongoing campaign against the infidels. The men who gave them to me are half a world away and have nothing to do with our purpose for meeting here today."

Hicks had to admit he was impressed with Kamal's ease with bullshit, but Omar didn't sound totally convinced. "You should be in hospital, receiving care."

"Perhaps, but our uncle's concern about the well-being of your noble cause exceeds any concerns about my condition. Your request drew his attention, my brother, and his interest."

"And, I hope, his support?"

"His support depends entirely upon what you have to show me today." Hicks heard something, maybe the bag of money he'd given Kamal, slide across the floorboards. "But he does hope you will accept this gift as a small token of his praise of your noble efforts."

Hicks clapped his hand against the wheel. That's it. *Hook him and reel him in.*

Omar was quiet for a moment as Hicks supposed he looked in the bag. "It appears to be most generous and very humbling," Omar said, though Hicks heard disappointment in his voice.

Kamal must've heard it too because he said, "His support will be far more generous once we learn more about what you propose to do."

"Our uncle's concern is both appreciated and justified. As you will soon see, his support will be vital to the success of our cause."

"Although I don't doubt the sincerity of your words," Kamal said, "our uncle has heard many such claims about many ideas. He remains dedicated to supporting Allah's work against the infidels, but he must also be cautious."

Hicks swerved as he got cut off by a moving truck as he tried to get off the highway. *Good for you, kid. Keep pushing him. Don't kiss his ass. You've got the money he needs.*

"You will see evidence of this and more this very day, my brother. And I am sure you will agree that our efforts will bring great glory to our uncle and to Allah himself, all for very little expense. Our plans are grand in scope but humble in their execution. But I'm afraid that we must take certain precautions."

"What kind of precautions?" Kamal asked.

"My people did not ask to search you when you got in their car as a courtesy to you and our uncle. But I'm afraid now I must insist. I must also insist that you not only leave your phone here but you dismantle it as well."

Hicks prayed: *Don't let them smash that fucking phone. Don't...*

"I will remove the battery and leave it here as you ask," Kamal said, "but as it is my only contact with our uncle, I suggest that you instruct your people to not destroy it."

Omar seemed to agree. "Then I will make sure my men leave it alone, but it must remain here."

Hicks remembered to breathe. Now that he had them isolated, he could program OMNI to track their thermal signatures wherever they went.

Unfortunately, he wasn't near his computer and the traffic was moving too fast for him to program OMNI himself. He could've eyeballed them as they left the building, but he was still eight miles away and Kamal needed protection now.

Hicks activated the car's speakerphone and said, "Communications Department."

OMNI recognized the command and dialed the pre-programmed number over the secure private network.

A bland male voice came through the Buick's speakers. "How may I direct your call?"

Hicks used the standard Urgent All-Clear (UAC) code. "This is Professor Warren and I need to speak to a supervisor, A.S.A.P."

"I happen to be a supervisor, Professor. What is your emergency?"

"I need a thermal tracking protocol established on an Asset. I'm in transit and can't do it by myself."

Hicks heard the click of the supervisor's keyboard. He knew he was pulling up Hicks' surveillance profile so he could see what Hicks was seeing. An icon appeared on the lower right hand corner of his dashboard screen, showing him the Communications Department had logged into his system. By then, Omar and Kamal had gotten up and headed for the door. The screen switched to thermal.

"Are these the two signatures you want to track, sir?"

"I need them tracked and his phone to stay recording as well. The phone doesn't have to be a live feed if bandwidth is a problem. Thermal tracking of the subjects is the priority."

He heard the man's fingers clicking across a keyboard. "One moment."

A space between two cars opened up on Hicks' left side. It wasn't much, but just enough and he floored it, shooting the gap and getting around the ass-dragging son of a bitch in the Prius in front of him. He was only halfway across the Brooklyn Bridge and needed to make up time if he was going to be of any use to Kamal. Omar and his men might be taking Kamal upstairs or on a three hour drive some place. OMNI would track where they went, but couldn't do much remotely if shit went sideways.

A bus drifted from the left lane into the center lane without signaling. Horns blared and tires screeched. Hicks floored it and shot past the whole mess, hoping to gain precious seconds to Midwood.

The supervisor asked, "Are you okay, sir?"

"Worry about securing that tracking protocol, ace. I'm fine."

More keys clicking and then, "Protocol is up and good. Passive surveillance on the cell phone is continuing. Are you watching the feed live?"

"In between avoiding getting run off the road by a fucking bus, yeah."

"Very well. OMNI will also send you an alert if the targets separate. We've got a heavy demand on the feed today, so we may not be able to track two of them live at the same time."

Hicks didn't like it, but saw no point in arguing. He could remember a time when they had three satellites parked over the US alone. Now they only had four spread out throughout the globe. Luckily, one was all his.

"Identify the larger of the two men. He's my Asset. Make sure the satellite tracks him as a priority. We can't lose him."

"Understood, Professor. Will you require Varsity assistance with your research?"

The last thing he wanted was those gung-ho assholes kicking in doors and killing off leads. "Not at this time, but I'll let you know if I do. Thanks for the assist."

Hicks killed the connection and went back to passively watching the drama play out on his dashboard screen while he kept an eye on the traffic.

He tapped the screen and changed it to the standard GPS view. OMNI tracked Kamal and Omar as they left Midwood—just the two of them in the car according to the satellite. That fit with Omar's cautious nature. The system tracked them as they drove to a building near the Barclays Center in Brooklyn. Hicks followed at a distance.

He tapped the building they'd entered, which automatically called out an information bubble that gave him details of the structure. Who owned it and when it was built. It's general purpose. It was a former warehouse that had been converted into a modern self-storage facility a few years before.

Omar obviously had something to show him. Something that had to be kept away from the place where they'd just met. Something that needed to be protected under lock and key.

Hicks tapped the screen and changed the satellite settings to read radiological signs from the building, but OMNI wasn't picking up elevated radiation levels. That didn't mean it couldn't be in a lead container. It just meant that if it was radiological, it was well protected.

Without Kamal having his cellphone, Hicks couldn't hear what was going on, but he could still track them from above. He switched the screen from radiation detection to heat signature and over-laid that image with an X-ray of the building's structure. The floors appeared to be solid concrete, so the satellite wouldn't be able to give him a definitive lock on their position once they were inside. It was a minor setback. He would just have to wait until he debriefed Kamal to learn what he'd seen.

So close, but yet so far should be the motto for intelligence work.

Kamal and Omar had been in the facility for twenty minutes by the time Hicks was able to find a parking spot around the corner from the storage facility. There'd been no sign of them since they'd gone inside and he was beginning to get worried. He tried to access the facility's security systems, but the system—if they had one—wasn't hooked up to the Internet. The place also didn't have Wi-Fi because he couldn't find a trace of a signal. The facility billed itself as state of the art protection for its customers' valuable goods. The place hadn't been state-of-the-art since Reagan had been president.

But as the amount of time that Kamal had been inside

dragged on to thirty, then forty minutes, Hicks began to think maybe he should call in a Varsity squad to at least seal the place up and raid the unit before Omar could get away. Omar could be showing Kamal a tactical nuke or a dirty bomb. He could be showing him plans for the bomb they wanted to build if they had the money for parts and someone who could help them build it. He could be torturing him right now, but there was no way for Hicks to know. And a lack of knowledge could get you killed in this business.

Hicks knew Omar was protecting something; something that was in that facility. He needed to know what it was, but he couldn't let the Varsity come in and kill his one true lead before he knew more. Roger's ego aside, interrogation was always a risky choice.

Forty minutes became an hour and the satellite image hadn't changed. Just a bland image of the bland roof of the bland storage facility hundreds of miles below the satellite's lens. Hicks watched people walk by the building via OMNI, only to see them cross the street in front of him a few seconds later. He could remember when VCRs were cutting edge technology. Now he could watch someone walking in front of his car from space at the same time as he saw them in real life.

Hicks could also remember a time before all this; back when many things had been new to him. When he used to think people were basically good and had the best interests of their fellow man at heart. But gradually, he learned that people generally only had their own interests in mind and would often do anything to further their own goals. Whether it was to get in good with their boss or bang some girl or get a thumbs up from Allah, people were often willing to do whatever it took to get what they wanted. It didn't matter if you were after a better job or better karma or forty virgins in paradise; it was all about getting that shiny medal at the end of the race.

And once Hicks had come to understand that's how people worked, he was able to see the world for what it really was: a cold and desolate fucking place.

Hicks checked the time on the satellite feed. It had been over an hour and their car hadn't been moved. There also hadn't been any other vehicles anywhere near the place. No one else had gone in or out of the facility, either.

Then, the image on his dashboard screen blinked to life as the satellite picked up Kamal's and Omar's heat signatures as they walked out of the building. Hicks changed the zoom on the camera and switched it from heat signature to tactical. He focused in on both men.

Kamal had kept his beard, but shaved his head completely bald and wore a white skull cap. He looked nothing like the federal fugitive Hicks had seen the day before. Instead, he looked like a slightly underfed man who had something on his mind.

Omar's appearance never changed. He was a slight man and walking next to a bruiser like Kamal made him look even smaller. He was bone skinny and bug-eyed. The few teeth he still had were small and crooked. His black skin was marked with lighter patches and pockmarked from acne. He had the haunted, hunted look of a man who'd been held down most of his life, probably because he had been.

In Somalia, Omar had been an orphan who didn't have

any friends and he'd never had any formal education, at least none the University could verify. Yet somehow, this man—who'd been forgotten since childhood—had managed to scrape together enough money to leave his country and head to America. He'd started his own business and now wanted to be a major player in the jihad against his adopted country.

Men like Omar scared the hell out of Hicks because they had nothing to keep them going except the hatred that fueled everything they did. That hatred gave them strength and motivation and purpose. God help whoever found themselves on the other side of men like Omar, because the only way to stop them is with a bullet in the brain.

And Hicks would be glad to put a bullet in his brain, but only after he found out what he was doing.

As he watched Kamal and Omar come out of the storage facility, he looked to see if either of them was carrying anything or had anything tucked under their shirts. Both of them looked completely normal, except for Omar, who was fiddling with something in his hand, probably his car keys. He switched to the thermal feed to see if they were carrying anything that had changed their heat signatures. A bomb or something chemical but nothing abnormal came up.

They looked like two regular guys getting back into a car on a quiet Brooklyn morning. Kamal rode shotgun while Omar climbed in behind the wheel, started up the car, and pulled away. The car was a faded blue Corolla from the late nineties with a good amount of rust where the paint had shipped away. Hicks saw they were heading his way, so he quickly ducked, making like he was looking for something in the glove box.

Hicks knew OMNI would track them wherever they went, so there was no need for him to follow too close behind. Besides, he had other things to do.

He tapped the dashboard screen and rewound the OMNI footage to get a closer look at what Omar had been holding in his hand when he left the storage facility. Hicks stopped the playback at the point where Omar and Kamal had first left the building, then zoomed in on Omar's hands. The image was blocky and pixilated at first, but Hicks knew the software would scrub the image until it became much clearer.

And as the image came into focus, Hicks realized that Omar had been holding a key, but it hadn't just been a car key. One key had the Toyota logo on it. But the other was a storage locker key. And the small label on the face of the key read 338.

"Bingo," he heard himself say. "Got you, you son of a bitch."

Hicks wasn't surprised when his handheld began to buzz. He knew either the Dean or Jason had been watching the feed and saw what he'd been analyzing. He just hoped it was the Dean. But unfortunately, it was Jason.

"Good work," Jason said when Hicks allowed the call to go through. "It appears Omar has taken our friend into his confidence."

Hicks knew he was looking for a pat on the back for picking Kamal, but he wouldn't give him the satisfaction. "Ten grand in cash helps buy a lot of confidence with a rookie like Omar, but we won't know what he told Kamal until we debrief him."

"Too bad Omar made him leave his cellphone back at the

house or we might've had an idea on what he'd shown him in there."

"But at least we know which storage unit is his."

"It certainly does. Because even though the storage facility doesn't have their security cameras hooked up to any external network, they do back up their computer to a remote server twice a day. I was able to access those records and found out that number three-three-eight is a large locker that is registered to a John Smith of 505 Fifth Avenue in New York. The bill is paid in person in cash each month."

Hicks wasn't surprised Jason had gone ahead and looked up the record. He also wasn't surprised it was a phony name and address or that Omar paid for it in cash. "What size is the unit?"

"The largest they have available. Ten-by-ten-by-eight. No inventory on what's in there, unfortunately, but there never is in those kinds of places."

Hicks didn't expect there to be one. "I'll worry about the unit later. Now that we know where they are…"

"…we can keep an eye on the facility through OMNI," Jason said. "We'll watch all emails in and out, cell and web traffic, customers, everything. You're not the only one around here who knows what they're doing, James. I'll also send in a Varsity unit to look around Omar's storage unit and see what they find."

"No you won't," Hicks said. "Not until I get the chance to debrief Kamal. Omar could have anything in there. He could also have rigged the unit to explode if tampered with."

"We're not talking about a bunch of rookies here," Jason said. "We've got some of the finest technicians in the world.

I think they can safely figure out if the storage unit presents a threat."

"I know they're the best because I trained half of them," Hicks reminded him. "But a proper infiltration in a building like that takes time. The walls are too thick for OMNI to read, so any threat assessment will have to take place on site. That takes time and draws attention. Right now, there's no sense in risking discovery until Kamal tells me what went on in there."

Hicks could hear the disappointment in Jason's voice. His checkmate had been short-lived. "Very well. When will you debrief Kamal?"

"As soon as I can." He checked OMNI feed and saw Omar was, indeed, heading back toward Queens. He probably wanted to drop off Kamal himself. Maybe see where the man was staying to make sure it wasn't too expensive. Like the Waldorf Astoria. "In the meantime, did the Dean have any more luck getting a match on the man from the camera's SD card?"

"In a matter of speaking, yes. We can talk about it after you debrief Kamal."

Hicks hated stone walls, especially in a fluid field op like this. "No, we'll talk about it right now. If he's part of this somehow, I can get Kamal to keep an eye out for him when he's with Omar."

Jason said nothing.

And Hicks was getting frustrated. "Jesus. This guy can't be that important, can he? We would've had something on him ourselves if he was that big."

"We don't know for certain and that's the problem," Jason

admitted. "The Dean reached out to our British cousins who practically admitted they'd embargoed the image and the identification but they're refusing to let us know why. Whoever this man is, he's very important to Her Majesty's government."

Hicks swore as he put his head back against the headrest. He'd been hoping the French had embargoed the image. They were usually inclined to share information after a fair amount of posturing. They enjoyed reminding fellow intelligence agencies that they still had extensive networks in Africa and the Middle East.

But the English were different. Movies and espionage books liked to show the British intelligence forces as inferior to their American counterparts. They were often portrayed as the handsome, oblivious older brother who'd fallen to drink and now depended on his younger brother for support.

Hicks knew that wasn't the case now and never really had been. While America's intelligence services had gotten bogged down fighting Communist expansion in Korea, Vietnam, and elsewhere around the globe, Britain had quietly protected its networks and more than held its own in the intelligence community. Their empire may have crumbled after the war, but their intelligence capabilities didn't. American bluster had its place on the world stage, but British resolve was still every bit as formidable as it had ever been.

And Hicks knew there must be a damned good reason for protecting that image he'd gotten from the SD card.

"Is the Dean at least hopeful he can get some traction with them?"

"Hopeful, but not optimistic. He's willing to call in a lot

of favors if we need him to, but we'd better be damned sure we need him to."

"We should know more after I debrief Kamal later," Hicks said. "I'll be in touch as soon as I can."

"See to it that you are." Jason killed the connection.

Hicks looked at the blank screen. Last word freak. He grabbed a dark baseball cap from the glove compartment and put it on before stepping out of the car. Investigating the storage facility was too dangerous for the Varsity team. Five guys with bags roaming through the place was bound to raise suspicion they couldn't afford. But one man dressed like a guard might not.

Hicks got out of his car, intent on testing his theory.

THE BACK DOOR of the storage facility was little more than window dressing. The security camera they'd set up to watch it had been ripped off the wall long ago. Only a few dead wires hung rusting against the stonework. The door was a heavy duty fire door, but the lock had been damaged and repaired several times. Picking it was a piece of cake. Getting inside was easier than it should've been.

By looking at the company's cleaning bills, Hicks had determined what the guards at the facility wore and dressed accordingly. Hicks' dark blue jumpsuit and baseball cap wasn't an exact match for the guard uniforms, but close enough so that if someone spotted him on camera, he'd blend in better. He knew there were no cameras in the stairwell, so he wouldn't be spotted until he reached Omar's storage room.

The fire stairs area was a dump. The body of a large rat

was slowly decomposing against the wall of the first floor landing. The image reminded him of Kamal rotting away in a tarp beneath the water tower. The irony wasn't lost on Hicks.

The storage area, on the other hand, was brand new with sparkling linoleum floors and florescent lights bright enough to perform surgery under. A smoked globe was set into the ceiling panels above every storage unit. Since the cameras weren't fed to any server off site, Hicks wondered if they even worked. At least they looked impressive enough to the customers. Anything to give people the illusion that their possessions, most of which they didn't need, were more secure.

Omar's storage unit was bigger than some Manhattan apartments—big enough to have a steel roll down gate similar to the type that stores used. And, just like those kinds of gates, the lock was set on the right-hand side. He checked to see if anyone was around, then pulled out his pick set again and went to work on the lock. It was more challenging than the backdoor had been but not challenging enough to keep Hicks from opening it.

He popped the lock and set it on the floor. He remembered what he'd said to Jason. Why he told him the Varsity shouldn't just charge into the facility and open the unit. Biohazards and booby traps were always a possibility. But this was only his life he was talking about, and the situation with Omar was already in hand if something happened to him. Besides, Jason would welcome the opportunity to shine.

Hicks grabbed the handle at the bottom and slowly pulled the door up. Nothing happened.

The inside was a large space, just like the company records

showed. Dark and mostly empty. Hicks turned on the light and saw… nothing.

Absolutely nothing except dust.

No furniture. No desk. No filing cabinet or anything that would justify renting such a large room. Just a large unit as empty as the day it had been built. He metal shelving built into the wall was equally as empty.

He'd watched the OMNI feed and knew Omar and Kamal were the only two who'd gone into the room and they'd been the only two who'd left. No one had interacted with them while they'd been in there. Neither of them had been carrying anything when they left. At least, nothing Hicks could see.

Hicks sank against the wall. Everything had been spinning so damned fast since Central Park that he felt like he wasn't seeing all of the details of this all at once, only bits and pieces and glimpses. He sat on the floor with his back against the wall and tried to slow it all down. He tried to take everything in pieces instead of the whole because the pieces gave him the best way to solve this thing.

He concentrated on his breathing and made his mind a blank; as empty and still as the metal shelving across from him. He needed to concentrate before this became unmanageable and…

And that's when he saw it.

The metal shelving was empty of everything except dust. A thick layer of dust had formed on the shelves, except for one square outline on the bottom shelf.

Hicks got to his feet and walked over to take a closer look. The outline of something, maybe a box or some kind of square container, was clearly visible on the bottom shelf. The rest of the shelves had a fair amount of dust on them, so it wasn't a fluke. Something had been there, and recently.

Something that neither Kamal nor Omar needed to carry out in a box. And since neither of them had been carrying anything when they left the building, it meant they must've taken it out of the container and left it behind.

Whatever the container had been, it was still close by.

Hicks took another look around the unit, but there was no sign of anything except more dust.

He left the storage unit open and went into the hallway. He spotted a large trash bin at the end of the hall and looked inside. The bin was filled with torn papers, plastic bags and other trash, but only one thing stood out—an oversized padded envelope at the top of the pile.

Hicks slid on his gloves and pulled the envelope from the trash. He saw that the envelope had been slit open at the top, but still sealed at the lip. That meant any DNA on the seal would be intact. A good sign.

He turned it over and saw a label had been ripped off it except for something that looked like part of a circular logo of a mailing label.

Hicks knew if there was any way to glean any information from the envelope, the University lab would get it.

He went back and locked up Omar's storage unit before taking the back stairs down to his car. No one had paid any attention to him. Then again, most people didn't.

CHAPTER
17

Hicks put the envelope in a forensic evidence bag he kept in the trunk of his car. He had figured he'd bring it to the University facility after he had the chance to debrief Kamal. But things didn't work out the way they were supposed to. They rarely did.

OMNI showed that Omar hadn't brought Kamal straight back to Queens after the storage facility. Instead, he drove him all over the city; visiting various parts of Brooklyn and Queens where extremist Muslims from various African countries congregated and prayed for death to America. There weren't as many such places as people might think, but there were more than enough for Omar to have made a day out of it.

Hicks trailed as close as a quarter mile out to avoid being

spotted. He knew Kamal wasn't in any danger. This was all a dog-and-pony show for his benefit and, ultimately, for the benefit of the man Kamal was supposed to be working for.

Everywhere they went, Omar and Kamal got a warm greeting from Nairobis and Nigerians and Kenyans and Senegalis alike. Hicks' surveillance had shown that Omar had visited many of these places before, but the extent of their affection for him was troubling. Omar had obviously been very busy; quietly making a lot of friends.

He had OMNI scan for cellphones and tablets everywhere they went, but none of the principles had any devices on them. Smart boys. Many were smart enough still to stay inside or at least keep their heads covered. This made it more difficult for OMNI to identify them from above, but not impossible. The old girl made due and indentified a fair number of them. Now they'd been tagged, they'd be tracked for the rest of their lives.

At one stop in Queens, one of Omar's men met them and brought Kamal's phone and battery back to him in a plastic baggie. The footage from the cellphone Hicks pulled off the system showed the bag had been sealed since Omar and Kamal left the house. Although the OMNI signal still powered it despite the lack of a battery, all it picked up was blurred images and muffled sounds through the baggie. Not even the University's equipment would be able to make much of any of it.

Not that there'd be much worth learning anyway. Hicks doubted the stooges who Omar had left watching the safe house would have been trusted with anything vital. But now they had a location on Omar's safe house, which was more than they'd had before.

As he watched Omar and Kamal finish glad-handing their new comrades, Hicks ordered OMNI to begin running identity checks on everyone they'd met that day. A full report would be waiting for him at Twenty-third Street by the time he got back there later that night. By that time the next night, the University would have a better idea of who they were, where they were living and why they were there by this time tomorrow. A fairly productive day by that alone, but Hicks hoped Kamal's intel would be able to put the icing on the cake. Hicks liked icing.

A T TEN O'CLOCK that night, Omar dropped off Kamal at the apartment. Hicks parked around the corner and watched the satellite feed while he listened to Omar's parting words through Kamal's cellphone. Until then, their conversations had been about the people they'd met that day and how they were all faithful servants of Allah.

In French, Omar said, "Will you be reporting back to our wise uncle about what you have seen here today?"

"I will," Kamal said, "and I know he will be very impressed by what I tell him."

"Do you think he will be impressed enough to aid us in our worthy cause?"

"If he—and Allah—wish it, it will be so."

"Yes, of course," Omar said immediately. Hicks was glad Kamal had picked up on Omar's deference to the Almighty whenever the situation presented itself. "If you wish to discuss the matter further, I am at your disposal."

"Good, because I will need you to be at my disposal tomorrow morning at ten. Have you or your men pick me up at the same place you'd picked me up this morning. I hope to have an answer for you by then."

Via the OMNI feed, Hicks watched Kamal get out of the car and walk into the building. He watched the car pull away from the curb and drive down the street, only to stop next to a parked car on the other side of the street.

Hicks zoomed in on the image and saw Omar speak to someone in the other car, before driving away.

So Omar had someone watching Kamal's place after all, Hicks thought. Smart. Like the old saying goes: trust but verify. Omar had learned a lot since losing two men in the park.

Hicks assigned the satellite's software to detect the black box in Omar's car and had the system track it passively, not visually. Satellites, even OMNI, had a limited bandwidth and he might need it for something else before the night was out. From now on, they'd have a record of everywhere that car went.

Hicks listened to Kamal's labored breath as he walked up the four flights to his apartment. Prison life had clearly eroded his stamina. Hicks didn't want to risk calling Kamal in case Omar's men had snuck in and bugged the place since they'd left, so he sent him a text message instead:

YOU'RE BEING WATCHED FROM THE STREET. CHECK FOR BUGS, THEN CALL ME.

Kamal's response:

K

Hicks listened to Kamal enter the apartment. He heard him put the keys and the

phone somewhere, possibly on the table. He activated the phone's camera and got a great view of the apartment's ceiling. He heard what sounded like Kamal checking around the apartment. After a few moments, he saw Kamal pick up the phone, open the flip and text him back:

PLACE HAS BEEN SEARCHED. DIDN'T FIND ANY DEVICES, BUT THEY COULD BE LISTENING. DON'T COME UP. SOMEONE IN THE ALLEY BEHIND THE BUILDING.

That was why Hicks hadn't placed any cameras in the apartment. If they'd been found, Kamal would've been killed. Hicks texted back:

WE NEED TO DEBRIEF. EMAIL ME A REPORT.

Kamal's response:

NOTHING TO REPORT. I SAW A DINER AROUND THE CORNER. MEET ME AT 0800. TALK THEN.

Hicks didn't like that. He texted back:

NO. LEAVE NOW.

He waited for a response like some goddamned teenager waiting for a girl to text him back. But no response came.

Hicks knew he had options. He could've gone into the building next door, gone up to the roof and entered Kamal's building that way. But Omar might be expecting that, so Hicks ruled that out.

He could call him anyway despite Kamal's warnings, but decided not to do that either. He doubted Omar's operation was sophisticated enough to have planted listening devices in the apartment. But he hadn't expected Omar to have such an extensive network, either.

Even in times like these, University protocol was clear. An experienced Asset had waived off the debriefing and he didn't have enough information to overrule that call. Protocol was there for a reason because, more times than not, it worked.

Besides, he needed to get that envelope analyzed. Hicks hit the ignition and put the car in gear.

CHAPTER 18

AFTER DROPPING OFF the storage unit envelope for analysis at the University's facility in Washington Heights, Hicks stayed up half the night analyzing the OMNI reports on all the people Omar had introduced to Kamal earlier that day. Most of them were African ex-pats who'd come into the country legally and held regular jobs. A few were clerics who had peaceful congregations. None of them had any warrants or raised any red flags except through their association with Kamal. Hicks ordered tacit tracking on them anyway. Now, for the rest of their lives, they'd be scrutinized by OMNI.

He also checked the footage from the camera in the TV in Kamal's apartment. He wanted to see who'd searched the place and when. And when he watched the footage, Hicks did not like what he saw.

HICKS WAS ALREADY on the move when his handheld started buzzing at seven that morning with text messages from Kamal:

SEE YOU AT THE DINER AT 0800

Then, a few minutes later, Kamal texted:

YOU THERE?

At eight o'clock:

WHERE ARE YOU?

At eight thirty, he texted:

MISSED YOU AT THE DINER. MEET ME
AT THE PARK AROUND THE CORNER.

And thirty minutes after that, at just after nine in the morning, Hicks was sitting on an ancient metal chair in Kamal's kitchenette when Kamal opened the door. He was aiming the .454 Ruger at the center of his chest.

Kamal just smiled as he shut the door behind him. "There you are." He jerked his chin at the pistol. "That the jazzed up .38 you had on you the other day? All that little thing is gonna do is make me mad." He looked at the long Islamic wall calendar Hicks had taken off the wall next to the door and placed on the kitchen table. "At least you did some redecorating while you were here."

Hicks kept the Ruger level. "You've disappointed me. I told you what would happen if you disappointed me."

Kamal nodded at the gun. "What are you gonna do? Kill me? What'll that get you? I'm supposed to meet Omar's boys with the money in an hour."

"Why did you lie about the place being searched?"

"What made you think I lied?"

"Because there's a camera in the television set, asshole. And I ran the footage, so I know the only one in this room yesterday was you. Omar's boys should've searched the place, but they didn't. Not a bright group of boys you've joined up with, Kamal."

"Who says I joined up with them?"

"You did, the moment you jerked me around about meeting for the debrief. Did you think I'd just show up at the diner? I'm running this operation, Ace. I choose the rendezvous points, not you."

"So that's what this is about? A pissing match about who's in charge here, you paranoid motherfucker? I'm in the field, man. It's my call where to meet and that diner was as good a place for a debrief as any."

"Which is why you picked a nice public, local place to tell me the bad news."

Kamal folded his arms. "Well, now you've just gone and lost me boss, because I don't have the first damned clue what you're talking about. And I don't think you do, either."

"Sure you do," Hicks said. "Whatever Omar showed you yesterday was big. Big enough for you to change your mind about cooperating with me. You wanted to meet at the diner, thinking I wouldn't try to kill you in a public place. You were right. I'm going to kill you here instead."

Kamal laughed again. "Damn, man. You've gone field crazy, you know that? Seeing boogie men and bad guys at every turn. You need help and a shitload of serious R and R."

Hicks picked up a dirty rag from the kitchen table. "I found this on the table when I walked in. It wasn't here when I left, which means you brought it in with you last night when Kamal dropped you off." He made a show of sniffing the rag. "Gun metal's got such a great smell to it, doesn't it?"

Hicks watched Kamal's Adam's apple bob up, then down. He made a slight move for his pocket and Hicks adjusted the Ruger. "Don't."

Kamal slowly raised his hands. "This is still a pretty public place, even all the way up here. We're being watched, remember?"

"Man in the car out front and one in the alley," Hicks told him. "Both trailed you to the diner, and the park, then back here." He nodded at his handheld on the table. "Satellite surveillance is a wonderful thing."

Kamal smiled. "But it's not everything, is it? Because even with all your technology and all your eyes in the sky, you assholes still can't hack what Omar's cooking up. And that's the beauty of it. You won't find out, either, unless I decide to tell you."

Hicks smiled, too. "So it's like that."

"That's the way it's got to be, boss man. Because what my man Omar is working on is just that big. And when you find out what he's planning, it'll blow your fucking mind."

"But you're not going to tell me unless I pay you what you want, right?"

214

"You're smarter than you look, boss man," Kamal said. "I had a damned nice nest egg in Afghanistan when those bastards took me down. I'd say five million ought to be enough to make me whole. Cash, of course."

"Of course."

"Oh, and you'll throw in clemency. Clean record, shit like that. All of that might come in handy somewhere down the line. None of that's what you might call unreasonable, is it?"

"Or I could just bring you in and have the information dragged out of you for free."

Kamal shook his head. "I've been through all that in training. None of that Guantanamo shit ever worked on me."

"Son, my people have places that makes Guantanamo look like a summer camp. And methods a hell of a lot worse than waterboarding. More effective, too."

"All of which takes time, boss man. And time is something you and whoever you're working for don't have. Omar's scheme is so goddamned simple, it's perfect. It's golden and it's ready to pop. You won't even know what's happening until it's already too late. Not unless I tell you all about it, which I'm willing to do, provided I get what I need to make me whole."

"You're going to have to prove you've got something worth selling first," Hicks said. "Tell me about Saudi Arabia."

"I know where it is," Kamal said. "Even spent some good times there."

"You and Omar took a large manila envelope from his storage container yesterday. It was on the bottom shelf against the wall. My people are analyzing it now but we were able to figure out the manufacturer had shipped that lot number to a distributor in Saudi Arabia."

Kamal shook his head. "Damn, you guys are good. Who the hell are you people anyway?"

"Right now, one of us is a guy with a gun to your belly. And you're the guy who's going to tell me what was in the envelope."

"I'll be glad to tell you everything you want to know as soon as you meet my price."

"Omar told you a lot, didn't he?"

Kamal nodded. "That money you gave me put me in real good with him. Spilled most of the operation to me, but not all. Give me what I want and I'll make sure that cell phone is on the whole damned time when I give him the rest." He checked his watch. "Clock's ticking, boss man. We've got less than fifty minutes before Omar's men come pick me up. So do we have a deal or not?"

"No," Hicks said, "we don't."

Kamal reached back for something under his coat as Hicks fired twice. Both flat-head rounds from the Ruger punched through the left side of Kamal's chest; lifting him off his feet and sending him to the wall.

Kamal collapsed to the floor and sagged to one side.

Kamal struggled to prop himself up on an elbow. Hicks planted his foot on his chest and pushed him back down to the floor. He showed him the Ruger. "Cored a charging Grizzly, remember?"

Hicks pulled on his gloves and patted Kamal down for weapons. He found a .9mm tucked in Kamal's belt and showed it to the dying man. "This a present from Omar?" He put it in his coat pocket. "Lot of good it did you."

Kamal gurgled as he patted at his chest wound, but Hicks pinned his hand to the floor beneath his shoe. "Don't fight it. Just let it happen."

Kamal gasped one last time before his eyes went vacant; fixating on that indeterminable point in space where people always looked when life finally left them.

Hicks pulled Kamal's corpse onto its side to check for exit wounds. Both rounds had exited his back and went into the wall without much splatter. Hicks took the calendar Kamal had hated from the table and hung it back on the wall where it belonged. It covered the holes nicely. Just like he'd planned.

There wasn't too much blood, either. Less splatter meant less time spent cleaning up. And Kamal had been right about one thing: Hicks didn't have much time.

He picked up his handheld and Jason answered on the first ring. "Is he dead?"

"What do you think?"

Jason sounded like he stifled a curse. "I hope he told you something before you killed him."

"He told me more than he thought he did. Whatever Omar's working on is low tech, which explains why we can't hack it or track it. That rules out radiological, so it's probably biological. We'll know more when we track the money and get the lab results on the envelope."

"We should have those within the hour," Jason said. "Did you place the isotope with the money?"

"I did that before I gave it to Kamal two days ago," Hicks said. Unless Omar's men ran the money through a Geiger counter, they would never know the bills had been marked. "Time for our African financier to contact Omar directly.

Have him tell Omar that Kamal had to tend to other business and already left the city. He should still have his men come by at ten to pick up the money Kamal left behind. I'll make sure everything is cleared out by then."

"But they're watching the building," Jason said. "They saw Kamal enter, but not leave. How will he explain that?"

"Omar wants the money. He's not going to give a shit about what might've happened to Kamal. They seem to be on a tight a timeframe to pull the trigger on whatever scheme they're planning. Too tight to worry about some stranger they met yesterday."

"I hope you're right, but I still don't like the idea of letting them leave with the money."

"If Omar comes for the money himself, I'll grab him, Hicks said. "But he'll probably keep playing it cautious and send someone else for it, probably armed. In the meantime, get a Varsity squad to sit on Omar's safe house in Midwood. We don't have to protect Kamal's cover anymore, so we should be sure they're ready to hit the place at a moment's notice."

"A Varsity squad has been in place at Omar's house since last night," Jason told him. "I took the liberty of ordering them in place when Kamal refused to meet you."

Hicks should've been angry, but wasn't. It was a sound move that had put them in a better tactical situation. He only regretted that he hadn't thought of it earlier. "Who's leading the team?"

"Scott. He and his men have been fully briefed on the tactical situation and have been watching the building from a converted truck a block away for hours. A few people have gone in and out, but none of them Omar. The house reads at least thirty heat signatures, so if they're planning something, they may already have all of their people in place."

Hicks couldn't add anything to what Jason had just told him. "Let me know when our friend contacts Omar. In the meantime, I've got some work to do."

HICKS HAD ALREADY been on the roof with Kamal's corpse for fifteen minutes when Omar's men reached the apartment. He was glad the fourth floor was the closest to the roof because moving Kamal's dead weight up the stairs had damned near killed him.

Hicks had wrapped Kamal's body in a blanket from the hall closet and placed the corpse under the building's water tower. It wasn't a perfect hiding spot, but it didn't have to be. It just had to keep him out of sight until he could get a Facilities squad to come retrieve the body later. But University resources would be busy with the Omar business until it was resolved. There was a very real chance that the birds or rodents might get to Kamal first, in which case the body would most likely be discovered. By then, it probably wouldn't matter.

He sat with his back against the door leading to the roof while he watched the scene unfold on the street on his handheld via satellite. A late model Honda—not Omar's Corolla—double parked in front of the building. The man who got out from the passenger side was tall and lanky and bald. He certainly looked Somali, but he looked nothing like Omar.

Hicks was about to assign the satellite to pick up in

the Honda's black box signal, but he could see Jason had already done that. The young man was beginning to overstep his bounds. First sending the woman to study him, and then ordering the Varsity into the field without consulting him. Now this. He was using the fog of war to broaden his boarders. When the Omar mess was over, Hicks would make it a point to knock him on his ass.

Through the thin wood of the roof door, Hicks could hear the man from the car running up the stairs. He tried to get the satellite to focus in on the driver, but the angle wasn't right. It wasn't Omar's car, but he still could've been behind the wheel. The angle was too steep to see for sure.

A text message from Jason appeared in a thin band at the bottom of Hicks' screen:

LESSON PLAN AMENDED. TERMINATE
ALL PARTIES ON SCENE.

Now Hicks saw Jason's incursion for what it was. He'd probably been lobbying the Dean until he got approval for the bloodbath he'd wanted all along. Kick in doors, guns blazing. Sift through the wreckage and write a report. Jason would look to come out of this a hero and expand his influence in the University.

Not if Hicks could help it.

Hicks typed back:

WE NEED TO KNOW WHO OMAR SENT
FIRST. STAND BY

Hicks heard the passenger bound up the stairs. Hicks switched the OMNI image to thermal and saw the heat signature of the man only a few feet below Hicks' position on the roof. The man stood outside Kamal's apartment, to the side of the doorframe. He turned the knob. He let the door swing in on its own. He stood with his back against the wall, listening, waiting, before looking around the doorframe and entering the apartment. This man wasn't one of Omar's rookies.

A new message crawled at the bottom of Hicks' handheld:

TERMINATION LETTERS APPROVED. IMMEDIATE ACTION REQUIRED.

But Hicks ignored the text. Killing Omar's messengers wouldn't do anything except scare off Omar and make him change his plans. Omar still had a man watching the apartment and a man in the alley. There was no way Hicks could kill all of them without it turning into a bloodbath. Omar had already gone underground once after Colin got killed. Hicks knew he was too close to uncovering Omar's plot to let him get away now. They had to know what kind of threat they were dealing with.

Hicks ignored the text and kept watching the feed.

Via the satellite's thermal imaging camera, Hicks saw the man exit Kamal's apartment.

The man held the bag of money in one hand and closed the apartment door with the other. But instead of heading downstairs to the car, he surprised Hicks by simply standing still for a moment. Quiet once more. Listening.

Hicks didn't move. He was already sitting with his back flat against the roof door. He didn't have to worry about the gravel moving under his feet and giving his position away.

Hicks watched his thermal image; he saw the man had his head down; maybe closing his eyes as he listened for any sudden sounds that might tell him where Kamal might be. He probably knew that none of Omar's spies had seen him leave the building. He had to be somewhere close. Where could he have gone?

And then Hicks saw the man look up the stairs toward the door to the roof.

Hicks pulled the Ruger from his belt. Jason just might get his bloodbath after all.

THE MAN LOOKED down the stairs, then back up toward the roof. He shifted the bag of money from his right hand to his left, clearly trying to decide what he should do. Take the money back to the car, or take a look around. He probably knew Omar would ask him questions, and he didn't want to lie. Hicks knew from surveillance that Omar was very good at spotting lies. His men knew it, too.

Hicks knew what the man was thinking because he would've been thinking the same things in the same situation. The money was important, but at what cost? Knowing where Kamal was would help erase lots of question marks later on.

The satellite's thermal image showed the man had drawn a weapon. Details were tough to see, but it looked to Hicks like it might be a nine millimeter. He heard the creak of the old wooden treads as the man began to walk upstairs to the roof.

Hicks pocketed his handheld and quietly got to his feet; slowly stepping away from the door. One sound could set the man firing, or worse, running. Hicks didn't want to risk either if he could avoid it.

Hicks slowly put one foot behind the other as he kept the Ruger aimed at the door. The other side of the door was plastered with warning signs that the door was alarmed and would emit an alarm if opened. A red sign on the alarm bar said an alarm would sound if the bar was pushed.

But Hicks knew the door hadn't been locked and no alarm had gone off when he had come in that way to surprise Kamal in his apartment. The signs were all bullshit. All Omar's man had to do was turn the knob and pull it open. It would be the last thing he ever did.

He could imagine his handheld was full with messages from Jason telling him to TERMINATE as he watched the whole thing from the safe comfort of his den in Maryland or wherever the hell he lived. But Hicks wanted the money man alive. He wanted him to bring the money to Omar so they could track it and learn whatever they were planning. But all of that depended on the money man leaving here alive.

If possible.

Hicks carefully backed up far enough away from the door so he couldn't be seen when the door opened, but not close enough to the edge to be seen from the street. A delicate balance, but one he was used to walking.

A cold wind picked up, filling his ears. He couldn't hear if the man was close to the rooftop door or if he'd given up and gone back downstairs. But as the wind died down, he didn't hear anything.

He stole a quick look at his handheld. The man was still on the other side of the door, looking at the signs about the alarm.

He didn't know if the man could read English, but he'd probably seen warning signs before and knew what they meant. An alarm sounding would bring attention—maybe even police—and an armed man holding a bag with ninety grand in cash didn't need attention. He needed to get that money to the man who was waiting for it.

The wind finally died down enough for Hicks to hear the stairs squeak again as the man went back down to the car. Via the handheld, he watched the man put away his and pick up his pace.

Both of them had come within the width of a door of having a bad day.

Knowing Jason was watching, Hicks thrust a middle finger up at the satellite. *Terminate that, you son of a bitch.*

He stayed on the roof until the moneyman got in the car and drove away. He knew he'd get a lecture from Jason about disobeying orders, but that didn't matter. They had a solid lock on Omar and where he was going to be and when. Now, all they had to do was find out what that bastard was playing at.

CHAPTER
19

"**W**HAT THE HELL was that?" Jason's voice caused the Buick's speakers to tremble as he drove back into Manhattan.

But Hicks was still too charged to even let Jason dampen his mood. "That what a successful operation looks like, Ace. Now that you've actually seen one in real life, you'll recognize it next time it happens."

"I demand to know why you disobeyed a direct order to terminate all suspects on sight."

"Because it was an order that made no sense based on the realities in the field. I'm not going to start a running gun battle in a crowded apartment building. All that would've done is drawn a hell of a lot of cops, blown our entire operation, and maybe get me killed in the bargain. Besides, this isn't just

SYMPATHY FOR THE DEVIL

about stopping Omar anymore."

"It's about finding the extent of his network by watching what he does with the money we gave him. He was treated like a rock star yesterday by people we didn't even know he knew. That means Omar's been carefully building up some kind of network even while we were watching him. Grabbing Omar right now is like mowing the lawn to kill the weeds. It'll all grow back in time. We need to rip them out at the root."

"If only everything was that simple," Jason admitted. "We're still trying to trace the logo on the mailing label, but our lab has come back with the initial test results on the envelope, and it's not good news."

Hicks had been afraid of that. "They didn't find anything?"

"Just the opposite. They found traces of several viruses on the inside of the envelope; among them SARS, MERS, and even the Ebola viruses."

Hicks grabbed the wheel to keep from driving off the road. Sometimes, he hated being right. "How much of a trace?"

"None of them were large in and of themselves, but all traces were exactly the same amounts. I'd say Omar is playing with something he doesn't fully understand."

Hicks knew Severe Acute Respiratory Syndrome and Middle Eastern Respiratory Syndrome were deadly diseases that had threatened to turn into pandemics for years, but hadn't. Yet. Ebola was difficult to catch, but equally deadly when someone caught it. There'd always been rumors of scientists in the Middle East and elsewhere who'd tried to weaponize these diseases, but failed.

Hicks wondered if Omar had found someone who'd finally been able to make it work. And he wondered if the image of the man from the camera wasn't involved in this somehow.

"Has the Dean been able to get the British to release the identity of the man I found on the SD card yet?"

"No, but that's not a priority now," Jason said. "We need to hit Omar's house and hit it now before those viruses get out in the open."

"Bad idea, Ace. We don't know how much he's got or where the viruses are now. We have the place under surveillance and a go-team in place. If this mystery man on the SD camera is important enough for the British to hide, he's important enough for us to know who and where he is."

Hicks wasn't surprised to hear the Dean's voice break into the conversation. "Unfortunately, they're not cooperating."

Hicks had been afraid of that. Since Snowden, once the British dug in their heels on an intelligence matter, they were damned difficult to budge. "Fortunately, I think I know someone who might be able to tell us."

"I was hoping you might," the Dean said. "How long would it take you to get in touch with this someone?"

"Let me make some calls and let you know," Hicks said. "In the meantime, have Scott's people ready to hit Omar's place if the situation warrants it. Keep me apprised of what happens."

"Wait a second," Jason said. "Who are you calling? Where are you going?"

"Quiet, Junior. The adults are talking."

Hicks killed the transmission and gunned the engine.

He had another phone call to make on his way back to New York. He knew he couldn't afford to be late.

The British were sticklers for punctuality.

HICKS HADN'T MET his British counterpart in New York yet. There hadn't been a reason until now.

The British referred to their version of the University as The Club. They preferred to rotate the assignment to their New York Office every couple of years or so. They viewed the posting as something of a joke; a reward to agents in good standing who were close to retirement and looking to run out their string. They were men and women who'd been put out to pasture in the concrete jungle; given a chance to go to the Big Apple for a bit before they hung up their cloak and dagger for good. Enjoy the city, old boy and, while you're at it, see if you can't pick up a few things. Report back should you hear anything interesting. There's a good chap.

Hicks checked his watch again to make sure he was early. Postings to the Club might have been something of a joke to Her Majesty's government, but ten minutes early was still on time as far as the British were concerned. Old habits died hard, even among spies approaching the last stop on the train.

Hicks found his counterpart already waiting for him at the agreed upon rendezvous point: a wire bench in a park off Bleeker Street. The snow hadn't shown any signs of melting and there were still large piles of it clumped on one side. The Brit had only cleared off enough snow for himself.

The man Hicks knew as Clarke filled the entire other side of the bench meant for two people. He wasn't simply big, but incredibly obese and seemingly happily so. The fleshy rolls of his body were evident even beneath his green parka; the zipper's teeth appeared strained to the limit. Tufts of unruly reddish hair going an unseemly gray tucked out from beneath a faded black ski cap. His fleshy face may have been reddened a bit from the cold wind but Hicks would have bet that ruddy was his usual color.

Watching him work his way around the falafel wrapped in tinfoil almost turned Hicks' stomach. Bits of lettuce and meat had flecked on to his parka and he showed no signs of noticing them. They were cleared by a sharp wind blew up Sixth Avenue.

The fat man glanced at Hicks from head to toe before going back to his falafel. "You the Yank?"

Hicks nodded at the snow next to him. "Thanks for saving me a seat."

"I'm not your fucking butler, Yank. Clear it off yourself and have a seat. Standing up talking only draws attention."

Hicks pulled his gloves on tighter and shoved a mound of snow off the other section of the bench.

"I'll admit you're not what I expected," Hicks said as he settled on the damp bench.

Clarke grunted as he took another bite out of his falafel. "You were expecting some poofter in a tuxedo, sipping a martini." More bits of meat and lettuce fell on his parka as he spoke. "You bastards really make me laugh sometimes."

"I was actually expecting a professional who knew enough to pick a better location than this."

"What's wrong with here?" Clarke said with a full mouth. "Park bench out in the open just after a snowstorm? No one around. Who's going to bother with a couple of dodgy looking fuckers like us, gabbing on a park bench in the middle of winter? Besides, if you know what you're doing, this won't take long. You'll be sipping hot cocoa in a fucking coffee house in no time."

Hicks knew he was being tested and tried not to let the fat man get to him. "I've been around a long time and I've never heard about you or anyone like you in the Circle."

"The Circle," Clarke laughed. "You still call yourselves the University and your chief the Dean, don't you? Awfully collegiate for the kind of work we do, isn't it? All ivy and marble, but no blood or guts. Christ, you bastards are kind to yourselves with your fucking names."

For the sake of progress, Hicks held his temper. "I said I never heard of you."

"That's because I haven't been in this bloody Circle of yours very long, least your idea of it anyway. Don't worry, though. I've heard plenty about you. That stunt you pulled in Guatemala last year was the real thing. Some real Cold War stuff, that. I respect a man who can think on his feet and save his man's life."

Hicks wasn't in the habit of talking about his career with total strangers. "How about you tell me about the image your people embargoed? I want to know why."

"Sure you do," Clarke said, wiping his mouth with the back of his hand, then folding the tinfoil over the rest of his falafel. "Damned good, this. The fuckers might not be able to govern themselves, but their food is right tasty."

"The man in the photo," Hicks repeated. "What about him?"

"Watch the imperious attitude, cousin. We taught it to you, after all. And that goes for your Dean goes for you, too. I'm not telling you fuck all about him until you tell me why you want to know who he is."

Hicks kept it vague to see how far it got him. "We need him for questioning on a matter that's come up."

"Oh, fuck off," Clarke spat. "You'll need to tell me a damned sight more than that. Your Dean called my minister directly, demanding that we lift our hold on his information. That kind of call wouldn't have been made if you were just looking for general information. Now, you play nice and tell me why you care about this man or I'm leaving."

Hicks had never heard of Clarke before. He didn't know who he was or where he'd worked. He had no idea if he was capable or if he was just another fat man with a big mouth. He also didn't have any choice but to trust him.

"We think he's involved in some kind of event that'll take place in here in New York, probably in the next few days."

"Not good enough." Clarke got up, but Hicks grabbed his arm.

"It involves a small time Somali hack named Omar and some men working with him. This Omar turned two of my agents and it looks like they're planning something big."

Clarke stopped moving away. "How big?"

"Probably biological," Hicks said.

Clarke's eyes narrowed. "What do you mean 'probably?'"

"It means we found traces of MERS, SARS, and Ebola on the inside of an envelope we know was in Omar's possession. They were only trace amounts of each virus in the envelope, but they were all exactly the same amount of contamination.

We think they might be samples but that's just guess work at this point."

Clarke sat back down on the bench without any prompting from Hicks. "You said SARS, MERS, and Ebola."

"Did you get anything on the envelope itself?"

"It was an oversized padded envelope with a mailing label that had been torn off it. But we were able to trace the manufacturer and that the particular batch of envelope had been shipped to Saudi Arabia."

"Madinha," Clarke muttered more to himself than to Hicks. "Those lying bastards."

"What about Madinha?"

"I think you've found more than you know, Yank. More than any of us thought you had."

"So cut the shit and tell me why you guys embargoed the picture I sent for analysis."

"Because the man in the image is an Algerian national named Rachid Djebar. He's someone we've lost track of and want very much to find again."

Finally, Hicks thought, a name. Too bad it was a name he'd never heard before. "What does this Djebar have to do with Madinha?"

"If you'd asked me that same question three minutes ago, I would've said he had nothing to do with it. But when I put it together with your envelope and his disappearance, I think he may be the link between the two. And that is very bad news for all of us, believe me."

Hicks waited for him to keep talking, but he didn't. He simply sat there, going from ruddy to pale despite a steady cold wind.

Hicks knew pushing a man like Clarke wouldn't do much good. In this game, the importance of not panicking is often more important than rushing things.

The fat man was probably deciding what we should say as he looked out at the traffic mulling up Sixth Avenue instead. Despite the snow and the slush, bicycles darted alongside cabs and cars and trucks and buses as the autumn sun's harsh glare hurt his eyes. Several deep puddles had formed in potholes and at crosswalks, sending dirty water into the air every time a car or bike drive through one. It was a bland scene on a bland day that should've been forgotten as soon as it happened.

But judging by Clarke's reaction, Hicks had a feeling this was a moment he'd remember for a long time to come.

"Anything I tell you stays between us, yeah? I'm talking about operational detail shit. We don't like seeing our dirty laundry on CNN like you."

"All I care about is Djebar."

When Clarke spoke, his tone was quiet and clear. "Rachid Djebar is an Algerian national who burned one of our assets in Morocco during a joint operation with the French. This was about six months ago. The French have largely forgiven him for it, but we're not as understanding and we've been hunting him ever since. The bastard has been completely off the grid until your picture hit the wire and set off all sorts of bells in a variety of places."

"Who is he?"

"He fashions himself a dangerous man who shouldn't be crossed. You'd do well to keep that in mind when you come up against him, because he's every bit as dangerous as he thinks he is."

"So am I," Hicks said. "What about him?"

"At heart, he's nothing but a common street peddler from Wahran; albeit an exceptionally good one. Over the years, he's expanded his practice and network to the point where he'll peddle anything he can get his hands on. Arms, information, state secrets, drugs, contracts on people's lives. Lately he's been peddling what he calls relationships; putting two particularly nasty fuckers together so they can do whatever their black hearts desire. Weapons and munitions mostly. He gets a finder's fee for introducing them and brokering the deal, then goes on his way."

"Who does he work for?"

"Anyone so long as they're willing to pay his fee. Mexican cartels looking for arms. Drug dealers looking for new outlets. That sort of thing. No product for him to worry about and it's very, very profitable. Little risk for a lot of reward." Hicks realized he may have seen the name mentioned in a few intelligence reports over the years, but not specific details. If he'd been tied to a threat on American soil, he would've remembered. "What the hell is an Algerian like Djebar doing with a low-level Somali punk like Omar?"

"Haven't you been listening?" Clarke frowned. "I just told you he's a Matchmaker now. If that's what he's done with your man Omar, then there's two things you'd do well to consider and none of them pleasant."

"The first," Clarke explained, "is that this Omar isn't the punk you believe him to be. Djebar doesn't come out of his fucking hole for less than a hundred grand, plus a small percentage of whatever the action is. Since he was on Omar's camera shagging some whore, that can only mean Omar has money."

Hicks had seen Omar's travel activity. He'd gauged his spending and his contributions and he had a fair assessment of how much he raised at the cabstand. He could've raised that much if he squeezed the drivers and ran a little credit card fraud on the side. Drunks wouldn't notice an extra couple of miles on the odometer until the next morning, if then.

The Djebar connection would also explain how Omar had gotten the numbers for the financiers he'd contacted. He'd probably spent every cent he'd raised on whatever meeting Djebar had arranged for him. The question was why.

"What's the second thing?" Hicks asked.

"Given that you found an envelope with trace amounts of diseases inside mean Djebar was probably involved in helping Omar acquire them. There's not really much of a commission in that sort of arrangement."

"So?"

"So, it means your friend Omar really is planning something major. Because Djebar has always said his biggest regret in life was that he wasn't connected enough to help Osama and his pals fund their grand show." He nodded his fleshy face down Sixth Avenue toward the new Liberty Tower. "Right down there."

Hicks didn't have time to think about past attacks. He was too focused on stopping the next one. "You said something about Madinha before.""I hope your stomach is empty because you're not going to like this."

"My stomach's my problem. Tell me about Madinha."

"You may have read that there's been a rash of small, but rather nasty, outbreaks of MERS, SARS, and Ebola in small villages throughout the Middle East for the past couple of years. The Saudis, being good neighbors, have taken the lead on studying the outbreaks and have their laboratories searching for ways to treat and cure these diseases. One of those labs is in Madinha."

Hicks didn't like where this was going. "Go on."

"The Saudis believed these outbreaks were suspicious and so did we," Clarke explained. "We helped them track down who might be behind the outbreaks and traced them back to three scientists in the Saudi lab in Madinha. Two of them were French and one of them was American. None of them were Muslim and all of them had passed extensive background checks before being employed at the lab. They'd apparently been contacted by some ruthless bastards who'd paid them well to look into ways to weaponize the viruses they were studying. The outbreaks were trial runs."

Hicks knew there'd been several attempts to figure out how to turn these viruses into biological weapons for years, but none had been successful. Yet. "Why haven't I heard any of this before?"

"Because the Saudis were embarrassed by the whole thing happening at one of their labs and moved in to quickly arrest all three scientists. All three were said to have been killed while resisting arrest. Forces fired upon their car, which conveniently exploded as it ran off the road. Bodies were burned beyond all recognition but authorities assured us they'd killed all three men. That was two months ago. They assured us all samples of all the viruses were present and accounted for. As they're our allies and prickly about having their honor questioned, we took their word for it. Given this business with the envelope in Omar's possession, I'd say they lied."

Hicks felt his hand begin to shake and not from the cold. "If we'd known about all of this, we could've been on the lookout for something like this. Maybe could've prevented it."

Clarke smiled. "I'm sorry, old boy, but American secrets have a habit of winding up on the front page of the New York Times."

Hicks didn't smile. "The University is different, and you know it."

"So you say. Well, that's all in the past now. Little we can do about it now except put a lid on Djebar and Omar. I trust you're tracking Omar?"

"We've got a go team sitting on his residence right now, but I need Djebar first."

Clarke's eyes narrowed. "Why? You know where the fucker is. Grab him right now."

"Because Omar's got more means and money than we know, and I need to know how much before I pull him in. I have a feeling Djebar can tell me that. And that's why you're going to release his information to me. And the information on the three scientists who were supposedly killed by the Saudis."

"Agreed," Clarke said. "But only on one condition."

Hicks wasn't in a bartering mood. "Name it."

"We get Djebar after you're done with him. He won't be easy to break, but you have to agree to not kill him or hurt him to the point where he's useless to us. You honor your end of the bargain, my office works with yours in the future. You don't, I never answer your phone calls again. Not even if your president himself calls the Queen."

"Fine," Hicks said. "But we have to get Djebar first, don't we?"

Clarke held out a gloved hand to him. "Do we have a deal?"

Hicks shook it. "We have a deal."

"Right. I'll have the information you're looking for released to you and only you. If I find out you shared it with those fucking brie eaters, I'm going to be furious."

Hicks assumed he meant the French. "You have my word. But he's not going to be pretty when you get him back."

Clarke smiled. "I wouldn't expect him to be."

CHAPTER 20

A S SOON AS Clarke released the information on the scientists and the embargo on Djebar's file, the full resources of the University's system went to work.

It was times like these that made Hicks appreciate the true power of the University's ability to digitally reach into any life it chose.

Hicks had been with the organization for over a decade and not even he knew the full history or the reasons behind what the University was or even what it was. Where agencies like the NSA were only beginning to get their footing in the electronic landscape, the University had been in it from the beginning; from a time when microprocessors and wireless technology and the Internet were mere ideas on a classroom chalkboard.

Hicks was interested in the Saudi scientists, but Djebar was the more immediate priority. Within thirty seconds of Clarke lifting the embargo on the image, OMNI began comparing it to millions of images taken in the New York area in the past week. Airport security cameras, social media pictures, even cell phone pictures from all over the New York area were examined.

Within five minutes, OMNI had discovered fifty incidences of where Djebar had been before and after Colin's murder. More hits on more images came in each second.

The first viable hit came off a security camera at JFK airport a week before. It was a picture of Djebar as he stepped off a plane from Mumbai. Hicks made a note to tell his friends at the Indian Intelligence Bureau that he had been in their country for a time.

Hicks noted the resemblance on Djebar's forged passport to the blurred image they'd gotten from the SD card, only this one was much clearer. Djebar had a thin face and now sported a pencil thin mustache. He had deep set eyes and a light tan that probably helped him pass for Latin, Turkish, Mediterranean, Arabian, or even Persian if he'd wanted. Ambiguity was invaluable in the shadows.

The next hit came at a surprising place: a traffic cam in Long Island City. The image showed a clear image of Djebar and Omar in the back seat of an Escalade. Two men in the front were stocky black men and vibed hired security. Hired security meant they were probably armed. Hicks didn't waste time or effort searching for their identities because they were probably not part of Omar's plans.

The Escalade's license plate was clearly visible and showed

it was registered to Shabazz Security in midtown Manhattan. Another search for the car's black box showed it was parked over at the Millennium Hotel in Times Square. That didn't necessarily mean Djebar was there, too, but it was worth looking into.

The University had long been tied into the lodging and security systems of all the major hotel chains in the world. He checked the Millennium's lodging information to see if Djebar was registered under his own name or any of the aliases the British had provided.

When all aliases came up negative, Hicks went old school and put OMNI to work searching the hotel's security cameras for any matches of Djebar's likeness.

He had a hit from two nights before at the check in desk. Hicks matched the time on the image to the entries made in the hotel's system and found that a Francois Andabe of Zaire had checked in at that exact moment. And he was scheduled to check out the day after tomorrow.

Hicks' mind flooded with questions. If Omar had the money to bring a man like Djebar to New York, then why the hell had he made a panicked phone call for funding? It didn't make any sense.

Not yet, anyway. And he hoped Djebar could tell him why.

Hicks knew he had two choices: go straight after Djebar and find out why he'd met with Omar. Clarke had said Djebar wouldn't go quietly, so getting him could draw attention they didn't need and might tip off Omar. Omar was already probably on edge because of the Kamal mystery. And even if he grabbed Djebar, Roger might not break in time before

Omar hatched whatever he was planning.

The second option was to put Djebar on electronic surveillance while the Varsity raided Omar's safe house. But the safe house was in a crowded Brooklyn neighborhood. If Omar was working on something like a dirty bomb, a lot of people could get killed.

Hicks decided grabbing Djebar could answer a lot of questions. It was worth the risk.

He called Roger and told him to get ready.

CHAPTER
21

As soon as he reached Times Square, Hicks checked his handheld to get an exact lock on Djebar's location. Djebar's security detail's Escalade was still parked on the street next to the hotel and hadn't been moved since Hicks had first located it on OMNI. A high roller like Djebar was above taking cabs or subways. He'd prefer to roll deep with an armed posse and a fancy car to take him where he wanted to go.

Hicks liked to take down his targets while they stayed at hotels. If you went in at the right time of day, security paid no attention and the magnetic key card locks were a joke. Reaching a target in a huge place like the Millennium Hotel was a piece of cake. Djebar would be no different.

The only tricky part would be the security detail he had with him. The fact they were twice his size didn't bother him.

From what he'd seen on the traffic camera, they were muscle bound and slow. Street thugs in suits who used to their size as their best deterrent.

But the fact they were armed would make it harder to avoid a firefight and Hicks wanted to avoid a firefight at all costs. Gunfire would bring cops and cops would shine more light on this thing than Hicks could not afford, especially now.

He'd have to do this the old fashioned way—fast and by hand.

THE LOBBY OF the Millennium Hotel was too crowded for any of the staff to notice Hicks take the elevator upstairs. He'd checked the car as he'd walked by it and wasn't surprised to see it was empty. That meant Djebar still only had a two man team with him; both either in the hallway outside the room or inside watching the door. He'd find out soon enough. Killing them wouldn't be a problem. Not killing them would be the challenge. He'd have to hit them hard and fast before one of them started firing.

Hicks had changed into the same blue coveralls and blue hat he'd worn to the storage facility. He knew there were cameras in the elevator, so he kept his head down as he subtly slipped his hand in his pocket; wriggling his right hand into a pair of brass knuckles he liked to use on such occasions. He knew there was a chance the footage from the elevator camera would be viewed before OMNI would scrub it if things went sideways. He didn't want to give them a better look at him if he could avoid it. No sense in doing the cops' jobs for them.

As soon as he got off on Djebar's floor, Hicks spotted one of the security men standing in the hall; the bigger, balder of the two from the Escalade. He was sitting on a chair at the far end of the hall.

Hicks waived as he quickly walked toward him; yelling, "Hey! You the guys who complained about the water pressure? Room 1040?"

The guard began walking toward him and motioned for him to be quiet. "Not so loud, my man! Some people are trying to sleep."

Hicks kept walking toward him. "I don't mean no disrespect or nothin', mister, but I got a job to do here." Ten feet away now. "I didn't ask for this job, you know? I ain't even supposed to be here today. This was supposed to be my day off, and I ain't even gettin' time and a half for this shit."

The guard squared up to block Hicks' path. Three feet away. "I told you once to be quiet and I'm not gonna tell you again. I don't know…"

Hicks fired a straight right hand and buried the brass knuckles into the bigger man's face; shattering his nose. Hicks grabbed the bigger man before he fell over and slammed him face-first against the wall. He dropped the knuckles in his pocket and pulled the .9milimeter Glock from the holster on the guard's belt. He chambered a round and placed the muzzle against the back of the guard's head. "Open the door and go inside like nothing's wrong. Do what I say and everyone goes home. You get stupid or brave; I blow your fucking head off." He pushed the barrel harder into the man's neck. "Do you understand?"

The big man was busy trying to stem his bleeding nose

with his fingers. "You broke my fucking nose, man."

Hicks grabbed him by the back of the collar and pushed him toward the door. "Inside. Now."

The guard put his key in the lock and opened the door. Hicks put a shoulder into the guard's back and sent him stumbling forward. As the big man fell into the room, Hicks heeled the door shut and aimed the Glock at the first man he saw.

It was the other guard, the shorter and leaner of the two, caught flat on his ass on the couch watching television. As surprised as he was, he was smart enough to hold up his hands. "We're cool, baby. We're cool."

"Where's Djebar?" The man on the couch looked genuinely confused, so Hicks said, "Your boss. The man you're protecting. Where is he?""He ain't here. He's out with a friend."

"Bullshit. If you're here, he's here." Hicks lowered the gun until it was aimed the guard's crotch. "Last chance. Where is he?"

The guard motioned toward the closed bedroom door. "In there. Sleeping it off. Had some company last night and he hit it pretty hard. Ain't been out of his room all day."

The guard with the broken nose was trying to get to his feet, but Hicks put a shoe to his ass and pushed him down again. "Go crawl to your buddy over there on the couch." And to the guard on the sofa, he said, "I could've killed both of you by now, couldn't I?"

The man swallowed; nodded.

"But I didn't, did I?"The man shook his head.

"That's because I don't want you dead. You play this

smart, everyone keeps on living. That's why you're going to open your jacket real slow and take your gun out with your thumb and index finger. Do it real slow, then toss it on that chair over there."

The guard did exactly as he'd been told to do. Hicks said, "Now give your friend a hand and help him up on the couch. Make sure he keeps his head back. It'll help with the bleeding a little."

Hicks kept the Glock aimed at them as he went over to the bedroom door. He was just about to put his hand on the knob when the door opened and a smiling Rachid Djebar came out, already dressed in tan pants and a white shirt. Clean shaven, too, like he was walking into a board meeting.

"Good morning, my friend," the Algerian smiled. "I take it you have come here to discuss something with me."

Hicks grabbed him by the collar and pulled him into the living area. He pushed him against the wall; keeping his gun on the guards with one hand as he patted down Djebar for a weapon.

Djebar laughed the entire time. "Why would I spend money paying these men to protect me if I carried a weapon of my own?" He looked over at the two men. "Given how easily you got in here, though, perhaps it is something I should consider."

Hicks knew he should've checked the bathroom and the bedroom to make sure they were clear, but there was only one of him and three of them.

Instead, he took his handheld off mute, and said, "All clear. Get up here right away."

Djebar straightened out his rumpled shirt. He wasn't

a large man, but his clothes made him look bigger than he really was. But it was clear they were expensive, maybe Saville Row if Hicks had time to check the labels, which he didn't.

"Ah, I see you have brought friends," Djebar said, his English clear with just a hint of a French accent. He looked like an alert, eager young man, not like the conniving fifty year old power-broker Hicks knew him to be. "That is good as I always like meeting new friends."

Hicks stepped far enough away so he could cover all three men from a good angle. "We're not friends, Ace. And you're going to find that out soon enough."

"Don't be silly," Djebar smiled. "I get along with all sorts of people, as I'm sure you know well."

"What makes you think I know anything about you?"

"Because I am still alive and if you were here to kill me, all of us would be dead by now. You said so yourself to these men here. And if you were a policeman come to arrest me, there would've been far more of you. That leaves only one logical conclusion: you must be interested in my line of business. Perhaps my matchmaking abilities? Either you want me to serve as a matchmaker between you and another party or you wish to discuss my past previous clients." The Algerian shrugged. "As I profit from both making and telling, I see no reason why I should be concerned."

And Hicks saw no reason to tell him anything. "Just shut your mouth and stand there."

But the Algerian was undaunted. He leaned on the back of the large chair that faced the couch where the two guards were sitting. Behind them, a corner view that looked out ten stories above Times Square. Djebar looked back at the view over his shoulder and flashed Hicks his best salesman's smile.

"A million dollar view, is it not? Maybe more since a million doesn't buy as much as it once did. From here, we have a clear view of where the ball drops on New Year's Eve and the daily hustle and bustle of Times Square; the Crossroads of the World. We have the exceptional above and the mundane below, none of which can be fully appreciated by being in the middle of it. One must see it from a distance in order to appreciate the dichotomy, doesn't one? A distance, for example, which those of us up here can enjoy. A distance—a perspective, if you will—that can only be attained through money. That's all it takes in your country. In most of the world, really? Have enough money for a suite like this and you can have it. Have enough money and enough influence and you can have this suite whenever you want it. But without money, where are you?" He pointed to the street. "Down there with the rest of the people, crawling around like ants, looking up; never knowing just how insignificant they are until its too late. This is your America, Mr. Hicks. The country you kill for. And the country you'll one day die for."

Hicks should've guessed Djebar might've known his name. "You know who I am."

"How could I not?" Djebar said. "You dealt with an old mentor of mine in Karachi years ago. When I was still an apprentice and you an American operative. You wouldn't remember me, but I certainly remember you. And that is why I know you are an honorable man with whom I can work. So let us get down to business and discuss why you have come to see me today."

Hicks had been in Karachi several times, but didn't

know which mentor Djebar was talking about and he didn't remember Djebar. There were always young people around; all of them listening and hoping the American will notice them. Maybe give them a job and a way back to America.

He heard a knock at the hotel door, followed by two knocks. The signal he'd agreed upon with his partner. "You might want to hold off on the praise. I've got a feeling your opinion of me is about to change for the worse."

Hicks opened the door and stepped aside to give Roger Cobb enough room to push a wheelchair into the room. A black medical bag was on the seat.

And Djebar was not smiling any more.

But Hicks was. "You might remember Roger from Karachi. He was with me."

Djebar looked at the wheelchair and the medical bag and subconsciously took half a step back.

"He was there?" Roger appraised him from head to toe, then smiled. "Handsome boy. I would've remembered. Did we party?"

Djebar looked at the bag on the wheelchair and took another step back. "Whatever you are planning to do to me, it won't work. I've been trained to resist all forms of interrogation."

"Good. I love a challenge." Roger took a syringe out of his pocket and removed the plastic top. "This is just a little medicine to help you relax. We're old friends from Karachi, remember? We're going to get real close, you and me. Very, very close." As he began walking toward Djebar, the Algerian took one step back and then another until he was against the wall with nowhere to go.

Roger's tone was almost soothing. "Oh, come now. It's not as bad as all that. Just one little pinch and we'll all be on our way."

Djebar pushed off the wall and tried to run, but Roger caught him by the throat; as quick and clean as a cobra striking a rat. The Algerian gagged as Roger pulled the smaller man toward him and injected the clear contents of the syringe into his neck.

Hicks pushed the wheelchair forward in time for Djebar to fall into it. Within a few seconds, Djebar's chin was on his chest, drooling.

Roger took a thin hospital blanket from his bag and wrapped it around Djebar. "That should keep him upright for the ride ahead."

The guard whose nose wasn't broken asked, "Where are you taking him? What are you doing to him?"

"You don't want to know that," Hicks said as he took the guard's gun off the chair and began to strip it. "In fact, we were never here and none of this ever happened."

The guard thought about it for a moment. "My man here needs help. His nose is busted and bleeding bad." He looked at Roger. "You some kind of doctor? Maybe you can help?"

"Healing isn't exactly my forte," Roger said as he grabbed his bag and approached the guard with the broken nose, but I'll see what I can do." He reached into his bag for some forceps and gauze and began to tend to the broken nose.

Hicks spoke to the other guard. "We've already closed out Djebar's account with your company. I made sure he paid it in full with a damned generous tip for you guys for doing such a good job. We've also seen to it that Djebar has paid for this room through the weekend. And his AmEx Black Card is still wide open, so make sure you enjoy it."

Roger laughed as he began to pack the other guard's nostrils with gauze. "Ah, to be in your shoes, friend. One can have a good time getting into a lot of trouble with one of those cards. Believe me, I know."

"But why do all of this for us? Why not just kill us?"

"Because I already know all about you, Miguel Reyes, and I know you're not part of this. You're just a nice Dominican boy from Washington Heights who loves his mother, his two sisters, and his nieces. I know you're not going to interfere in our lives, because I know you don't want us interfering in yours."

"Shit," Reyes said as he looked from Hicks to Roger, then Hicks. "Shit."

"Here's what's going to happen next. Roger's going to set your friend's nose and we're going to wheel this asshole out of here. You're going to spend the rest of the day here ordering room service and putting it all on your pal's Amex card. As far as your bosses are concerned, you dropped him off at JFK and that's the last you saw of him."

"I just hope this is the last time I see you."

"Keep your mouth shut about what happened here today, and you'll never see me again. If you make it about more than that, if you tell anyone what happened here or about me or my friend, I'll be the last person you ever see. Your family, too. Understand?"

Roger set the guard's nose in a crude splint and injected him with something for the pain. He made a show of using a new needle. "Don't worry. It's not the same one I used on Djebar. No telling what potpourri of social diseases are battering around his system. This will make you sleepy for a while and dull the pain for a day or so."

Roger closed up his bag and got up from the couch. "I was right. Healing isn't as much fun as hurting."

The guard with the broken nose dozed off, but Reyes said, "What about my gun, man? That's mine, not the company's."

"It'll be waiting for you when you get home tomorrow. Don't forget, I have your address." Roger dropped his medical bag in Djebar's lap, but the man was too out of it to notice.

As they wheeled Djebar to the elevator, Roger said, "Leaving them alive was a mistake."

Hicks disagreed. "I'm not killing two guys for doing their job. They worked for the company Djebar hired to watch him, not Djebar himself."

"Well if you were going to leave his black card with them, the least you could've done was tell them about the Jolly Roger. The club can always handle more customers."

Hicks looked down at Djebar. His head was slumped forward and he'd begun to drool on his blanket. "You've already got one."

CHAPTER 22

AN HOUR LATER, Hicks watched Roger prep Djebar for questioning via the television set in the waiting room he'd set up for such sessions. Roger referred to the interrogation chamber as his 'studio.' It was actually a former dentist's office in an old building in the West Village. The years hadn't dulled the smell of awkward desperation and fear that most dental offices had. Roger's activities in the years since had only added to it.

The place was still outfitted with late seventies furniture, complete with a glassed in receptionist's area where patients could make their payments. An old sticker on the window still read: 'MasterCharge The Interbank Card Accepted' and 'Your BankAmericard Welcome Here.'

Only Roger's patients didn't make payments in cash,

check, or credit card. They didn't have to present proof of health insurance either. They paid by telling Roger the truth. And if the truth was currency, then Roger was often well compensated.

Roger had strapped Djebar's arms and legs to a dentist's chair. The chair had been re-covered in soft rubber to make for easier clean up after a session. A drain had been installed in the center of the floor and florescent lights powerful enough for surgery hung down from the ceiling. The small dentist's tray had long since been removed in favor of a proper surgery table that held scalpels and sutures. Much heavier equipment, too, like steel bone saws and spreaders that sparkled in the strong light.

Many of Roger's patients often laughed at the equipment when they saw it, trying to convince themselves it was all just for show. But by the end of their session, they'd learned that Roger never wasted time on theatrics and, quite often, put all of the tools at his disposal to good use.

Through the old television in the observation room, Hicks watched Roger slip the heavy rubber coroner's apron over his head before he injected Djebar again. Hicks knew the last injection had been a sedative, but this would be just the opposite.

Djebar snapped awake just as Roger pulled the needle from his neck. His eyes instantly bright and alive.

Hicks watched Roger pull up a stool and sat next to Djebar; smiling down into the Algerian's face. "Welcome back, my friend. How was your sleep? Restful, I trust?"

Djebar now squinted at the light and tried to look away, but realized he couldn't. His head was secured in a vice that

Roger had attached to the chair's headrest long ago.

"Where... where am I?"

Roger reached up and dimmed the light just enough to stop it from shining into his eyes. "Where are you? That's a very interesting question. I like to think of this place as a threshold of new beginnings and new truth. You're in a place where a precious few people have enjoyed the rarest of opportunities to shed the bonds of their old lives and embrace a rebirth. To become something new and clean and pure."

Hicks watched Djebar struggle to look anywhere but at the light. He managed to move his head just enough to get a glimpse of the bone cutter glinting on the operating table on his left. "Oh God. Please. I'll tell you anything. Anything at all. Just don't hurt me."

Roger placed a finger to Djebar's lips. "Of course you'll tell me anything, my friend. Anything at all, especially whatever you think I want to hear. But I'm afraid that won't be good enough for our purposes, because I don't want you to tell me just anything, Djebar. I want you to tell me the truth. The pure, unadulterated truth about your friend Omar and why you're here and what you were hired to do for him."

Djebar began to speak, a panicked jumble of English and Arabic and French but Roger gently placed a finger on his lips again. "Everything's going to be fine, Djebar, because the truth isn't just an assemblage of facts. It's a process of discovery that can't be rushed. Anything you tell me now will only be a hint of what I really want to know, and I want to know everything about everything. About Omar. About why you're here and about all your other dealings all over the world. And together, you and I will help you remember things you thought you forgot. We're going to remind you of things you never thought you knew. It's a journey we're about to take together, my friend; a journey that, for you has been oh so very long in coming."

"No," Djebar whispered; his voice as small as his eyes were wide. "No, please. We can deal. We..."

"Our destination on this journey is the purest truth we can know, and you and I will arrive at that glorious place together very soon."

Hicks watched Djebar dry swallow. He began to tremble in his restraints as he saw Roger tie a thick rubber surgical mask under his nose.

"Why? Why are you doing this?" Djebar whispered. "To me? I told you I'll tell you anything. You don't have to do this to me! And for whom? For your country? For your own people who hate you and despise you for what you are?"

Hicks watched Roger reached for his rubber gloves. "But this isn't about me, my friend. It's about you and what you are now and what you're going to become in such a short amount of time."

Through the old speakers of the television set, Hicks could hear Djebar begin to whimper and pray in Arabic as Roger snapped on the rubber gauntlets that came up to his elbows. He saw Djebar's surprise when Roger joined him word for word in his chant of a passage from the Quran. In Arabic. It was a passage Hicks had heard prayed in these interrogations many times before. In English, it meant:

"The righteous shall return to a blessed retreat: the gardens of Eden, whose gates shall open wide to receive them. Reclining there with bashful virgins for companions, they will call for abundant fruit and drink."

Roger smiled down at Djebar from behind his rubber mask. "Such a beautiful sentiment in such a sacred book used by such ugly, ugly people for devious purposes. People like you who want to exterminate people like me."

Djebar shut his eyes and whimpered when Roger stroked the side of his cheek with the cold rubber glove. "In pain, there is truth and beauty to be found. And if that is true, by the time you and I are done here today, you will be the purest, most magnificent man alive."

Hicks watched Roger pick up a scalpel and let Djebar watch the light dance along its sharpened edge. "To paradise."

Hicks turned off the television as Roger brought the scalpel down on Djebar's sternum. He could still hear the gurgled screams though the thin walls. It was, after all, an old building.

CHAPTER
23

Hicks had smoked two Churchill cigars before the examination room door opened. Djebar's screams had gone hoarse before they had ended and that had been longer than Hicks wanted to remember. The screams had been followed by a heavy silence, then gasping whispers and tears and muffled words. He had even heard laughter coming from the room, but not for a long time.

Hicks could've gone somewhere else while Roger conducted his interrogation, but he never did. The idea of going for a walk or grabbing coffee at Starbucks while Roger cut into someone struck him as cold and odd, even more so than the torture itself.

Conventional interrogation wisdom said torture didn't work. But as Roger was fond of saying, "If it doesn't work, you're doing it wrong."

Roger had already removed his rubber surgical mask and gauntlets when he walked into the waiting area. Except for the rubber apron, he looked as refreshed as someone who'd just woken up from a long afternoon nap.

"My," he sighed as he sat in an ancient metal and pleather chair across from Hicks. "That was *quite* a session. Glad I had the recorders rolling for that one. He became quite cooperative after a while."

Hicks noticed a sliver of something bright pink on the belly of Roger's apron and quickly looked away. "Jesus, Roger."

Roger noticed it and picked it up with two fingers. "Ah, how Merchant of Venice of me. Sorry about that. The price of progress, I suppose. A pound of flesh, as it were, only this one was just a couple of ounces."

Hicks felt the bile rise in his throat. He was no stranger to blood and carnage, but Roger's interrogations were always something more than that. He didn't just work on the body. He worked on the soul. Hicks had never believed in things like souls until he'd seen the results of Roger's work. Because only damaging someone on a spiritual level could count for the results he was able to get. It was less about the pain and more about the use of it to get what he wanted.

Hicks swallowed down what was rising in his throat and said, "Did you get anything out of him?"

"Oh, quite a bit. Your friend Clarke was right about our Djebar, you know? He's been exceptionally well trained to hide information. He's spent a lifetime hiding behind several walls in his mind. Selective memory, disassociation, and the like. I made him remember things he didn't think he knew or thought he'd long forgotten. He's far more complex than your typical run of the mill Matchmaker, and now I can see why he's so well paid."

"I'm glad you're impressed," Hicks said. "What did he tell you about Omar?"

Roger took the piece of tissue and tossed it in a small trash can between the tables. It made a wet smack off the side and a small puff of dust rose as the flesh struck the bottom. "Omar had hired Debar to put him in touch with some scientists who've been working on weaponizing SARS and MERS and Ebola in a lab in Saudi Arabia. According to Djebar, the Saudis told their allies that all the scientists were killed. They weren't. In fact, they all got away. Their deaths are just a cover story the Saudis are using to cover their mistakes."

Hicks hadn't told Roger about the envelope because he didn't want him to lead Djebar in that direction. As good as Roger was, he was still human and humans are prone to being influenced. "Did he say who Omar is working with?"

"You said there were three scientists. Which of them did Djebar put in touch with Omar?"

"He mentioned something about a Samuelson who'd been working at the lab. By then, Djebar was a little tired, so the details were foggy. He mentioned something about shipments and samples and keeping everyone on program, whatever that means. He said there were three scientists, but didn't tell me anything about the other two."

"Did he tell you how much of the viruses this Samuelson had given Omar?"

"Twelve vials in plastic containers," Roger said. "He was very specific about how the containers were plastic, but I couldn't get him to tell me why."

"Because they were transported in a padded envelope," Hicks said. It was all coming together and none of it was pretty. "Did he tell you anything else about Samuelson?"

"No, but before he passed out, he kept confusing phrases. Instead of payment, he kept referring to 'his people' and 'us' and his 'reward.' I thought you said he worked alone."

"I did," Hicks said. Then again, he'd once thought Omar was just a cab driver with a big mouth and no network. The rest of what Djebar had said could've been babble or it could be everything.

Hicks pulled out his handheld in hand. "Did you upload your session with Djebar to OMNI?"

"It was a live feed the whole time," Roger said. "The system should be combing through it now. Why?"

Hicks dialed the Dean. "Did Djebar give Omar the samples already?"

"He said the bulk of the shipment is scheduled to arrive today or tomorrow, but he did give him several samples on account when they gave their deposit. Samuelson is supposed to give him the rest today."

Hicks began dialing the Dean. "How?"

"That part was handled directly between Samuelson and Omar via email. It's all part of the security procedures the scientists insist upon and it's pretty effective."

The Dean answered Hicks' call on the second ring. "OMNI is already analyzing everything he got out Djebar. Tell Roger he hit the mother lode with this bastard."

Normally, Hicks would've been happy that the Dean was pleased, but he didn't have that kind of time. "We need to pour everything into finding Samuelson and the other two scientists from the lab. We need to know where he's been since the Saudi raid. Where he is now. We need to find out how he's sending them the rest of the viruses and we'd better find out fast."

"I'll make sure it's a priority," the Dean said. "In the meantime, Scott's Varsity team is ready to hit Omar's facility at any time. According to his field reports, no one has moved from the building all day. No one in, no one out, so maybe they're waiting on that delivery you mentioned."

Roger heard the entire conversation and said, "Make sure they have gas masks with them before they go in. That should be enough to protect them in the event of contamination, so long as they get out of the building as quickly as possible after they hit it."

Hicks heard a few more clicks from the Dean's keyboard. "We should play it safe and just send in a drone to level the whole building right now. We can claim it was a gas leak or a meth lab that blew up. Christ knows that excuse has worked in the past for less dangerous circumstances."

"That might kill Omar and the existing samples, but it won't help us find out where the next batch of samples is coming from or who Omar's working with. These guys have managed to stay off the grid for this long. Anything we get out of him will have to be through interrogation."

"I'm scrambling a drone anyway," the Dean said. "It'll be in the area within two hours. In addition to Scott's team, I've already another team en route to cover the perimeter while Scott's team goes in. Either by land or air, that building gets hit in two hours. Hicks, I take it you'll want to be there when we go in."

"If I get there in time," Hicks said, "but if Scott has cause, tell him not to wait. I'd rather keep them contained in the building than risk letting them go."

"Understood," said the Dean. "I'll let them know you're in route. I'll send details on the drone to your handheld as they come in. And, for what it's worth, Hicks, you were right all along."

Hicks wasn't in the mood for praise, either. "Don't let Jason hear you say that. Let's just hope we can stop this damned thing before it spreads."

The connection went dead and Hicks pocketed the handheld. To Roger, he said, "Are you sure you got everything out of Djebar about Omar?"

"Everything relevant, yes. But I think there's still enough paste left in the tube for at least one more scrubbing. I know our friends across the pond want him back." He suddenly looked like a sad child asking to stay up past his bedtime. "Can I keep him? Just a little while?"

The way he looked when he said it made Hicks grateful they were on the same side. "Just a little while, then fix him up and call that number I gave you. And make sure they get access to everything he said. But if you kill him, Clarke's going to be pissed and so will I."

Roger brightened. "It'll be my pleasure."

Hicks didn't know what to say to that, so he simply closed the door quietly behind him.

CHAPTER
24

HICKS DIDN'T HAVE any trouble locating the Varsity observation post in Midwood. They'd been stationed in the back of an old delivery truck with the faded signage of a fruit vendor on the side. The white paint on the cab was peeling and gray, showing the rusting metal underneath. Graffiti covered most of the exterior. The truck looked like it belonged in a junkyard instead of playing a role as a forward observation post, which was the general idea.

A man Hicks knew by the name of Scott was in charge of the Varsity team who'd been watching Omar's safe house for the past day. Hicks had worked with Scott in various parts of the world for the better part of a decade, but still didn't know if Scott was his first name or his last name. He really didn't care, either.

The inside of the cargo area had been outfitted as a cramped forward observation post. The truck had four bunk beds for operatives to sleep in while two others monitored the equipment. Everything was hooked up to OMNI via the network, making the whole set up a mobile version of his Twenty-third Street station. A state-of-the-art ventilation system made the truck cool in the summer and warm in the winter, but the air still smelled like stale coffee.

"What's the play?" Scott asked Hicks when they were inside the truck. "The Dean called direct and said this was a potential Level One scenario, but that's damned near a given. We don't exactly get called out to fetch cats out of trees."

Hicks saw no reason not to level with them. They were risking their lives right along with him. They were entitled to know what they were up against. "We just learned that Omar is working toward bringing in weaponized versions of the SARS, MERS, and Ebola viruses into the country. We have good reason to believe that he already has several samples of each in his possession with an untold number on the way. We don't know if they're in the building or elsewhere. We don't know who is delivering them or when. But we suspect that Omar is scheduled to receive delivery of these samples at some point today. If it looks like the delivery is taking place, we go in."

The five other men looked at each other, then at Scott. Kicking in doors and killing bad guys was one thing. Doing it with a lethal biological agent in the building was another story.

Scott said, "I am not sending my men into a goddamned HazMat area without proper equipment."

"Suspected HazMat area," Hicks said, "and it's probably a small enough amount for your gas masks to protect you."

One of the other men asked, "What about a drone strike to take out the building? Hell, we've nailed targets tighter than this one before."

"The Dean is prepping that option as we speak, but it's still more than an hour out. But if we blow the building without knowing what's inside, we run the risk of missing delivery of the shipment and finding out who Omar is working with. Not to mention the virus might not even be there and we'd be killing every lead we have in finding out where the new shipment is coming from."

Scott spoke for his men. "I say level the building and sift the rubble later. I'll take a building full of dead Hajis before I let one of my men get scratched." The men grunted their agreement. "There's some potentially bad shit going on in there and lighting it up is the best for all involved."

Hicks didn't think so, but he didn't want to disagree with Scott in front of his men. "Like I said, it's being considered."

One of Scott's men asked, "Any idea about what kind of weapons they have? We've been watching them since yesterday and haven't seen shit."

"I've watched the guys for a while and never seen them with anything bigger than a nine millimeter. But I didn't know Omar was capable of running a bio-terror ring, so we should be prepared for anything."

"If we go in," Scott said.

"If we do, what's your plan for hitting the building?"

Scott turned it over to his man at the computer who brought up a three dimensional rendering of the building from the University satellite. "When the second team arrives, we'll have a twelve-man force, so we'll set up a containment and breach scenario. The second unit will cover us with two men in the front, two in the back, and one sniper stationed at the front of the building and one at the back. With the front door covered, we'll breach through the back door where they're least expecting it."

The tech switched screens to a thermal read of the building. "We're looking at a three-story structure that has been modified several times recently. Scans show twenty people moving freely through the building and basement since yesterday. About six of the twenty have been on the top floor and appear to be in bed. Judging by what we've been able to see through scans, they're all running fevers and they might be sick."

"Or infected," Hicks observed.

"You catch on fast," said Scott. "If Omar is still inside—and we've got no reason to think he's anywhere else—that means they all know him and are probably part of whatever he's planning to do with those diseases. That means there are no innocents in that building and if we go in and start shooting, everyone is a legitimate target."

Hicks told the computer tech to pull up Omar's photo. "I know you've been looking at this bastard's photo for a few days now, but I need you to memorize his photo. He's our main target and you wound him if you have to. Even cripple him, but don't kill him. We need him alive so we can find out where the viruses are and what he's done with the samples he already has. We need him to tell us where the shipment is and where the samples he already has are. And he can't tell us a damned thing if he's dead."

One of Scott's men asked, "What makes you think he'll talk."

Hicks flashed back to the sounds and smells he'd just left at Roger's studio. The piece of Djebar he'd thrown in the garbage. "Don't worry. He'll talk."

The computer tech said, "Then you boys better work fast because it looks like something's going on."

HICKS LOOKED AT the OMNI thermal feed on the monitor. Inside the building, he saw several heat signatures blurring into one as they massed in the hallway by the front door.

"God damn it," Hicks said. "They're coming out."

One of Scott's other men put his hand up to his earpiece and repeated, "Sir. The second team is a block out."

"Good. Have them stay in their vehicles and stay ready." To Hicks, Scott said, "If they move, I say we hit them in transit. It'll be public, but it'll be clean and final."

Hicks asked the computer tech for the mouse and took the feed off thermal, switched it to normal vision and zoomed in on the front door of the building. His handheld began to buzz. It was either the Dean or Jason calling for a status report now that things were heating up. Hicks decided it must be Jason. Only that numbskull would be dumb enough to call just as an operation was about to pop.

Hicks watched the line of men stream out of Omar's house into the street. OMNI automatically scanned each face and would run identity checks within a matter of moments on each man it saw. The all had the gaunt leanness of Somalis, but none of them looked like Omar.

Hicks knew if he hit them now, he could prevent everyone from getting away. Keep all the bad guys in one place. But he would risk killing Omar in a firefight and lose the one man who knew about his plan. Omar had always led a compartmentalized existence. Hicks knew no one would know enough about his plans to tell him much.

Hicks and the others watched as the men from the building piled into five cars that had been parked on the street in front of the building.

"Time's wasting," Scott said. "Make the call."

Hicks knew what he should do, but decided what was best for the broader mission. "Our group is Team One and your other group is Team Two. Team Two will follow and track those five cars. OMNI is our eye in the sky but those boys are our boots on the ground. No matter what happens, they stick with the cars and report back where they go. If we're not available, they report to Jason. Team Two stays cocked and locked unless they see something funky going on. Until then, they are to report back only."

Scott clearly didn't like it, but was too professional to say it, especially in front of his men. He nodded at his radio man, who relayed the instructions to Team Two. Then Scott said, "Then you still want to hit that building."

Hicks clicked the screen back to a thermal image of the building. "I counted ten people who came out of that house. That leaves ten more still inside. Five on the top floor, many of whom appear to in bed and quite possibly sick, and five who look like they're in the basement. Any of those men who just came out look like they were carrying any lab equipment to you?" Scott shook his head, so Hicks said, "Me neither. The samples of the virus are still in there. That's why Team Two tails the ten men and the rest of us go in."

Scott looked at the monitor. "I don't like it, but I'm not paid to like it, am I?"

"I'm open to suggestions," Hicks said, though he'd planned enough of these operations to know there were no other options.

They watched as the ten men who'd left the building pulled away in five cars. Team Two—in a Chevy Trailblazer—followed ten seconds behind.

Hicks stepped away from the computer. "It's your team and your call, but either way, I'm going in. Alone if I have to."

One of the other men spoke up. "Wait a minute. What about the drone strike?"

Scott answered for him. "Drone like that's at least an hour out. Those men leaving the premises give us the best chance of going in with minimal resistance." He reached into a supply drawer and handed Hicks a gas mask. "If you're coming with us, you're wearing one of these."

Hicks took the mask. "Then let's go."

HICKS LED THE way out of the truck. Scott's men followed with Scott locking up and bringing up the rear. The street hadn't been shoveled and patches of ice had formed beneath the snow; making it slippery. None of the men stumbled.

Hicks led them through the path he'd staked out already; through an alley that led between two buildings that let out directly across the street from Omar's building. The alley was a popular pass through for kids going to and coming home from school, so the snow had trampled well and made for easier travel.

When they got to the mouth of the alley, Scott's men began to lever out the shoulder guards on their AR-15s. In the trot through the alley, Scott had managed to fall in right behind Hicks.

"How do you want to call it?" Hicks asked him. "It's your show from here on in."

Scott gave his men the orders. One stays behind and covers the rest of the team from the alley. Three work behind the house and come in the back door. Hicks, Scott, and the last man go in through the front.

Hicks spoke into the wireless earpiece. "Jason, you on the line?"

"I am and in position," he said.

He'd never had Jason bird-dog an operation like this. He hoped he was a better spotter than he was a Department Head. "I'm going to need a final thermal check before we go in. Copy?"

"Copy. I still count ten heat sigs remaining inside. Four in the basement. Six clustered upstairs from what I can tell. Sigs all register calm colors. Doesn't look like you're expected. First floor reads clear. Copy?"

"Copy," Hicks said. "Go team is ready. Scott is assuming command of the breach."

Hicks glanced back at Scott. "Just make sure Omar stays alive."

Scott tapped Hicks on the shoulder, signaling him to break from the alley. Hicks sprinted out fast and low. He didn't bother going for the Ruger until he got to the side of the front door.

Hicks had been conducting raids since he was eighteen years old, but the speed of Scott's team impressed even him. They'd already broken around the back by the time Hicks turned to see where they were. He pulled the Ruger from his hip holster and looked to Scott for what he wanted to do next.

"Since the first floor shows blue on thermals, the two of us will clear out upstairs," Scott said. "You take care of the basement."

"That's four on one," the other man said. "That's a lot for one man to cover."

"But he ain't just another man, now is he?" Scott grinned. "He's Faculty and that makes all the difference. Isn't that right, Mr. Hicks?"

Hicks pulled on his gas mask and reached for the doorknob. "Goddamned right it is."

CHAPTER 25

THE DOOR SWUNG in silently and slowly. It didn't creak or bang into the wall.

Scott went in first; his AR-15 leading the way. He paused at the foot of the stairs. His second came up behind him and began sweeping the first floor. Hicks trailed in after him and went for the basement stairs.

The first floor was covered with area rugs, so there was minimal chance of the men downstairs hearing a cracking floorboard above their heads.

Hicks found the door to the basement beneath the stairs was open and headed down; the Ruger at his side. The stairwell was well lit by a single yellow bulb; the basement just as dark.

The stairs were flimsy and creaked beneath his weight as

he descended, but he kept moving at a good clip. He heard the din of excited chatter coming from deep within the basement so he doubted any of them could hear him anyway.

The landing at the base of the stairs was dark and the windows were boarded over. The only immediate light came from the broken wooden walls on his right.

Despite what he'd seen of the official building plans on the city's database, the basement looked as if it had been sectioned off into rooms some time ago. But now, the plaster was cracked and all of the walls had gaping holes.

Hicks took cover behind a fractured wall and looked through the holes at what was happening in the center of the room.

He saw Omar holding a syringe as he stood in front of five men lined up in a row. All three men were black and short and painfully thin; probably Somali. Their clothes were faded t-shirts and cheap jeans that didn't fit them right. Not baggy in a fashionable gangbanger way, but in a poverty way. Like a missionary handed out a garbage bag full of clothes from the back of a truck in a village a long time ago.

One of the men moved off to the side, rubbing his right arm. The other three held their right arms, veins-side out, waiting for Omar to inject them.

Hicks braced himself against the wall. The son of a bitch was injecting them with the virus. Making them carriers. Signing their death warrant and the death warrants of anyone who came in contact with them.

Through the cracked wall, Hicks scanned the room for guns or guards. He saw neither. He came around the wall and stepped into the light behind the others. He brought up the

Ruger and aimed at Omar's chest.

Omar saw him and froze; the needle and vial still in his hand.

The other men turned to face him and slowly backed away.

"Don't do anything stupid," Hicks said. "Just set it down on the table, nice and easy and we can all walk out of here alive."

Omar gave him that crooked, gaping smile Hicks had seen in countless surveillance images, but had never seen in real life. He still held the syringe and needle. "Walk out of here? And walk into what? A cell? Guantanamo? One of your black sites?"

"I'm not with the CIA and neither was Halaam," Hicks said, using Colin's cover name. "No Guantanamo and no jail cell. Just the two of us working this out as soon as you put that shit on the table and step away."

Omar surprised him by laughing. "How do I know?"

"Because if I wanted you dead, we wouldn't be talking."

He caught the glint in Omar's eye; the quiver of the needle and vial in his hand. If he dropped that vial, everyone in the room would be infected, including him. For his own sake, he added, "I don't want to kill you."

Omar wasn't smiling anymore. His eyes flat; committed. "How wonderfully American of you. As if the choice is your own. But it isn't. It's mine. A purposeful death is glorious and far better than a life spent in…"

Hicks fired.

The round tore into Omar's right shoulder; the impact lifting him off his feet and spinning him back. The syringe stayed in the vial and flew out of his hand. Both the vial and the syringe hit the floor, but neither of them broke. Hicks remembered what Djebar had told Roger: the vials were plastic.

The five men bolted through a doorway on the other side of the room. Hicks brought his gun around as he called for them to wait, but they were too panicked to hear him and ran up a flight of stairs. He stepped over Omar's body as he ran to see where they were going.

He watched them trip over each other as they scrambled up the back stairway that led to the small yard behind the house. Where Scott's men were already in position, waiting for them.

Hicks heard the muted coughs of the silenced AR-15s as the men hit daylight. The poor panicked bastards ran right into a wall of lead fired at eight hundred rounds a minute. They never had a chance.

One of the Somalis scrambled back down; the same man he'd seen Omar inject with the virus. He might've been the first he'd injected or he might've been the last. It didn't matter. He looked at Hicks, then at the stairway up to the house. Hicks was standing between him and that doorway.

Between him and freedom.

"We have a vaccine," Hicks told him in French. "We can cure you. You don't have to die."

But the man either didn't speak French or he was too scared to understand. Instead, he screamed as he ran straight at Hicks, teeth bared and hands flailing. Hicks fired before he got two steps. The shot caught him right between the eyes and took the back of his head with it as it left his skull. He was dead before he hit the ground.

Hicks went back to Omar. He was still splayed on the floor, unconscious. He'd hit his head when he fell and was out cold. The shot from the Ruger had obliterated his shoulder socket. He was pumping blood but still alive.

The vial and the syringe were safely out of his reach, but Hicks didn't take any chances. He dragged Omar over to the heater and slip tied Omar's left hand to a pipe.

He didn't know if Omar was infected with the virus. He didn't know if he might catch it by touching him, but he had to check his condition. He pressed two fingers against Omar's carotid artery and his pulse was strong. Hicks slipped on his gloves and quickly field dressed the wound to minimize some of the bleeding. He figured it would hold the Facilities group's HAZMAT team arrived.

Hicks stood up and hit the comm link to the rest of the team. "This is Hicks. Two down in the basement. Four more in the backyard. Prime target has been hit but stabilized. Over."

Scott clicked in from two stories above. "Top floor has ten souls. No hostiles. All of them appear to be sick. The stink up here is horrible. Team Beta, report."

But Jason overrode the frequency as Scott's men began reporting in. "Hicks, what condition is Omar in?

"He caught a round in the right shoulder, but he should last until Facilities arrives," Hicks said as he headed upstairs. "He's stable and secured to a radiator in the basement. How far out is Facilities?"

"Have you had the chance to question him yet?" Jason asked.

"Negative. He's out cold, and I'm not spending any more

time down there than I have to. We're evacuating the house now and will wait for Facilities to run their tests."

"Copy that," Scott said. "All teams evac to the street, then back to the van. Over."

"Facilities unit is en route under the guise of a ConEd team," Jason said. "They are less than thirty minutes away. Did the virus breach the perimeter, over?"

"No perimeter break," Scott said. "All targets contained inside the building. We are evacuating back to the van. All units: move out."

Scott met Hicks at the base of the stairs and they went off the tactical link to Jason.

"There's a shitload of sick women and children up there," Scott said as they went into the street, "and it looks like there's room for at least thirty more people. Many of them look like they might've been kids, but there's no sign of them up there or in the house. What the hell's going on here?"

Hicks had some ideas, but didn't want to waste time guessing. He pulled off his gas mask when they reached the street, glad to be able to breathe in fresh air. "Were you exposed long?"

Scott removed his mask as well. "Just long enough to sweep the area and boogie back into the hall, but we kept our masks on the entire time. We've got a hot dose of anti-virals back in the van which ought to kill anything we might've caught, but there's some real far-gone shit going on up there. I think a couple of them might already be dead."

The rest of the team was already crossing the street and heading through the alley, back to the van.

As they walked, Scott broke down the shoulder stock

of his AR-15 and carried it close under his arm. "Damn it, Hicks. What was that in there?"

"I think Omar was making the most of the samples he had," Hicks said. "He was using those people to breed the diseases. After he got the samples, he injected his people with it and used their blood to infect others. I saw him injecting at least one and possibly all five of the men your boys just shot coming out of the basement. The other thirty you said could be staying upstairs are probably out in the world somewhere. Schools. Work. Buses. Subways."

"Shit. They're probably all over the city by now."

Hicks didn't want to think about it. There was nothing he could do about it yet, anyway. All he could do was wait for the Facilities team to show up, seal the place and tell the Dean and Jason what he was dealing with. Until then, guessing could only lead to panic and panic would make a bad situation worse.

Besides, he still had one more plate spinning. "Check in with Team Two. Where are we with the ten bastards who left here?"

Hicks checked their position via the OMNI feed on his handheld while Scott raised them on the comm. "Team Two this is Leader One. What's your position?"

"Leader One, we are heading east through Brooklyn and we're heading toward the on ramp to the Belt Parkway. All five cars are still moving in a loose formation. We have eyes on the targets and are trailing at a fair distance with the OMNI feed as backup."

Hicks pulled up the live OMNI feed on his handheld. He saw the five cars moving along in the center and left hand lanes. None of them were moving particularly fast or particularly slow. They were driving slightly over the speed limit, but probably not enough to garner any attention from the cops.

Hicks wondered aloud, "Why the hell were they heading east onto the Belt Parkway? Manhattan is west. What the hell was east of the city? Where…"

Hicks stopped walking; stopping dead in the street before he reached the van.

Scott had already climbed inside, but jumped down again and came back to Hicks. "What's the matter?"

Hicks changed the OMNI feed to a map view of where the five cars were headed. He zoomed out and saw that heading east on the Belt Parkway could lead them to one of two places. And Hicks bet they were going to both.

"What is it?" Scott demanded.

"The bastards are in five cars on the Belt Parkway."

Scott shrugged. "We already knew that. So?"

"Belt Parkway is the best way to get to two places from here. One of them is JFK Airport and the second is LaGuardia Airport."

"You think they're looking to pick up the samples at the airport?"

"Either that or they've already been injected and sent out to infect people at the airports."

Scott looked back at his men in the van, then at Hicks. "What can we do about it from here?"

Hicks looked back through the alley at Omar's safe house. The house and the street were as quiet as they had been right before Scott's team had raided the place. There was no way of knowing there were five dead men in the basement or ten people coughing themselves to death on the top floor. "I don't know, but I'm going to find out. Until then, make sure your men keep those cars in range. We may need them."

CHAPTER
26

HICKS DRY-SWALLOWED THE anti-virals Scott had insisted on giving him as he walked back to the house.

Scott spoke to him via the comm on his handheld. "I'm telling you for the last time this is a bad idea. You don't know what the hell you'll be breathing in there."

"I just downed your anti-virals," Hicks said. The pills were horse pills and stuck in his gullet. "Given what we're up against, it's an acceptable risk."

"I've got five of my best men trailing those cars. We can intercept them right now and find out for sure."

Hicks knew if Scott said his men were good, they were. Scott had been trained by Tomczak and Tomczak had been trained by Hicks. But there were too many factors involved with stopping the five cars on a busy highway like the BQE.

Getting all five at once would be difficult, if not impossible for one car, even a car filled with highly trained men.

He knew he could have the locals stop traffic, of course, but all that would do is pen in ten desperate, possibly infectious men in a traffic jam with hundreds of civilians. Some would be bound to be killed in a shootout. Some of the infected would likely get away. If they weren't infected, the damage was minimal. But if they were, it could turn into a much bigger problem.

Hicks simply didn't know enough to make a decision yet. But Omar knew. And Hicks was going to make sure Omar told him everything.

Over the comm, Scott said, "You know we'll come in after you if you need us."

"Everyone in there is either dead, dying, or tied to a radiator. What the hell would you rescue me from?"

Hicks heard Scott call him a son of a bitch as he killed the connection.

HICKS WALKED UP the stairs and went through the front door, closing it behind him. Now that he didn't have the adrenalin coursing through his system, he could hear the wet, gagging coughing of the people upstairs. Women and children, from what Scott had told him, though Hicks had no intention of checking for himself. He didn't need to. He already had all the motivation he needed to throw Omar the beating of his life.

He'd left the door leading down to the basement open and walked downstairs, slowly this time, not worrying about making noise. He took out the Ruger and held it at his side; just in case.

But when he got to the bottom of the stairs, everyone and everything was just as he'd left it. And Omar's left hand was still slip-tied to the radiator pipe. His shoulder wound hadn't bled through the bandage yet. A good sign. It meant he'd probably live long enough to be transported to a University facility for a more elaborate interrogation.

Omar struggled to lift his head when he heard Hicks coming down the stairs. His thin face was even more gaunt than normal and his skin was slick with perspiration. But he still managed a smile when he saw Hicks. "Ah, it is you, American. You came back to finish what you started. I knew you wouldn't just walk away."

Hicks kept the Ruger at his side. "What did you inject those people with upstairs?"

"I injected them with a solution."

"What solution?"

"The solution to all of my people's problems," Omar laughed. "God (God? Not Allah?) will remember those who have brought about His justice."

Hicks knew Omar would waste half the day talking this gibberish if he let him, so he cut it off. "What about the ten men who left here a little while ago? Did you inject them with the same solution?"

Omar coughed a wet cough. "You will find out about them soon enough."

"You're not hurt bad enough to die, and there's still plenty I can do to hurt you." Hicks aimed the Ruger at Omar's right foot. "This is the last time I ask nicely."

"Or what?" Omar spat. "You'll hit me? Beat me? Shoot me? Don't be a fool. This is America, and I have rights. You are a policeman and policemen obey the law."

"What makes you think I'm a cop?"

"Cop, FBI, CIA, NSA, what difference does it make? You have rules about how you can treat me. So get out of here and bring me a lawyer. You don't scare me."

Hicks slammed his foot into Omar's left hand, smashing it against the radiator. Omar screamed as he tried to pull his arm free, but the tie held it in place.

Hicks grabbed him by the collar and pulled him up until he sat with his back to the wall. "I'm not a cop, asshole, and you're not going to jail. You've got no rights because you're never going to see the inside of a courtroom. You're not even going to jail. You're going to spend the rest of your fucking life with men like me who like hurting men like you. You're not going to get lawyer visits or be allowed to pray or any of that bullshit you see on the news. We're going to make sure you live long enough to die slow, but before you do, you're going to tell us everything you know. Because the less you tell us, the longer we keep you alive." Hicks let him go and his head banged against the radiator.

"Dirty Harry tactics," Omar said. "I'll never tell you anything."

"Why not? Djebar did."

Omar's eyes flattened, just as they had before Hicks shot him. "You lie."

"Nope. We broke your friend inside of fifteen minutes and he's a hell of a lot tougher than you. Better trained to hold up against that kind of thing. He told us about the viruses, Samuelson, and all about you and where to find you. So what do you think we're going to do to you unless you start talking."

Omar flinched when Hicks cocked the Ruger and aimed it at Omar's left foot. "You saw what this did to your shoulder. Imagine what it'll do to your foot. For the last time, tell me about the ten men who just left here."

THE FACILITIES TEAM pulled up in a ConEd truck just as Hicks was coming outside. Scott had brought the truck around and helped block off the street. They were less concerned about maintaining cover as they were about giving the Facilities team room to work. Jason would make sure the police and fire department would be warned off the area until the University's people had a chance to examine the building.

Scott got out of the driver's seat while his men opened up the back of the truck and grabbed some air. "So, did he talk?"

Hicks flexed his right hand. "Not at first, but he talked. The ten men in the cars have been injected with the virus."

"Which one?"

"A mix of all three," Hicks explained. "Omar says it eats through the host real fast, but it's easier to spread. He injected all of them with the virus and plans on sending them to meet the arrivals terminals at JFK and LaGuardia."

"What about the shipment of the other drugs you talked about?"

"He said he missed the window to give Samuelson the all clear to deliver it, so he's gone. I'm not worried about him as much as I am about those ten assholes on the BQE."

"My men are on that. What about the people who'd been living upstairs?"

"Omar said they've been sent all over the city, just like you thought. Nothing we can do about that now but alert the hospitals when we can. They've got protocols in place for this kind of thing already." Hicks pulled out his handheld and pulled up the OMNI feed on the five cars. "Those bastards still on the BQE?"

"Traffic has slowed to a crawl," Scott said. "Overturned tractor trailer in Queens, unrelated to our guys. Looks like we caught a break."

"Did Jason get back to you on the status of the drone?"

"At least an hour out. Took some time to get clearance to use it for domestic purposes. Observation is one thing, but arming them for targets on American soil is something else."

Hicks knew all too well about those limits. "Your boys really as good as you say they are?"

"They are," Scott said. "No bullshit. But, with that many civilians around, it won't be clean."

Hicks' handheld began to buzz and he wasn't surprised to see who was calling him. "It's the Dean."

Hicks answered it and the Dean said, "I read the manuscript you uploaded on your debrief with Omar and I've been monitoring the situation on the BQE. What do you want to do?"

"It's not my call to make, sir. It's yours."

"And I'm relying on you to make it. You're on the ground. I'm not. What's it going to be?"

"Then have the cops block all traffic eastbound on the BQE." Hicks looked at Scott. "Set your men loose. Kill all hostiles."

Scott was already on the comm to his men.

FROM INSIDE THE van, Hicks and the others watched the scene on the BQE unfold from ten thousand miles above the earth.

Just before the back door of Team Two's Trailblazer opened, a call went out over every NYPD radio in the area that a preventative Federal action was taking place on the BQE with information to follow.

The five men from Team Two knew they'd be spotted by Omar's men as soon as they hit the ground, so they moved fast.

The ten Somalis were scattered among five cars. The lead car was in the extreme left lane of the BQE, about four cars ahead of the Trailblazer. One Varsity member ran straight toward the lead car while his two partners from the back seat darted toward the rear two cars in the center lane. The passenger and driver of Team Two were designated as backups.

The four Somalis in the rear two cars of the informal convoy were too startled by the first Varsity man running along the left hand lane to notice the two men who snuck up behind their cars and shot them through the rear windshields at the same time.

Hicks could imagine the gunfire as it echoed on the packed stretch of highway as people hit the horns and screamed at the unexpected violence; ducking as best as they could.

Four Somalis dead. Six to go.

Hicks saw the first Varsity man had reached the lead car just as the driver realized what was happening behind him. Traffic wasn't locked in, but the driver jerked the wheel all the way to the left as he tried to get around the car in front of him. He smashed into the car's rear bumper and threw the car in reverse just as the Varsity man fired three times into the car. The vehicle smashed into the grill of the car behind it then idled.

Both occupants dead.

Six down. Four to go.

Hicks watched the three-man Varsity team close in on the two remaining cars from the front and back.

The drivers of both cars began to look for ways to drive away, but there was nowhere to go. At once, all four Somalis broke from their cars just as Hicks had feared they would. They began to run in every direction except where the Varsity men were.

The Varsity man who'd just killed the men in the lead car opened up on the two men nearest him. He dropped the first Somali as he leaped out from behind the wheel. He put down the passenger as he tried to open the driver's door of the car next to him.

Eight infected down. Two more to go.

The passenger of the last car slid over the hood of a neighboring car as the occupants cowered as low as they could get. One of the Varsity men came around a van and took him with a headshot. He slid off the hood and fell to the roadway between two cars.

Nine infected down. One to go.

The last Somali threaded his way through the cars;

bobbing and weaving; keeping his head low as he moved. Hicks watched the third Varsity member fire, but the shot hit a Volkswagen's side view mirror.

The man dropped to all fours and darted left between a minivan and a school bus. He saw a clear lane ahead of him and flat out ran as fast as he could. He'd almost reached the back of the bus when the Varsity man recovered and fired twice more. Both shots caught him in the back; sending him into the grill of a Mack truck before he fell dead on the roadway.

Ten Somalis down. All five Varsity members alive.

The official word came over the comm a second later. "Team One Leader, this is Team Two. All hostiles dead. The threat has been neutralized. No civilian casualties. Over."

Hicks didn't have to look at Scott to know he was all smiles. "And that, Mr. Hicks, is how we do that."

But Hicks didn't have time for high fives. "Have your men tell everyone to stay in their vehicles and make sure your men stay back from the dead. The Somalis still might be contagious."

Hicks' handheld buzzed. Jason was calling. "Fine job, Hicks. Damned effective."

Hicks didn't have time for compliments from that weasel either. "They're Scott's men, not mine. He deserves the praise. In the meantime, we've still got ten individual biohazards on our hands. Have the cops block off the BQE from the previous exit and start filtering traffic that way. Then have them clear out the traffic ahead so we can start getting cars out of there. Just make sure the cops know Scott's men are the good guys and to not question them about who they are and what they're doing there."

"Duly noted."

"And tell them to bring HAZMAT units with them when they do. God only knows what kind of shit Omar pumped into their system before he sent them to the airports."

He could hear Jason's fingers flying across the keyboard. "Didn't he tell you that when you questioned him?"

"He told me he injected his followers with bits from both samples Djebar gave him from Samuelson. Omar's no scientist and I've seen what it's done to the people he's injected, so whatever it is, it's lethal."

He heard Jason continue to type. "Did Omar or Djebar tell you where the scientists are or if they're in the country?"

"No," he lied.

Scott and his men were too busy celebrating their win to notice Hicks had left. And when they did notice, they didn't especially care.

CHAPTER 27

ICKS KNEW LYING to Jason about Samuelson's whereabouts should've bothered him, but it didn't. Besides, Jason was probably monitoring his activity on OMNI anyway. He'd figure out where he was going and what he was doing in time.

If they'd known he was going after the scientist, Hicks knew they would've insisted on sending Scott's men or another Varsity team with him. But Hicks didn't want that. He wanted to find Samuelson on his own and in his own way. It was up to him to bring down the son of a bitch who'd given Omar the weapon he needed to put his personal jihad into effect. The man whose actions had turned a good man like Colin into a threat all because his viruses gave Omar the most powerful weapon in the world—hope.

Before Omar had passed out from the pain, Hicks got

him to talk about Samuelson, or at least as much as he knew. About how he'd killed his fellow scientists from the lab and taken the viruses to sell on his own on the black market.

This had happened in his shop. And Hicks knew it was up to him to clean up the mess.

The antivirals Scott had given him started doing a number on his stomach halfway through the Lincoln Tunnel. He didn't have time to stop. He drank bottled water and kept going. His dashboard screen showed Jason had called several times since he'd left the crime scene at Omar's place.

He knew Jason could see he was driving to New Jersey. He'd seen his OMNI activity and knew who he'd searched for. He was supposed to be a smart boy. Let him fill in the blanks for himself. That's what Hicks had done, which is why he was driving to Philly.

Doctor John Samuelson had been an American biologist working in Saudi Arabia. He'd first been sent to the region by UNESCO as a biologist specializing in the study and treatment of infectious diseases. The Saudi government offered him far more than he was making to come work for them and he took the job. Everything was above board.

Hicks saw nothing in Samuelson's background to explain why he'd decided to conspire with his fellow scientists to steal the viruses and sell them on the black market. He didn't have any known religious or political affiliations. He'd never even registered to vote. He didn't have a family or any outstanding debts or expensive habits that made him need the money.

By all accounts, Dr. John Samuelson was a bland man of fifty with bad teeth and thinning hair. There was no reason in the world why anyone would think he would've broken the law until one day, he did. He'd crossed the line and tried to turn the world upside down. But he had. He was that bolt from the blue that institutions like the University feared. The one-off you couldn't predict. The man who shot up a playground one day just because he goddamned well felt like it.

Only Samuelson didn't use a gun. He used a test tube and a petri dish instead, and handed them over to some very nasty people.

Hicks intended on asking him why.

Omar had told Hicks Djebar had arranged for him to meet Samuelson in the food court in Penn Station, where Samuelson gave him an envelope with several samples of the virus. He went back home, injected the willing followers he'd recruited from all over the city to be part of his glorious jihad and watched them get sicker. He put the envelope with the samples in the locker at the storage facility and let nature take its course.

When Colin and the others didn't return from the park, Omar ran and began making phone calls to the financiers, courtesy of Djebar's little black book.

Hicks had Samuelson's name and file, but pictures on his company ID card were old. His passport and driver's licenses even older and finding him that way would've been near impossible. Even OMNI's ability to age modify a photo couldn't produce guaranteed results like a recent photo.

But when Omar said they'd met at the food court, Hicks put OMNI to work. It found Omar on Penn Station's security cameras, saw him talking to Omar and tracked Samuelson from there.

OMNI searched images stored from traffic cameras, NYPD security cameras and other services to track him back up to the Port Authority Bus Terminal on Forty-second Street and Eighth Avenue. Port Authority cameras showed him buying a bus ticket. By accessing the bus line's computers and matching transactions to the security footage, Hicks saw Sellers had paid cash for a bus ticket to Philadelphia and boarded the bus an hour later.

OMNI scanned the security footage from the time his bus had arrived at the Philadelphia Bus Terminal on Filbert Street. And there was Samuelson, last off the bus. Just another poor bastard down on his luck, trudging with his bag containing dozens of samples of deadly diseases into a cold Philly night.

Why Philadelphia? Hicks didn't know. But he was going to find out.

Security cameras tracked him through the terminal and out to the street and all the way to a Hilton Garden Inn a block or so away from the bus station. That had been three nights ago. He'd paid in advance for five nights and, in searching hotel records, OMNI said he was still there.

And that's why Hicks was driving to Philadelphia. He left the high fives and the celebration to Scott and his men. Their mission was over. They'd earned it.

He hadn't earned shit. Yet.

*****

It was after ten by the time Hicks pulled into the hotel's parking lot. He parked in the handicapped space next to the fire door stairs that were closest to Samuelson's room. It would make it easier to get out of there when the time came.

He knew he'd be on camera the entire time he was on the property, but that didn't bother him. Footage could always be deleted later.

He walked through the lobby as though he was a guest. He even waived at the night clerk on duty, though the man was too enraptured by the glow from his iPad to have noticed. Hicks noticed he wasn't texting, so he decided he must be watching porn.

Hicks knew the elevators were locked down after eight o'clock and could only be operated by a magnetic room key. He pulled out what appeared to be a standard hotel room key card and inserted it into the slot to call down the elevator. The card was an electronic version of a ghost key. He'd preloaded it with the hotel manager's codes so he could open any door in the building.

He took the elevator up to the fifth floor and walked down the hall to room 505. Samuelson's room. He paused outside the door and listened. He heard the TV was on, so he figured Samuelson must be inside. He had no idea if he'd thrown the security latch or not and the OMNI satellite wasn't in range to scan the room. He'd have to try his key and take his chances.

Hicks pulled his Ruger and slid the card key into the lock. He pushed in the door and it opened all the way. Samuelson hadn't used the safety latch at all.

From the doorway, Hicks could see the bed was unmade and empty. So was the chair on the other side of the room. The bathroom door was open, but the light was off.

The latch hadn't been thrown because Samuelson wasn't there.

Hicks went in and shut the door behind him. He began

searching the room for the messenger bag he'd seen Samuelson holding in his trek from New York to Philadelphia. It wasn't on the table or under the bed or in the closet.

But Hicks did find a mini-safe in the closet. And it was locked.

Luckily, it was a newer safe that allowed housekeeping supervisors to swipe their keys and open the safe in case a guest checked out and forgot to empty it. Hicks used his key card to open it. Samuelson's messenger bag was stuffed inside.

Hicks tucked his Ruger back in the holster and slowly eased the bag out of the safe. It was heavier than he thought it would be and moving it slowly only made it seem heavier.

Hicks laid the bag on the bed and undid the leather straps. He found a metal case roughly the size of a cigar humidor and slid it out of the bag. He opened the metal catches and slowly opened it. Inside were fifty plastic vials exactly like the one Omar had been holding in the basement when Hicks shot him. None of them was labeled except for a single red, green, or blue dot.

Hicks figured these must be the samples Samuelson was supposed to deliver to Omar. But he'd never gotten the chance. But he'd already been in Philadelphia before he was supposed to deliver the rest of the samples to Omar.

Something didn't make sense. Either Omar was lying or...

Hicks heard the gentle ping of the elevator sounding that it was stopping on the fifth floor. He shut the case and gently slid it and the bag under the bed. He didn't expect Samuelson to be armed, but he didn't know if he'd be alone. He didn't want a stray round hitting the toxin if all hell broke loose.

He backed up into the dark bathroom and aimed his Ruger at the door.

He watched the door open and Samuelson and another man walked into the room. A tall, dark skinned man. Painfully thin and bald with a wiry beard.

Hicks waited for Samuelson to close the door before he spoke from the darkness. "Don't fucking move. Either of you."

Both men put up their hands without being told to do it. Samuelson grew even paler than he already was, but the dark skinned man looked calm and cool. "I don't know what you're doing here," he said, a hint of a French accent, "but you have made a terrible error. And it will cost you your life."

"I've heard that before." Hicks stepped out of the bathroom. To Samuelson, he said, "Throw the latch on that door nice and slow. Don't do anything stupid."

Samuelson did as he was told. "We don't want trouble, mister. If it's money you want, I've got money right here in my jacket. It's yours if you just get out of here and leave us alone."

"I didn't come here for money, John Boy," Hicks said. "I came here for you." He looked at the tall man. "Who's your friend? One of Omar's buddies?"

The tall man's eyes narrowed. "You know of Omar. You are the man he fears."

"I don't know about that," Hicks said. "I'm a pretty nice guy once you get to know me. And he and I are going to get to know each other a lot better real soon. As a matter of fact, why don't you join us?" From his pocket, he took some of the plastic pull ties Scott had given him before the raid and tossed them on the bed. "I insist. Put those on. Pull them tight with your teeth."

Samuelson looked up at the tall man, then back at Hicks. "Look, you seem to know who I am and what I do, okay? We can make a deal, here, man. I'm not exactly dealing pot here, so I know we can talk our way through this."

"You're going to be doing a lot of talking." Hicks smiled at the tall man and decided to take a gamble. "Just like Omar. And Djebar."

The dark man didn't say anything, but his eyes said plenty. He knew exactly who Djebar was.

And suddenly, a lot of loose ends began to fall into place.

Hicks spoke to the tall man in French. "Who are you working for?"

The dark skinned man finally smiled. "I work for Allah. His will protects me."

"We'll see about that." Hicks shifted the Ruger from Samuelson to him. In English, he said, "Put the ties on. Now."

The man took one of the ties and handed one to Samuelson. "Let us do as he says, doctor. My men will free us when we get outside."

Samuelson watched how the tall man put the ties on his own wrists and did the same. "He's not kidding, man. He's got five mean looking bastards downstairs."

Hicks didn't let it rattle him. "Oh, I'm sure. Former Republican Guard types, too. I've been killing his brand of tough guy all week. Forgive me if I'm not impressed."

"They were necessary means to ends," the tall man said. "And as you will soon find out, I am not Omar and my men are not cab drivers."

"Neither am I. Now pull those nice and tight and put your hands against the wall."

Both men did as they were told and Hicks made them step back three steps from the wall so they couldn't swing at him while he frisked them.

Samuelson pled his case while Hicks patted them down. "This is bigger than you think it is, man. You don't need this kind of trouble. You CIA boys cut deals all the time, right? We can cut one here, believe me. You could walk away a wealthy man."

Samuelson's pockets came up clean except for a wallet, a hundred in cash and two condoms. Hicks tossed them all on the bed. "I'm already wealthy, asshole, and I'm not CIA."

As Hicks began patting down the tall man, the man said, "Don't waste your time trying to bargain with him, doctor. He is a zealot. A true believer. A patriot who believes in truth, justice, and the American way, even though his idea of the American way is far different than what you and I know it to be. He'll be dead in a few moments anyway, so save your breath."

Hicks finished patting down the man's leg and brought his fist up into the man's balls. The man's knees buckled and he fell forward into the wall. Hicks grabbed the tie that bound his hands and pulled it back until his hands were behind his neck and his head was flush against the wall. The man screamed.

"That's the second time you've threatened my life in the last five minutes, asshole. I don't like that. Maybe you've got guys outside and maybe you don't. Anyone shoots at me, you get it in the back. Because *that's* the American way."

Hicks let the tall man fall to the floor. He went back to put the metal case back in the bag and pulled it over his shoulder. Then he pulled out his handheld and had OMNI scan the area for security cameras. Anything that could tell him what might be waiting for him outside.

From the floor, the man said, "Are you calling the police? They'll never get here in time and my men will kill them when they do. Unlike you, we do not believe in leaving witnesses behind. Like you did with Djebar's men."

Hicks looked up from the handheld. The man said, "That's right. Those two guards you left alive were dead fifteen minutes after Djebar failed to check in with us. You have no idea how far we can reach, but soon you will. And by then, it will already be too late."

Hicks went back to the handheld. He couldn't let himself get sidetracked by talk of what may have happened. He had to focus on what was happening now and that meant getting a look at what was waiting outside.

OMNI searched for a wireless camera feed from a security camera across the street. Hicks selected a security camera from the building across the street. It was focused on the lot in front of its own building, but Hicks was able to readjust the focus to center on the hotel lot. He saw his Buick right where he'd parked it.

And a red minivan just inside the entrance to the lot. A minivan that hadn't been there before and didn't look like it was staying there long. The resolution on the cam feed was shit, but he could see thin trails of smoke coming from the exhaust. The windows were tinted, and he couldn't see how many people were inside. But the headlights were on and someone was keeping the motor running.

Hicks put the handheld away and adjusted the messenger bag's shoulder strap over his shoulder. "Time to go boys and girls." He pulled Samuelson off the wall and told the tall man to get up.

He rolled over onto his knees and stood. "If you are a religious man, you should make your peace with your God now because you will not have time when we get downstairs."

Hicks shoved him toward the door. In Arabic Hicks said, "To Him we belong and to Him we shall return."

"Fuck you."

"Nice language." Hicks smiled as he opened the door. "How American of you."

CHAPTER
28

HICKS PRODDED THE tall man and Samuelson down the hallway faster than they would've liked to go. He kept them side by side, making sure they provided him with cover if anyone got off the elevator.

Halfway down the hall, the elevator began to move downstairs.

The tall man said over his shoulder, "Your time is running short. My friends are coming to check on me."

Maybe they were, and maybe they weren't. Hicks didn't care. He planned on taking them down the fire stairs anyway.

He dug another tie out of his pocket. "Stop moving." They did as he told them to do and he slipped a tie through both their belts and pulled it tight. He didn't want them splitting up in case any shooting started. "Now you two assholes are literally tied at the hip. Move to your right and head down the stairs."

"You can't expect us to go down stairs tied like this," Samuelson said; struggling to get away from the tall man. "What happens if one of us trips and falls?"

"Then you get up," Hicks said, "Because if you can't, I put a bullet in both of your bellies because you're no good to me anymore." He shoved the tall man by the back of the head. "Keep that in mind before you pull any shit. You'll get your virgins, but you'll be screaming a long time before you get there."

The man said nothing. He simply opened the door to the stairway and walked in tandem with Samuelson down the stairs; one step at a time.

As the stairwell door closed, he heard the whir of the elevator starting up on the other side of the stairwell. Hicks saw the smirk on the tall man's face and prodded him forward with the barrel of the Ruger. "Keep moving."

They made decent time going down the stairs; the sound of the elevator coming back up stayed with them the entire time. The sound stopped just as they made it to the bottom of the stairwell. One door led out to the lobby. The other back to Hicks' car just to the left of the doorway. The door said an alarm would sound if it was opened, but he pushed the two men through it. No alarm sounded.

Samuelson and the tall man regained their footing in the parking lot and Hicks grabbed hold of Samuelson's belt before they strayed too far. His Buick was right next to the door, but the red minivan was still parked to the left about fifty feet away.

The engine was still running and now two men were standing by the sliding door. They were just as dark as the tall man, but shorter and broader. And they'd already spotted their friend standing next to Samuelson, but not Hicks. He was crouched behind them.

The two men called out to the tall man in Arabic. He responded and they began walking toward him; reaching under their coats as they moved.

Hicks came out from behind them and shot the gunman on the left; center mass through the chest. The impact knocked him off his feet and sent the gun he'd just pulled flying. The second man broke to dive behind a car, but Hicks shot him through the back before he made it. The man landed on his belly, yelling in Arabic.

Samuelson and the tall man tried to move, but Hicks grabbed Samuelson by the belt and pulled them back from the Buick and away from the fire door, knowing he still had the men upstairs and the driver of the minivan to worry about.

But the driver never tried to get out of the van. Instead, he threw the minivan in reverse out of the parking lot.

Hicks pulled his hostages to the side and squeezed off two shots at the minivan. Both rounds punched through the windshield just above the steering wheel. The van rolled out into the street, popping the curb and backing into a stop sign, where it jerked to a halt. Hicks heard the blare of a car horn just before another car heading east slammed into the side of the van.

He knew whoever had gone up to Samuelson's room would be on their way down in a hurry now that they'd heard the shots. He'd never be able to load these two into the Buick in time to get away before they came down. Best to end this now while he could do it at a place of his choosing. And while he had the two men as cover.

The tall man began yelling in Arabic and Hicks banged him in the back of the head with the butt of his Ruger. Not hard enough to knock him out, but enough to daze him while he reloaded.

Hicks knew he still had two rounds left in the Ruger and a nine millimeter tucked into his belt, but he wanted the stopping power of the Ruger. He broke the cylinder, dumped the spent shells, and used his speed loader to reload. In less than three seconds, Hicks was back in operation.

Hicks pulled them back even further as he heard yelling coming from the stairway. It could've been scared hotel residents running from the hotel, but Hicks doubted it. People tended to hunker down when they heard gunfire. They didn't run outside unless they had to.

The two men who came through the fire door into the parking lot were no hotel guests. Both were as dark skinned as the three men he'd just shot, but leaner, more athletic. They looked at the wrecked minivan first as the tall man called out to them once more.

Hicks came out from behind the tall man and drilled the first gunman through the chest. Center mass again with the same result as before. One more dead bad guy.

The second man got off a shot in Hicks' direction as he darted back inside behind the fire door. The shot went wide and shattered the rear windshield of a car parked two spaces away. But the car alarm went off, making it harder to hear what was happening.

Hicks' instincts kicked in, and he followed his training. He focused less on what he heard and more on what he could see. Everything slowed down for him as it always had in situations like this. Close to the finish line. One bad guy left. Don't fuck it up by getting careless. Work what's in front of you and shoot.

Samuelson and the tall man tried to break right, but Hicks grabbed a handful of the tall man's shirt and kept him in place. He aimed at the glass of the fire door as the men struggled. He held them with his left while his right hand adjusted for their movements. The Ruger was steady as Hicks waited for the shot.

He saw the gunman take a quick look out the door's thick fireproof glass. The glass was too thick to shoot through. Hicks knew the door was fireproof, but it wasn't bulletproof.

Hicks fired twice into the door and saw the man buckle and fall back from view.

The tall man tried to turn on him; trying to push Samuelson into Hicks to knock him down. But it's tough to toss a man around a man who's tethered to you as closely as Samuelson was.

Hicks sidestepped the move and brained the tall man in the temple again, this time knocking him out. He grabbed him before he fell and told Samuelson, "You'd better pull him, too, or I'll leave you both here like the others."

Hicks slammed the trunk and pushed both men inside; still tethered to each other. Samuelson was crying when Hicks slammed the door. It was of the best reasons why Hicks drove a Buick. Plenty of trunk space.

Hicks could hear the din of police sirens over the blare of the car alarm as he climbed in behind the wheel and started the engine. He could hear Samuelson kicking the trunk lid as he pulled out of the lot and into South Philly traffic.

Just another car on a busy night in a big city.

Except for the two terrorists he had in the trunk.

CHAPTER 29

ONE WEEK LATER

THE CHEAP PLASTIC chair groaned and popped beneath Hicks' weight as he stretched his legs. He wasn't surprised to see a rat scurrying along the base of the wall only a few inches from his shoe. The rat looked well fed and didn't pay Hicks any mind.

He had no idea why Jason had insisted on meeting in a dump like this; an old pizza joint in Alphabet City that had gone out of business more than a year ago. The place looked as dirty and tired as the day they'd closed up shop. Not even the junkies and other undesirables who made up the social fauna of the Lower East Side had bothered to break into the place since it closed. If only Jason had been as wise.

In fact, Hicks didn't know why Jason had insisted on calling a meeting at all. Hicks hated University meetings.

He hated the waiting. He hated not knowing how a meeting would turn out. And he didn't like walking into a room full of people who'd had the same training he'd had. They might not have his level of skill, but they usually knew who and what he was. Hicks had spent a good portion of his life being ambiguous. Certainty, especially when it came to himself, made him anxious.

An emailed response to a report was easier than attending a meeting. Far more antiseptic. Even the harshest email was better than biting his tongue while some son of a bitch yelled at him from across a table. And Hicks hadn't been yelled at in a long time.

He looked over at Roger, who was perched on an old bar stool against the wall. Hicks thought about starting up a conversation to pass the time, but Roger was busy tapping away at his phone; smiling and biting his lip at whatever image someone just sent him. Hicks had neither the urge nor the stomach to ask what he was looking at.

That's why he was surprised when he said, "I don't know why you're so worried. You're a fucking hero, after all."

"Who said I'm worried?"

Roger finally looked up from his handheld. "Maybe worried is too strong a word. Perhaps tense is more accurate or pensive, even. Either way, there's no reason to be worried or tense. Not with all the information you've given them. They're probably going to give you some kind of medal."

Hicks watched a rat descend on a cockroach struggling across the floor. "If they were giving me a medal, we wouldn't be meeting in a shithole like this."

Roger watched the rat begin to eat its catch. "I don't know.

I think the place has a certain charm to it."

"You would."

"Maybe they're not going to give you a medal, then," Roger offered. "Instead, maybe it's a special meeting with the man himself. Our elusive Dean. Ever think of that? Ever wonder what he looked like?"

"No." And Hicks never had. The man's appearance didn't mean a damned thing to him because he'd seen what the man could do. He could coordinate an embassy evacuation or a drone strike or make a multi-million dollar transfer with a few keystrokes. In his experience, men like that were best kept at a distance.

Jason came out of the kitchen and quietly beckoned them to follow him. He was wearing a charcoal gray suit and a dark red tie; looking very much the banker. That worried Hicks. Jason was a J. Crew boy at best and never one for formality. If he was wearing a suit, whoever they were meeting with was important enough to warrant the sartorial effort.

Four plastic chairs had been arranged around a high stainless steel preparation table in the middle of the pizzeria's kitchen. Three of chairs were empty.

One of them was not.

The man sitting in the chair had his back to the door and didn't turn around when they walked in. He was a black man, maybe sixty years old; neither thin nor heavy. His hair was still mostly black, but silver highlights had begun to creep in at the sides and back.

Jason motioned to Roger and Hicks to take the two chairs on the other side of the table, which they did. As Hicks sat down, he saw the stranger's face wasn't as full as it should've been and his brown eyes looked tired, like the color had been washed out of them long ago. His shirt collar looked like it used to fit him well, but he'd since lost enough weight to make it look just a little big on him. His hands were folded on the table, but Hicks still noticed the slightest tremor in his left hand.

Hicks had never seen the man before, but he knew exactly who he was.

And that's why Hicks knew this conversation wouldn't end well.

As soon as Jason sat down, the stranger began, "You know who I am, don't you?"

"I thought I did when I walked in," Hicks said, "but now that I've heard your voice, I'm sure."

The Dean neither smiled nor nodded nor unfolded his hands in order to make himself accessible in any way. "Let me guess. I sounded taller on the phone, right?"

Hicks knew what he was implying, but didn't take the bait. "I never cared what you looked like, sir. And I still don't."

"No, I suppose you wouldn't." He looked at Roger. "What about you?"

"Makes no difference to me," Roger said, "though I always think men in your position should look like Donald Sutherland for some reason. Perhaps it's the stoic vulnerability, especially around the eyes."

The Dean looked at Jason. "You were right about him."

Roger laughed. "No one's ever been right about me, sir. Not now. Not ever."

Hicks knew the banter was meant to break the ice. But all it did was make him feel more anxious.

The Dean looked back at Hicks. "I know how much you hate these face-to-face meetings. You think they're a big waste of time and energy. Besides, a voice on the phone or an email in an inbox is easier to deal with than flesh and blood. Anonymity in an anonymous world."

Hicks hated that he knew what he was thinking. He hated being easy to read most of all. "It is, sir."

The Dean's gray eyes narrowed just a bit. "How long have you been working for us?"

"Going on fifteen years, sir. I believe you hired me."

"Thirteen years and four months to the day, to be precise," the Dean said. "One of the smartest hires I've ever made. But in all that time we've never met, not even once. You never asked for a meeting, and I never offered one. Why do you think we're meeting now?"

"Because something has changed."

"Correct. Now what do you think that something is?"

"The intelligence we got from Omar and Djebar and Samuelson and the Moroccan is probably starting to generate some results."

Since interrogation had begun on the tall man Hicks had grabbed with Samuelson, the man had refused to give his name. The University hadn't been able to get a fix on his identity because his finger prints had been burned off. Facial recognition programs came up empty, too, so the interrogation teams had taken to calling him The Moroccan. He'd let that much slip during interrogation.

"Everyone you've brought in has started to talk in their own way," the Dean said, "but you've nabbed important targets many times since you started working with us. Albeit, never like this, but I never asked for a meeting then. Why do you think I wanted to meet now?"

"Because, like I said, something has changed."

"You already said that, son. I want you to tell me what else has changed."

Hicks looked at the Dean's skin. The size of his collar. His eyes. The sense he got from him. "You're dying."

Jason slapped the table. "Goddamn you, Hicks. You'll have some respect for..."

But the Dean held up his left hand. It didn't tremble much, but enough for Hicks to notice it better this time. For the first time, he smiled. "You're very perceptive, James. Always have been." He folded his hands on the table again. "You're right. I am dying."

Jason sat back in his chair. "You're what?"

"Cancer in my brain and damned near everywhere else it can go. I've fought it for a long time and now, but now I've nothing left to fight it with. It's only a matter of time."

"It's always a matter of time, sir," Hicks said. "Some just have a more finite deadline than others."

He could feel Jason glaring at him, but the Dean was all Hicks cared about. "That's very true and it happens to be the reason why we're having this meeting today. The University will go on well after I'm dead. It's been around since before I was born, and it'll carry on after me. This institution is much more than just one man and arguably, it's never been more needed than it is right now."

"This has to do with what we've pulled from Omar and the Moroccan," Hicks said.

The Dean motioned to Jason who took it from there.

"The Moroccan's name is Mehdi Bajjah. He's a thirty-five year old Moroccan whose family moved to England when he was an infant. He was educated at Eton and later Trinity College before coming to the United States as a software engineer. Like Samuelson, he'd never been particularly religious and he didn't have any pronounced political beliefs. Married a nice Irish girl living in London at the time and had three children with her. He had the life any man in his right mind would envy until, one day six years ago, he simply disappeared."

"What do you mean disappeared?" Roger asked.

"Dropped completely off the grid," Jason said. "Walked away from his wife, his family, friends. Just went to work one morning and never came back. No note, no contact of any kind with his family. The poor woman wound up on public assistance when the money ran out. She had to move back with her family in Ireland. They had him declared legally dead a year ago."

"No trace of Bajjah at all?" Hicks asked. "Not even once in all those years?"

"No credit cards, no bank accounts, nothing. He simply vanished until you saw him walk into that hotel room last week with Samuelson. We have no idea where he's been or who he's been with for the past six years."

"How much have you been getting out of Samuelson?" Hicks asked.

"Oh, he gave up everything before we even touched him," Jason said, "but I'm afraid he's a dead end."

"How the hell is Samuelson a dead end?" Hicks asked. "He's the link to Djebar, to Omar, to this Bajjah asshole."

"No he's not," the Dean said. "Because Samuelson didn't

steal the viruses to sell them on the black market. He stole them because that was his job. And he was working for…"

"Djebar." Hicks dropped his head in his hands. He rubbed his fingers along his scalp and squeezed his head until his knuckles popped. It was all so simple, so clear, he should've seen it the whole time. "Djebar wasn't working for Omar. Omar was working for Djebar."

"Not exactly," the Dean said. "They're all working for someone else. Djebar was their front man, but Bajjah and Omar are merely cogs in a greater machinery we're only beginning to understand. We'll find out more in time, but it'll be slow going. Samuelson doesn't know many details and Omar is close to cracking completely. Djebar and Bajjah were the better trained of the bunch and are much harder to break, though we're making progress."

"Bajjah's the toughest of the bunch," Jason added.

Roger smiled. "Give him to me for the weekend, honey, and we'll see how tough he is."

"We want him functional," Jason said. "The British say you damned near turned Djebar into a catatonic. He's only just beginning to regain his senses."

Roger shrugged. "I got what I wanted, didn't I?"

Hicks' head was spinning. He'd been wrong about everything from the beginning and only saw it now. He'd had everything upside down. About Omar and Djebar and everything. He wanted to be anywhere but there. He would've gotten up and left if he didn't think he'd pass out before he reached the door. He wouldn't give Jason the satisfaction of seeing him faint. He'd already embarrassed himself enough.

The Dean said, "Stop kicking yourself in the ass, Hicks.

We wouldn't have known any of this was going on if it hadn't been for you and Colin. Christ knows how far those diseases could've spread if we hadn't gotten a lid on it as fast as we did. You saved a lot of lives."

Hicks knew it was supposed to make him feel better, but it didn't. He hadn't saved Colin's. "We got lucky."

"We got lucky because we're good," the Dean said. "You were good and you stopped the immediate threat. And your instincts led us to a wider operation no one knew existed and I mean no one. CIA, NSA, FBI, or anyone overseas. They're all banging at our door now and we're sitting on it because it's ours." The Dean slowly sat back from the table. "Unfortunately, no good deed goes unpunished."

Hicks knew all of this was too good to be true. "What does that mean?"

"You've stopped the immediate threat here in New York and whatever Bajjah was planning to do. We think he was looking to start an outbreak in D.C. when Omar's New York operation fell apart, but that's just speculation at this point. What's clear is that all of these bastards are part of a much larger network we didn't know existed. And I'm going to need you to go after them."

"In New York?" Hicks asked.

"Anywhere they are in the world," the Dean said. "And we can't waste much time. Now that they know someone's on to them, we'll have a harder time finding them. They've enjoyed obscurity for a long time."

"The stunt they pulled here was flawed," Jason added, "but not by much. Samuelson and his team had been able to hone the viruses to breed quickly, but they didn't count for them incapacitating the host before they could spread the disease. We know they're bound to try again and soon. That's why we need to act quickly."

Hicks didn't doubt they'd be anxious to try again. The only thing he doubted was the role he could play in stopping it. "What do you want me to do, sir?"

"I'm dying, James," the Dean said. "But determining what we're up against here is a bigger job than anything the University has undertaken before. You've been on it literally from the beginning and I need you to make sure we get off on the right foot. I need someone who will resist whatever winds of change that might come after I'm gone and make sure we don't lose sight of finding out everything we can about whoever is responsible for this. Your contempt for bureaucracy is well documented and I have a feeling it'll come in handy before all is said and done."

Hicks read between the lines. "You're not just talking about internal bureaucracy, are you, sir?"

"External forces will be even more severe than those coming from whoever replaces me," the Dean said. "Our sister agencies are annoyed we're not being as forthcoming with the information they're requesting. They've sensed there's something to this threat and our involvement in stopping it, but we've been able to keep them in the dark so far. They've never really valued our efforts to this point and I never saw any reason to prove them wrong. But now that we've got something they want, I'm afraid we may have to endure more scrutiny from them."

"And the fact that I'm blackmail proof makes me less susceptible to influence from outside forces."

"No one's blackmail-proof," Jason said. "Everyone's got a weakness."

"Everyone but Hicks," the Dean said. "He's one of the few who don't. He doesn't have a wife, or kids, or any relatives close to him worth mentioning. Certainly no one whose safety our colleagues could use to threaten him. All he has is the job and that's why I want him for this role."

"Understood, sir. I've kept other agencies at bay before and I can do it again. But what about my work here in the New York Office? I've got dozens of operations going on and I can't just drop them. I've got people in the field, assets to work..."

"You can work wherever you'd like," the Dean said, "but Jason here will be managing the New York Office while you're on this assignment. Now, I know you two won't be exchanging Christmas cards any time soon, but even you must admit he's the only member of the University system who knows what's happening with this office other than you."

Hicks hated to admit it, but the Dean was right. "I'll work to make sure it's a seamless transition, sir. What resources will I have in my new assignment?"

"Anything you require," the Dean said, "at least for as long as I am in office. I'll do my best to hang on for as long as I can until you have everything up and running, but as you know, that's not entirely in my control. But you're an industrious man. I'm sure you'll be up and running in no time."

"What are my parameters?"

"You're to find these people, learn everything you can from them and kill them. All of them, before they kill us. And I'm asking Roger here to serve as your Inquisitor in this effort, a role I know he'll appreciate."

Hicks saw Roger looked less than pleased. "I don't want to leave New York." He motioned to Jason. "And I sure as hell don't want to work with him."

"You may not have to, but you will if that's what's required," Jason said. "You've been allowed to operate your club with a fair amount of autonomy for a long time now. That will change if you don't cooperate. Oh, and the current level of funding you provide the New York Office will continue, of course."

"Oh, of course," Roger parroted, then blew him a kiss.

To Hicks, Jason said, "We won't need you to move out of your Thirty-fourth Street facility at the moment, but we'll broach that subject at a later date."

"I'm not going anywhere and it's not on Thirty-fourth Street," Hicks said. He saw his chance to tweak Jason's nose a bit. "Do I start right away or do I need to undergo any kind of evaluation process? Psych reviews, things like that?"

Jason fumbled with his notes as the Dean answered for him. "You were fit enough to uncover this plot single-handedly and pull down everyone involved. I think you're fit enough for this."

Hicks knew he should've been happy or at least proud, but he wasn't. He'd just been given his own command but it felt hollow somehow. "I just wish Colin was here to help me see it through, sir."

"We all do, James," the Dean said. "And for his sake, and for the sake of the people we protect, I know you're the best person for this assignment. I'll alert all the University Office Heads throughout the system that you have authority to call on them whenever you need it." The Dean tried a smile. "I'd wish you luck, but you make your own, so I'll save my breath. Just know you have my complete support and I look forward to seeing results."

"And soon," Jason added. "Very soon."

Neither of them offered to shake hands, so neither did Hicks. He and Roger simply stood up and walked out of the kitchen.

Jason always had been a last word freak.

ROGER TOOK A cab back to his club and offered to open a bottle of champagne to celebrate. He even offered to put the men in leather hoods in another room. But Hicks declined. He wanted to walk for a bit, anyway.

He'd heard everything the Dean had told him. He knew the support he'd thrown behind him. In all his years in the University, he'd never seen him do that for anyone.

He should've been happy or at least excited about all of this, but he wasn't. He didn't feel a thing and knew he never would. He rarely felt anything, which was what had made him ideal for the kind of work he did. The work was all he had. He'd never wanted anything else.

He pulled out his handheld and called someone he figured would understand. She picked up just before the phone went to voicemail.

"Why are you calling?" she asked. "What's wrong?"

"Who said anything's wrong? I know we didn't set the world on fire the other night, but I still wanted to call and thank you. This was the first chance I had to do it."

"A gentleman," she said. He heard the smile in her voice. "How chivalrous of you. How are you doing?"

"Busy week," he said. "Lot happened, but it turned out okay in the end, I guess. I was wondering if you were still in New York. Maybe we could meet for a drink, seeing as how well our last drink turned out."

"Now you're just being silly," she said. "You know I'm still in town. You know everything, remember?"

"No, I didn't know, but I'm glad you are. And you're wrong about me knowing everything. I don't know if you're going to say yes."

"I think you did. How does the Bull and Bear sound? Five o'clock?"

"Let's say the King Cole Bar at the St. Regis," Hicks said. "You know I don't like going to the same bar twice in a row."

"Of course. Proprieties must be observed. See you there at five."

She hung up the phone and Hicks put the handheld back in his pocket. Enough work for one day.

A light snow began to fall and some of it had already begun to stick on the cars and sidewalk. Another storm was rolling in.

He used to like the snow, but didn't anymore.

THE END

ACKNOWLEDGEMENTS

Thanks to Maura Lynch, Tessa Ruiz, Andrew Solomon, Debora Oliveira, Melissa Gardella and Tiffany Leigh for providing invaluable insight on this book in its earliest stages.

Thanks to my resident gun experts Blackie Noir and Derek Viljoen for their advice on the various weapons that appear in this book, especially Blackie who first told me about the Ruger .454 Alaskan. They had me at 'it can core a charging bear'.

Thanks to Lorin and Micheal Mask, Alyson Giller, Melissa Lomax, Eric Frank, Kathy English, Col. A.J. Copp USMC (ret), Col. Christine Voss Copp USAF, C.J. Carpenter, Brian Madden, William Donohue, Wesley Gibson, Liz Thaler, Steve Agovino, Dana Kabel, Charles Salzberg, Will D., Phyllis Sambuco, Mike Consani, Dana King, Mike Reyes, Mae Patel, Richie Narvaez, Anamaria Alfieri, Mark Mannix, Donna Evans, Tanis Mallow and Rob Brunet for their constant encouragement and belief in my work.

Thanks to Mike, Pat, Juan, the two Sams, Cliff, Jeff, the two Adams, Mark and all the gang at the Nat Sherman Townhouse in New York City for all the great times and all the great cigars.

Thanks to Todd Robinson, Matt Hilton, Ron Fortier, Rob Davis, Paul Bishop, Jack Getze and Les Edgerton who believed in me when a lot of people told me to give up writing. Each of you found me at a low-ebb in my writing career and pushed me to keep going.

Thank you to James Grady, whose work 'Six Days of the Condor' and the movie based on his work 'Three Days of the Condor' caused me to fall in love with this genre at an early age and inspired me to try my hand at this genre.

Thank you to Owen Laukkanen, Jeff Siger, Joe Clifford and Tim O'Mara for their generous support of my work.

Thanks to my agent and part-time therapist Doug Grad of the Doug Grad Literary Agency for knowing how to keep a mad Irishman on course. Thanks to Jason Pinter at Polis Books who was gracious enough to allow me to be part of the impressive, growing Polis family.

And thank you to Arcenia and Rita, without whom none of this would be possible.

My love and gratitude to you all.

ABOUT THE AUTHOR

Terrence McCauley is an award-winning writer living in New York City. In 2014, he won the New Pulp Award for Best Author and Best Short Story for *A Bullet's All it Takes*. His short stories have been featured in *Thuglit, Shotgun Honey, Atomic Noir,* and *Matt Hilton's Action: Pulse Pounding Tales Vol. 1 & 2*. He recently compiled *Grand Central Noir*, an anthology where all proceeds go directly to God's Love We Deliver, a nonprofit organization in New York City. He has written two acclaimed historical crime thrillers, *Prohibition* and *Slow* Burn, both of which are available from Polis Books.

Find him online at www.terrencepmccauley.com
and @tmccauley_nyc.